DEADLY

Deadly

A PRETTY LITTLE LIARS NOVEL

SARA SHEPARD

ATOM

First published in the US in 2013 by HarperTeen
First published in Great Britain in 2016 by Atom

13 5 7 9 10 8 6 4 2

Copyright © 2013 by Alloy Entertainment and Sara Shepard

alloyentertainment

Produced by Alloy Entertainment
1700 Broadway, New York, NY 10019

Typography by Liz Dresner

The moral right of the author has been asserted.

A CIP catalogue record for this book
is available from the British Library.

ISBN 978-0-349-00279-8 (paperback)

Printed and bound in Great Britain by Clays Ltd, St Ives plc

Papers used by Atom are from well-managed forests
and other responsible sources.

MIX
Paper from
responsible sources
FSC® C104740

Atom
An imprint of
Little, Brown Book Group
Carmelite House
50 Victoria Embankment
London EC4Y 0DZ

An Hachette UK Company
www.hachette.co.uk

www.atombooks.co.uk

To Lucy, Shay, Troian, and Ashley

No one here gets out alive.

—JIM MORRISON

THE GREAT AND POWERFUL ALI

Remember when you learned about *omnipotence* in English class? It's when a narrator is all-knowing and can see and hear everything. Sounds like a pretty sweet deal, right? Sort of like being the Wizard of Oz. Imagine what *you* could do if you were all-knowing. Like when you lost your journal in the locker room—you could see where it went. Or at that party last month: You would know if your boyfriend made out with your rival in the back bedroom or not. You'd be able to decipher secret looks. Hear intimate thoughts. See what's invisible . . . even improbable.

Four pretty girls in Rosewood wished they were omnipotent, too. But here's the thing about seeing and knowing everything—sometimes ignorance is safer. Because the closer the girls get to the truth about what happened that fateful night in the Poconos, when Alison DiLaurentis almost killed them and then vanished, the more dangerous their lives will become.

* * *

One chilly February night, on a secluded, wooded street in the Pocono Mountains, it was so quiet that you could hear a twig snap, a high-pitched giggle, or a gasp for miles around. But no one was in the area this time of year, which was why Alison DiLaurentis didn't feel the least bit worried as she and four girls she barely knew stood in a dark, upstairs bedroom in her family's vacation house. The walls might have been thin, the windows drafty, but no one was around to hear the girls scream. In just a few short minutes, Emily Fields, Spencer Hastings, Aria Montgomery, and Hanna Marin would be dead.

Ali couldn't wait.

Everything was set. In the past week, Ali had dragged not-guilty Ian Thomas, long dead, to one of the second-floor bedrooms of this house and hidden him in the closet. She'd placed an unconscious Melissa Hastings, Ian's once-girlfriend, next to his bloated body earlier today. She'd assembled the gasoline, the matches, the boards, and the nails, and called her accomplice to let him know the exact time and final details. And now, finally, she'd coaxed Spencer, Aria, Hanna, and Emily to this house tonight, leading them upstairs into that same bedroom where Ian and Melissa were stashed.

She faced the girls now, hands on her hips, watching them see her as their old friend Alison, a girl they'd loved—though in truth the "Alison" they knew was actually Alison's sister, Courtney. She'd switched places with the real Alison, sending her twin to the mental hospital and taking over her life. "Let me hypnotize you again for old time's sake?" she asked, giving them that winning, pleading smile. She knew they'd say yes.

And they did. Ali tried to contain her excitement as they closed their eyes. She counted down from one hundred, pacing around the small bedroom, listening for sounds on the first floor. Unbeknownst to the four others, a boy had sneaked into the house just moments ago. Right now, he was pouring liquid, locking doors, and placing boards against windows. It was all part of the plan.

Ali kept counting down, using a lulling, soothing voice. The girls went still. When Ali was almost to one, she crept out of the room, locked the door from the outside, and slipped a letter under the crack. Then she tiptoed down the stairs and rooted around in her pockets. Her fingers curled around her lucky matchbook. She struck a match, then dropped it on the floor.

Whoosh. Every wall, every exposed beam, and every ancient board game, musty-smelling Audubon Society bird book, and nylon camping tent burst into flames. The air grew pungent with gasoline vapor, and the smoke was so thick, it was difficult to see from one end of a room to the other. Alison listened to the girls' panicked wails rise through the house. *That's right, bitches*, she thought gleefully. *Scream and cry all you want, it's not going to help.*

But God, did the fumes reek. Ali pulled her T-shirt over her nose and hurried through the first floor. She looked this way and that for the boy of her dreams, the only person she trusted, but he must have already been headed to their rendezvous point. Quickly, she checked his work on the windows. He'd boarded almost everything up snugly, providing little chance of the others escaping, but she grabbed the hammer he'd left on the windowsill and gave one of the boards an extra pound, just to make sure.

Then she stopped and cocked her head. Was that . . . a *thump*? A voice? She glared at the ceiling. It sounded like footsteps were clambering down a set of stairs—only, *which* stairs? She stared at the foyer. No one. She didn't know the layout of this rambling, old house that well, as her parents had bought it just before Courtney had made the switch and sent her away.

Then something caught her eye, and she whipped around. Through the gray, billowing smoke, five figures rushed toward the kitchen door and out to safety. Ali's jaw dropped. Lavalike rage burbled in her chest.

The last girl stopped and peered through the haze. Her blue eyes widened. Her blond-red hair was a frizzy cloud around her face. Emily Fields. Emily rushed forward, her face a mix of rage and disbelief, and grabbed Ali by the shoulders. "How could you do this?" she demanded.

Ali wriggled out of Emily's grip. "I already told you. You bitches ruined my life."

Emily looked like she'd been slapped. "But . . . I *loved* you."

Ali burst out laughing. "You are *such* a loser, Emily."

Emily looked away, like she didn't believe Ali could say such a thing. Ali wanted to shake her. *Really?* she considered saying. *I don't even know you. Get a freaking life.*

But then a huge *boom* sounded, the pressure driving them apart. Ali's feet lifted off the ground, and seconds later she landed on her shins so hard, she almost bit clean through her tongue.

When she opened her eyes again, the flames were dancing around her even more hungrily than before. She pushed up to her hands and knees and crawled toward the kitchen door, but Emily had gotten there first. She had one hand around the knob. The other hand held a wooden plank, big enough to bar the door from the outside, keeping Ali in.

Ali suddenly had the same trapped, teetering feeling she'd felt at the beginning of sixth grade, when her twin was home for the weekend. Her mother had come upstairs, dragged Ali from her bedroom, and said, *Get out of your sister's room, Courtney. It's time to go.*

Now Emily met Ali's gaze. She stared at the plank in her hands as if she didn't know how it had gotten there. Tears ran down her cheeks. But instead of shutting the door tight, instead of propping the plank diagonally across the outside of the door so Ali couldn't escape, as Ali thought she would, Emily flung the plank onto the porch. It landed out of view with a heavy *thunk*. After one more ambiguous glance at Ali, she took off.

Leaving the door wide open behind her.

Ali limped toward the door, but as she tumbled over the threshold, there was another thunderous *boom*. What felt like two hot, heavy hands shoved her from behind, and she went flying again. A horrible stench of burning skin and hair singed her nostrils. Her leg exploded with pain. Her skin sizzled. She could hear herself screaming, but she couldn't stop. But then, all of a sudden, it was like someone hit a switch: The pain just . . . *vanished*. She floated outside her body, up, up, up over the inferno and into the trees.

She could see everything. The parked car. Roofs of the nearby houses. And under a huge tree in the front yard, those stupid bitches. Spencer wailed. Aria doubled over with coughs. Hanna patted her hair like it was on fire. Melissa was a limp pile on the ground. And Emily looked worriedly at the door through which they'd all escaped, a concerned expression on her face, before covering her eyes with her hands.

Then another figure shot out from deep in the woods. Ali's gaze moved to him, and her heart lifted. He ran right toward where she'd landed and dropped to his knees next to her body. "Ali," he said, suddenly so close to her ear. "*Ali*. Wake up. You have to wake up."

The invisible tether extending her into the sky snapped tight, and instantly she was back inside her body. The pain returned immediately. Her charred skin throbbed. Her leg pulsated with her heartbeat. But no matter how hard she screamed, she couldn't make a sound.

"Please," he begged, shaking her harder. "Please open your eyes."

She tried as best she could, wanting to see the boy she'd loved for so long. She wanted to say his name, but her head felt too fuzzy, her throat too ruined. She managed to muster a moan.

"You're going to be okay," he said emphatically, as if he was trying to convince himself. "We just have to . . ." Then he gasped. Sirens sounded down the hill. "*Shit*," he whispered.

Ali managed to open her eyes at the sound. "Shit," she echoed weakly. This wasn't how things were supposed to go. They were supposed to be far away by now.

He tugged her arm. "We have to get out of here. Can you walk?"

"No." It took all of Ali's strength to whisper. She was in so much pain, she was afraid she might throw up.

"You *have* to." He tried to help her up, but she just crumpled. "It's not far."

Ali looked at her useless legs. Even wiggling a toe hurt. "I can't!"

His eyes met hers. "Everything is in place. You just have to take a couple of steps."

The sirens grew closer. Ali's head lolled to the grass. Letting out a frustrated moan, he hefted her over his shoulder, fireman-style, and carried her through the woods. They jostled and bounced. Twigs scraped Ali's face. Leaves fluttered against her singed arms.

With all her remaining strength, she twisted around and stared through the trees. Those bitches were still huddled together, the lights from the ambulances flashing against their features. It didn't look like *they* needed medical attention at all. *They* didn't have any broken bones. *They* hadn't sustained any burns. But they were the ones who were supposed to suffer. Not her.

She let out a furious shriek. It wasn't fair.

The boy she'd loved forever followed her gaze, then patted her on the shoulder. "We'll get them," he growled in her ear as he carried her to safety. "I promise. We'll make them pay."

Ali knew he meant every word. And right then, she made the vow to herself, too: Together, they were going to get Spencer, Aria, Hanna, and Emily if it was the last thing they did. No matter who they took down. No matter who they had to kill to do it.

This time, they were going to do it right.

1

MORE ANSWERS, MORE QUESTIONS

"Hey." A voice floated over Aria Montgomery's head. "Aria. *Hey.*"

Aria opened her eyes. One of her best friends, Hanna Marin, sat on the coffee table across from her, staring at a steaming cup of coffee in Aria's hands. Aria had been so out of it, she couldn't even remember getting coffee before she'd dozed off.

"You were about to spill that in your lap." Hanna took the coffee from her. "The last thing we need is for you to land in the hospital, too."

Hospital. Of course. Aria looked around. She was at the Jefferson Intensive Care Unit, in a crowded waiting room on Monday morning. On the walls were winter forest watercolors. A flat-screen TV blared a morning talk show in the corner. Two of her other friends, Emily Fields and Spencer Hastings, were sitting on a loveseat next to her, wrinkled copies of *Us Weekly* and *Glamour* and paper cups of coffee in their hands. Noel Kahn's parents sat across the room, blearily staring at sections from *The Philadelphia Inquirer.* A horseshoe-shaped nurse's desk stood in the middle of the room, and a woman behind it talked on the phone. Three doctors in blue scrubs rushed down the hall, surgical masks dangling around their necks.

Aria sat up straighter. "Did I miss anything? Did Noel . . . ?"

Hanna shook her head. "He still hasn't woken up."

Just yesterday, a helicopter had brought Noel here from Rosewood, and he hadn't regained consciousness since. On the one hand, Aria couldn't wait for Noel to wake up. On the other, she had no idea what she would say when he did. That was because even though she and Noel had been dating for more than a year, Aria had just discovered that Noel had had a secret relationship with Alison DiLaurentis while she was in The Preserve. He knew the truth about the DiLaurentis twin switch, and he hadn't said a word to Aria—or anyone else. To say that Aria suddenly couldn't trust Noel was an understatement. She'd even gone so far as to wonder if Noel was Helper A, the secret boyfriend who'd been helping Ali torment the four of them. But then an A note had directed the girls to the storage shed. The girls were sure it was a trap Noel and Ali had set, so they'd called the police. They'd found Noel bound and gagged in a chair, close to death. And then there was a new note from A: Noel wasn't the helper. A—Ali—had manipulated them once more. Noel was just another victim.

"Miss Montgomery?"

A tall, bristly-haired police officer stood above Aria. "Y-yes?" Aria stammered.

The cop—who had Popeye forearms and a reddish crew cut—stepped closer. "Name's Kevin Gates. I'm with the Rosewood Police. Do you girls have a minute?"

Aria frowned. "We already told the police everything we know yesterday."

Gates smiled gently, making his eyes crinkle. There was something teddy-bearish about him. "I know. But I want to make sure my guys asked you the right questions."

Aria bit down hard on the inside of her cheek. Now that Noel had been hurt, she felt she needed to keep quiet about A again. She couldn't risk anyone else becoming a victim.

Gates led them to a more secluded part of the waiting room, next to a pot of very fake-looking lilies. After everyone sat down on a new set of scratchy couches, he looked at his notepad. "Am I correct that you received a text message that Noel was in the storage shed?"

Despite their more private location, Aria could still feel everyone in the room staring. Mrs. Kahn peeked up from behind the Food section of the paper. A boy in an Episcopal Academy sweatshirt peered out from under his hood. Mason Byers, one of Noel's buddies on the lacrosse team, who was sitting at a table across the room, stopped shuffling a deck of cards and cocked his head toward the group.

"I got a handwritten note, not a text," Hanna clarified. "And it said to go to the shed. I called the cops just in case the threat was real."

Gates made a mark on his notepad. "It's good you did. Whoever sent you that note most likely hurt Mr. Kahn—or, at the very least, saw who did it. Do you have the note on you?"

Hanna looked trapped. "It's at home."

Gates paused from writing. "Will you bring it to us as soon as possible?"

"Uh, sure." Hanna rubbed her nose, looking uncomfortable.

Gates turned to Aria. "Mr. and Mrs. Kahn said you called them several times that same morning, asking if Noel had come home. Did you have reason to be worried about him?"

Aria tried very hard not to make eye contact with her friends. She'd made those calls that morning because she was going to turn Noel in. As Ali's helper. "He wasn't picking up his phone," she said simply. "I'm his girlfriend."

Gates looked at Spencer and Emily. "You two were at the shed as well, correct?"

"That's right," Emily said nervously, peeling her paper coffee cup apart.

"Did you see anyone on the school grounds that

looked suspicious? Two people who might have put Noel there?"

Spencer and Emily shook their heads. "All I saw were a bunch of kids playing soccer," Spencer said.

"Wait." Emily leaned forward. "*Two* people?"

Gates nodded. "Our forensic team thoroughly inspected the photographs of Mr. Kahn in the shed. The complex way he was bound and gagged could have only been done by a two-person team."

Everyone exchanged a glance. Ali and Helper A, obviously. It was proof Noel really *hadn't* been Ali's accomplice.

"And you have *no idea* who could have done such a thing?" Gates pressed.

There was a long silence. Aria swallowed hard. Hanna's mouth twitched. Spencer and Emily looked anywhere but at the officer. It was probably obvious that they were lying, but it wasn't as if they could tell the truth.

Finally, Gates thanked them and walked away, his back stiff and straight. Hanna covered her face with her hands. "Guys, what am I supposed to do?" she moaned. "I can't give them that note!"

"If you don't give it, they'll think we're hiding something." Spencer slumped back on the couch. "Maybe we should just tell them what's going on."

Aria narrowed her eyes. "And risk someone else getting hurt?"

"What we need to do is figure out who Helper A is." Spencer glanced cagily at the cop, who was now talking to Noel's parents. "Then we can come clean about everything."

Hanna stared into her palms. "I can't believe Helper A isn't Noel."

Aria made a small, tortured sound.

"I didn't mean it like that," Hanna said quickly. "I mean, I'm *glad* it's not Noel. But we were so close to figuring it out. And now we're back to square one."

"I know." Aria plopped back onto the couch.

Hanna gazed across the room at the large water bubbler. "You know, before Graham died, he said the person's name who bombed the cruise ship started with *N*. There are other names that start with *N* besides Noel."

"True," Aria said. Hanna had been volunteering at the burn clinic so she could ask Graham Pratt, a boy they'd met on a cruise they'd recently taken, if he'd seen who had set off a bomb that had almost killed him and Aria—they were worried it might have been Helper A. But Graham was in a coma, so Hanna had to do a lot of sitting around and waiting. For the brief time Graham had gained consciousness, he'd told Hanna that the bomber's name started with *N*. But then he'd started seizing, and Hanna had run out of the room to grab a nurse. By the time she'd returned, Graham was dead—and Hanna's new friend Kyla was gone. That was because Kyla wasn't a burn victim at all . . . but Ali in disguise. The *real* Kyla's body had been found behind the burn clinic yesterday; Ali must have killed an innocent stranger, wrapped her own face in bandages, and taken the girl's place to prevent Hanna from finding out anything from Graham. It would have been easier to just kill Graham as soon as she had the chance, but Ali probably thought there wasn't any fun in that. This whole thing was just a game for her.

"There's also the possibility that Graham didn't really know the bomber's name," Spencer said in a morose tone. "What if Helper A gave him a fake name?"

Hanna raised a finger. "Why else would Ali have killed him? He obviously knew *something* important."

The door to the waiting room flung open, and a new nurse rushed in. She whispered something to the woman at the desk, and then both of them glanced at Aria, urgent looks on their faces. Aria's heart thumped against her ribs. Was it about Noel? Was he . . . *dead*?

The new nurse padded over to Aria. "Miss Montgomery?" Aria could only nod yes. "Noel is awake. He's asking for you."

Aria glanced around for Noel's parents, figuring they would want to see him first, but Mr. and Mrs. Kahn must have stepped out.

The nurse patted Aria's arm. "I'll be waiting by the door." The nurse spun around and strode to the entrance.

Aria faced her friends. "What should I do?"

"*Talk* to him!" Hanna urged.

"Ali couldn't have done it alone," Spencer said eagerly. "Helper A must have been there, too. See if Noel remembers anything."

Aria tried to take a breath, but her lungs felt cinched tight with string. Noel *could* explain everything. But after all she'd learned about him, and all they'd been through, she felt raw and unsteady.

Spencer touched her hand. "If things get too weird, just leave. We get it."

Aria nodded and stood. They were right: She *had* to do this.

She took deep breaths as she followed the nurse down the shiny, just-Cloroxed hallway and through a set of electronic double doors that led to the intensive-care unit. Just as she was about to pass through, a woman in jeans and a black sweater coat strode toward her. "Miss Montgomery? It's Alyssa Gaden from the *Philadelphia Sentinel.*"

Aria stiffened. Last night, the waiting room had been crawling with reporters asking questions about Noel, but the hospital staff had kicked all of them out. *Almost* all of them. "Um, no comment," Aria said. Mercifully, the doors to the ward locked behind her.

Halfway down the hall, the nurse turned into a small, bright, private room. Aria peered inside and gasped. Noel's face was covered in bruises. Stitches crossed from his jawline to his ear. There were IVs in both of his hands, and his skin was chalky white. His feet jutted straight out under the covers. He looked smaller and weaker than she'd ever seen him.

"Noel," was all Aria could manage.

"Aria." Noel's voice was gravelly, not his own.

The nurse checked Noel's IVs, then left. Aria sat down in a chair by his bed, staring at the checkerboard pattern on the floor. A machine measured Noel's pulse. By the number of beeps, it seemed like Noel's heart was beating very fast.

"Thanks for seeing me," he finally said in a small voice.

Aria's chin twitched. She almost said *you're welcome*, but then she remembered. Noel had lied to her. He'd loved a girl who'd tried to *kill* her.

She squeezed her eyes shut and turned away. "Everything you know about Ali could get you in major trouble."

"I know." Noel blinked at her. "But right now, you're the only one who knows what I know. So if someone is going to turn me in, it would be you." He cleared his throat. "You can, though. I get it."

Aria thought of Noel in a prison uniform. Sharing a room with a possibly violent stranger. Checking out books from the prison library. She wasn't sure if she wanted it, or if it was the worst possible outcome in the world.

"What happened to you in the cemetery?" she blurted.

"Someone came up behind me," Noel said slowly. "Whoever it was hit me over the head. At first, I thought it was Spencer, but it wasn't."

Aria nodded.

He stared down at his bony knees under the sheets. "I heard a deep voice, but I didn't see his face."

A deep voice. Helper A. "And then?"

"I was thrown into a trunk. Then someone dragged me through wet grass. I heard a latch open, then two people whispering."

Two people. "Was one of them . . . *her*?"

Noel's face fell. It was clear he knew exactly who Aria was talking about—in the cemetery during prom, Aria had explained, briefly, hysterically, that Ali was after them. "I don't think so."

Aria bristled. "Why? Because you love her so much and can't see how evil she is?"

Noel recoiled. "I *don't* love her, Aria."

Aria stared at him, waiting. He'd *said* he did.

"Look, I loved someone who didn't exist," Noel protested. "I stopped loving her when I fell in love with you." He choked back a sob. "I'm sorry. I know that doesn't excuse anything. I know we can't be together. But I want you to know that I'll always regret what I've done."

His voice was so small and scared that it made Aria's heart quake. "I want you to tell me everything," she said in the toughest voice she could muster. "How often you saw Ali at The Preserve. Who else you saw there. What she said to you. If she told you . . ." Aria took a breath, trying not to burst into tears. "If she told you what she was going to do to us."

"I had no idea what she was going to do to you, I promise," Noel said fiercely.

"Fine. Then tell me at least why you started seeing her."

He sighed. "I don't know. I felt sorry for her."

"How did you know she was at The Preserve?"

He shifted under the blankets. "My parents had me talk to someone after my brother committed suicide. It was a therapist who worked in an outpatient building at The Preserve. One day, I bumped into this girl going in when I was coming out—it was Alison. She was really cagey, and I thought it was, you know, the girl I knew from school. The next time I went, she was there again—and I was really confused, because the sixth-grade field hockey team had a game that day, and Mason, who was watching the game, had just texted me that Ali had scored a goal."

Aria nodded. "Got it."

Noel paused to take a breath. "I kind of put it all together in my head as I was looking at Ali come out of the therapist's office. She realized it, because she waited for me after my appointment and confessed who she really was. She told me she was Ali's twin, trapped in a hospital, blah blah blah."

"And you *believed* her?"

"Well, sure. She didn't seem crazy. Just . . . a victim."

Aria pinched the bridge of her nose. "So that's where you guys got to know each other? Outside the shrink's office?"

Noel looked ashamed. "No. After that, I . . . I visited her at the hospital."

A pain shot through her. "How often?"

"Regularly."

"Why?"

He twisted his mouth. "She made me feel heard. Important."

Sucker. Ali–*both* Alis–had a way of making you feel very, very special. But it was always for their own selfish needs. "And let me guess, she made it out like Courtney was the crazy one?" Aria spat.

Noel nodded. "Pretty much."

"You had no problem hanging out with Courtney, though," Aria pointed out, remembering how Noel had attended every party Their Ali threw. He'd sat at their lunch table and winged Cheetos at Ali's head. He'd partnered with Ali for a three-legged race during the sixth-grade field day, laughing hysterically when they'd stumbled over the finish line. "In fact, in seventh grade, you even went out with her!"

Noel cocked his head. "No, I didn't."

"You did, too! I know because Ali–*Courtney*–told you *I* liked you first–but you came back and said you liked her instead. She liked you, too–but then dumped you after a few dates." It was something she and Noel had never gotten into, but Aria could remember the incident as clear as day. Ali had broken Aria's heart when she'd announced Noel was into her.

Noel shifted in the bed, wincing as he twisted his torso. "Courtney never told me about you. I never liked her. She probably said that I liked her just to piss you off."

That *was* something Their Ali would do, but Aria didn't want to give Noel the satisfaction of being right. "If you really thought Courtney was dangerous, why didn't you warn anyone?"

For a moment, there were only the sounds of the beeps on Noel's monitors. "Because she didn't really seem dangerous. I stayed out of it. Besides, Ali told me not to tell a soul the truth. I kept my promise."

"And that's why you didn't tell me? Your *girlfriend*?"

Noel cut his gaze away. "I wanted to so many times. But . . ." He sighed. "I'm sorry."

She balled up a fist in her lap. *Sorry?* "So, at the end of seventh grade, did you know that the real Ali was out of the hospital for a few days?"

Noel took a sip from the plastic cup on the tray next to his bed. "I went to the DiLaurentis house the day before graduation. I only saw Ali, though. I didn't see Courtney."

Aria wondered if Their Ali had been home at the time. If she wasn't, she was probably out with Aria and the others . . . or else her new, older friends from field hockey. Had she been doing something completely innocent, like shopping at the King James Mall or hanging out at Spencer's? Little did she know she was going to die the next day.

"When Courtney went missing, did you suspect Ali?" Aria asked.

"No way," Noel said forcefully. "She seemed really happy that weekend, not like she was planning anything crazy. I really thought Courtney ran away. And when everyone found out about Ian, it made sense. I saw Courtney flirting with him. That guy could be a real asshole."

"Did Ali contact you when she was back in The Preserve?"

There was a loud *ding*, and Noel glanced at the monitor next to his bed. A heart flashed red, then vanished. "She wrote a letter saying that sending her back to The Preserve was a huge mistake," he said. "She seemed so worried about her sister going missing and so shocked that they couldn't find her. I fell for it."

"And you visited her again, for years."

"Yeah." Noel sounded ashamed. "Until Ian Thomas was convicted and Ali came back."

"Did you meet Tabitha Clark while you visited The Preserve?"

Noel swallowed hard. "I saw Tabitha around, but I didn't hang out with her except for this one time when Ali was released for a weekend. Her parents didn't want to see her, so she stayed with Tabitha in New Jersey. I took the train there and went to the movies with them."

Aria shut her eyes. Last week, she'd found a ticket stub for *Spider-Man* from a theater in Maplewood, New Jersey, where Tabitha was from. There had been handwriting on the back: *Thanks for believing in me.* So it *was* from Ali. "Did you meet anyone else at The Preserve?"

Noel raised his eyes to the ceiling. "A girl named Iris. Super-skinny, really blond."

That made sense. Last week, Emily had checked Iris out of the hospital for a few days to pump her for information. Iris was the one who'd explained that Ali had a secret boyfriend. When she saw a picture of Noel, she said she was sure it was him.

"How about any guy friends?" Aria asked.

Noel thought for a moment. "I can't think of a single one. Why?"

"Ali had a boyfriend."

She waited for the impact, expecting Noel to look shattered and betrayed. But he just blinked. "I never met him."

"Did she ever *talk* about him?"

"Nope." He shook his head.

She stared at her hands in her lap. "So last year, when Ian was arrested and they let Ali out, she contacted you again, right?"

"We met once before that press conference."

"At Keppler Creek?" Iris had told Emily that while Ali was still at The Preserve, she talked on and on about how she was going to have a secret meeting at a park near Delaware.

Noel tilted his head. "No. At my house. She said that everyone would know about her soon enough. And then you guys did. When all of you seemed so friendly with one another, I thought it was great. She seemed really happy, too. A happy ending."

Aria narrowed her eyes. "Did she tell you she lied to us? Told us she was *our* Ali?"

"Of course not." Noel very gingerly sat up in bed, his face contorting. "Like I said, I had no idea until after the fire."

"What about the kiss?" Ali and Noel had shared a kiss at the Valentine's Dance the night of the Poconos fire. Ali had acted like Noel had hit on her, not the other way around. Aria had been so mad at Noel, she'd joined Ali and her friends on their trip to the Poconos house.

"I wasn't helping her in her master plan, I swear," Noel urged. "She kissed *me*."

"And what about telling Agent Fuji I was lying?"

Noel squinted. "What are you talking about?"

"I saw an e-mail exchange between you and Agent Fuji."

"She let you read her e-mails?"

"No, I read *your* e-mails." Aria hated to admit it. "You told Fuji you thought someone had lied to her about Tabitha's murder. Why did you say that? Were you trying to get her to investigate me?"

Noel stared at her like a third ear had sprouted out of her forehead. "I had exactly one conversation with Agent Fuji where I told her I didn't know Tabitha and I didn't know anything. *I* was the one lying. And why would I want her to investigate *you*?"

Aria pretended to fix a kink in her pant leg. Could Noel honestly not know about Tabitha? "I'm supposed to believe that someone hacked into your e-mail account and wrote fake messages to Fuji?"

Noel threw up his hands. "I don't know. And while we're talking about it, who *is* this someone who's hacking into things and stalking you and beating me up? Do you really think Ali's still alive? Why didn't you tell me before?"

Aria scoffed. "I didn't tell you because I was trying to keep you safe."

"But . . ." Noel looked like he was going to say something else, then shut his mouth tight.

"But *what*?" Aria asked.

Noel shook his head. "Nothing. Forget it."

He was breathing hard by now, and his machine started to beep. Aria stared at it, grateful to have something to look at instead of his face.

A nurse swept into the room and checked the monitor. "I think you should probably get going," she said to Aria.

She ushered Aria toward the door. Aria peeked back at Noel's drawn expression, but she didn't wave.

She felt disoriented and dizzy. For so long, Noel had been the only thing in Rosewood that was keeping her going . . . but now he was a stranger. How could she continue on here? How was she going to live in Rosewood, go to Rosewood Day, even enter rooms in her house without a Noel memory rearing its head?

She needed to get out of this place, once and for all. Leave Rosewood behind and never come back. But as she took a few faltering steps, her knees collapsed and her legs felt heavy. Right now, it was a challenge just to get out of the hallway and back to her friends.

2

AN EMPTY ROOM

Spencer, Hanna, and Emily shot to their feet as soon as Aria returned to the waiting room. Aria avoided their gazes and trudged straight to the drinks station, her shoulders hunched.

"What did Noel say?" Spencer asked breathlessly, following her. "Did he see who hurt him?"

"No," Aria mumbled, grabbing a cup from the stack.

"Are you sure?" Hanna asked. "How well did he know Ali, anyway? Were they friends—or more?"

Aria busied herself at the coffee machine. Her eyes were red, and she kept making little hiccupping sighs like she'd been crying. Spencer hated pushing her for answers, but they needed to know.

Reluctantly, Aria relayed what Noel had told her, including how he'd visited Ali at The Preserve. When she got to the part about Noel not meeting anyone else there except for Tabitha and Iris, Spencer grumbled. "He didn't see one single guy? Ali *never* talked about someone she liked?"

Aria shrugged. "I think Ali wanted Noel to think she liked *him*."

Emily groaned. "That makes sense. It was her way of keeping him on her side."

Aria took a sip of coffee. "Noel said he heard a guy's voice when he was attacked. But that's it."

"I wish we could take down Ali and her helper once and for all." Spencer plopped into a chair.

"Maybe we could go back to The Preserve," Hanna suggested. "Ask them if there were any guy patients whose names started with *N*."

Emily looked unsure. "It seems so risky."

Hanna furrowed her brow. "You want to give up?"

"Maybe we should," Spencer said. Just last week, in an attempt to catch Ali and her helper, they'd gone rogue, putting away their phones, which A had hacked dozens of times, and buying burner cells. Then they'd met in a panic room in Spencer's stepfather's model home for Who-Is-A brainstorming meetings. They'd created a list of people who might have been helping Ali. They'd drawn lines through each name as they ruled people out. Finally, only Noel remained . . . and they'd thought they were one step ahead of A, until A's text yesterday included a picture of the suspect list. Spencer had no idea how Ali *found* the thing, as she'd had it hidden under her bed. *Noel as A? Not it!* the note had said.

"What about the cops?" Hanna reshaped her auburn ponytail. "Should I hand over Ali's note from the burn clinic?"

Spencer thought it over. If they showed the cops the note, Ali and Helper A might come after them. If they didn't, the cops might accuse them of obstructing justice. "What if you handed it over but told them nothing about A?" she suggested. "It's signed in Kyla's name, not Ali's. The cops don't have to know she's one and the same. To be honest, *we* don't even know for sure."

"That could work," Hanna murmured.

"What do we do about our burner phones?" Aria asked. "A hacked them, too. Do we keep them?"

"We might as well use our old phones," Emily suggested. "No matter what we do, she finds us. Let's just not make calls or send texts unless we absolutely have to."

"If we change our passwords on our e-mail daily, that could be okay to use," Spencer said. "But we shouldn't discuss anything about Ali or Helper A over e-mail or text."

"What if we get another A note?" Hanna whispered. "Can we still talk about it?"

Spencer glanced around the room, almost afraid A was listening. "Yeah," she whispered. "Maybe we could use a code word if we want to meet and talk about Ali. How about . . ." Her gaze clapped on the handsome, silver-haired figure on the TV screen. "Anderson Cooper."

"Done," Aria said.

Hanna leaned in closer. "What do you think A's next move is going to be?"

Spencer's stomach flipped over. How many times had they wondered *that*? "It could be anything. A's still watching us. We just need to keep our eyes and ears open."

Everyone nodded, looking even more terrified than before. But there was nothing else to say, so Spencer grabbed her purse, fished out her keys, and started for the elevators, eager to head home and take a long, hot shower.

She passed the cafeteria and staggered out into the bright morning. The street swarmed with people, including a bunch of ragtag protesters holding signs on the corner. ROSEWOOD, some of the signs read. SERIAL KILLER was written on another in big red letters. "Keep our children safe!" the protesters bellowed. One of them wore a Rosewood Day sweatshirt.

Spencer watched them for a while, feeling ambivalent. It was strange to have people care so passionately about something she was so directly and intimately caught up in.

Then she noticed a news van parked across the street, with a female reporter sitting in the passenger seat. Spencer ducked her head and strode quickly to her car, afraid that in seconds, the reporter would recognize her.

"Spencer?"

She gritted her teeth and whirled around—but it was Chase, a new sort-of friend. He was standing under the hospital awning wearing a black nylon coat and a gray baseball cap.

Spencer reluctantly crossed to Chase and pulled him into a more secluded nook near a service entrance. "What are you doing here?" she whispered.

Chase tugged at his mangled ear, a wound from a stalker in boarding school. "Weren't we supposed to meet today? I looked all over for you. Your mom finally told me where you were."

"Did she tell you *why* I was here?"

Chase shook his head.

"Okay," Spencer said, and told him everything. She knew she could trust Chase. He ran an unsolved-crime blog, and they'd met up when she was trying to track down Ali. There had been some identity confusion at first—Chase was trying to pass his brother Curtis off as himself because he was self-conscious about his ear, and for a while Spencer had even worried he was A. But he'd eventually come clean.

When Spencer finally finished telling him about Noel and the storage shed, Chase narrowed his green eyes. "So . . . Noel *isn't* Ali's boyfriend?"

Spencer sighed. "Nope. We're back to square one."

"Well then, we'd better get going," Chase said, linking his arm around Spencer's elbow.

Spencer planted her feet. "Where?"

Chase blinked. "We're going to stake out that town house on the surveillance video."

When Chase visited her yesterday, he'd shown her a grainy surveillance video of the outside of a town house in Rosewood. A girl who looked a lot like Ali was visible in a few frames. They'd made plans to investigate it today, but after everything that had happened with Noel, Spencer had forgotten.

A city bus whooshed by, spewing out exhaust. "Someone's boyfriend ended up in a storage shed because of us," Spencer said nervously. "Ali knows we're on to her. I can't let anyone else get hurt."

"But what if this is where she *lives*?" Chase asked. "If we could find proof that she's still alive, we could turn it in to the cops and put an end to this, once and for all. And then no one else *would* get hurt."

Spencer twisted her mouth. A shadow flickered across the window of a car parked across the street, for a moment looking like a person.

Chase *did* have a point. What if they found something at the apartment? What if they could end this whole nightmare today?

She looked up at Chase and nodded ever so slightly. "Okay. Let's do it."

Twenty minutes later, as low clouds rolled across the sky, Spencer and Chase steered into a housing complex in

West Rosewood, the low-rent part of town. Of course, low-rent was relative: A big FOR SALE sign in the development entrance boasted hardwood floors and marble countertops in every unit. A brand-new community swimming pool glistened in the distance. And the local grocery store was Fresh Fields, where you couldn't buy a quart of milk for less than five bucks.

"There it is," Chase said, pointing at a block of town houses. Each unit looked the same, with a fake, old-timey gaslight in the front yard, a faux dormer window set into the roof, and gingerbreadlike scallop details around the windows. In the surveillance photos, Ali had been walking into the unit on the corner.

Spencer pulled the car into park and stared at the house, shivering in the suddenly cold air. The house had a red-painted door and dried leaves all over the front porch. There were no blinds on the windows—she'd have thought Ali would insist on absolute privacy. Could this really be Ali's secret lair?

Then she peered at the units next to it. The grass in all the front yards hadn't been cut in a while, and newspapers were piled up on a front porch. There wasn't a single light on in any of the windows, and no dogs barked from inside. Before Spencer and Chase had left Philly, they'd checked the county courthouse records for information on the housing complex and found that most of the units hadn't yet sold. The house Ali was entering in the photo had been on the market since its construction last year.

A couple in their seventies named Joseph and Harriet Maxwell had bought the unit next door two Novembers ago, right when Ian Thomas was arraigned for Courtney DiLaurentis's murder; but the plant on their front stoop was withered, and there were a bunch of flyers wedged inside the storm door.

"This seems like the perfect place for Ali to hide out," Spencer murmured. "It's so deserted. No one would ever see her coming and going."

"Exactly." Chase started to get out of the car, then paused and turned back to her. "Spencer. Are you sure you're ready for this?"

Spencer's stomach swirled. *Was* she? She looked around the parking lot. Though it was empty, it still felt like she was being watched. She stared at a thick line of shrubs on the other side of the lot, then peered worriedly at a locked-up realtor's office across the street. Could someone be hiding inside?

"Yes," she said, getting out of the car and slamming the door firmly behind her. She needed to do this.

The sky was ominously gray, and the air felt thick and electrified. Something made a scraping sound behind her, and the hair on her arms stood on end. "Did you hear that?"

Chase stopped short and listened. "No . . ."

Then something fluttered in the woods that bordered the lot. Spencer stared hard at a splotch between the trees.

"H-hello?" she stammered. Nothing.

Chase's swallow was audible in the eerie silence. "It was probably a rabbit. Or a deer."

Spencer nodded shakily. She tiptoed up the corner unit's front walk and peered through the window, but it was too dark to tell what—or who—was inside. She inspected the front door. There were no scuffs, no footprints, and no welcome mat. Then, sliding on the gloves Chase gave her—they didn't want to leave prints—she touched the metal doorknob tentatively, as if it were wired to set off a bomb. Her skin tingled. She glanced over her shoulder again toward the realtor's office. Thunder rumbled. The wind gusted. A few raindrops landed on Spencer's head.

"Excuse me?"

Spencer yelped and spun around. A man walking a dog approached them down the sidewalk. He seemed older, a bit stooped. The collie's tongue lolled out of its mouth. Spencer couldn't tell if the dog was on a leash or not.

The man gazed from Spencer to Chase. "What are you doing?" he asked sharply.

Spencer's mind went blank. "Uh, we thought our friend lived here."

"No one lives there," the man said, squinting at the house. "That place has been vacant since they built it."

It didn't seem like he was lying. It also didn't seem like

he had any idea who they were—he was just an old guy out for a walk with his dog. "Have you ever seen anyone coming and going out of this place?" she dared to ask. "Anyone at all?"

"Nope, not even a light on," the man said. "But it's private property. You should move along." He gave them another long look, and for a moment, Spencer wondered if she'd trusted him too quickly. But then he whistled at his dog, and the dog stood. As they passed, the dog stiffened and turned its head toward the realtor's office across the street. Spencer sucked in her stomach. Did the dog sense a presence? But then it loped off and lifted its leg on a clump of dandelions. The man and dog disappeared, all footsteps and jingling tags.

Spencer waited until the man was a safe distance away before turning to look at Chase. "This was definitely the unit in the photo."

"Do you think Ali knew we found it?" Chase whispered, his eyes wide. And then, suddenly, a terrified look crossed his face. "Do you think it was possible that Ali *planted* that video? Maybe she was never here in the first place. Or maybe she sent us here to hurt us."

Spencer couldn't believe it hadn't occurred to her. She darted off the porch, certain something horrible was about to happen. It didn't, but for a split second, she swore she could hear someone snickering. She squinted hard at the trees, then peered worriedly at the realtor's office, desperate to make out Ali's shape at the window. What if she was close? What if she realized what they'd discovered—and she was furious?

Spencer took Chase's hand. "Let's get out of here," she said hurriedly, darting back to the car. She hoped, suddenly, that they hadn't made a horrible mistake.

3

HANNA LOSES IT

An hour later, Hanna Marin and her boyfriend, Mike Montgomery, sat in Hanna's Prius, in bumper-to-bumper traffic on the way from the hospital back to Rosewood. Mike fiddled with the radio, first choosing a rap station, then flipping to sports. He let out a sigh and stared out the window, looking just as exhausted as Hanna felt. He'd hung around for a long time at the hospital last night, partly for Noel and partly for Hanna. Hanna wasn't even sure when he'd left, but she was pretty certain it had been after midnight, and he'd showed up again shortly after Noel had woken up this morning.

Hanna's phone, which was connected to the car's Bluetooth system, bleated loudly. She pressed the ANSWER button on the center console without looking at the caller ID. "Hanna?" a familiar voice rang out. "It's Kelly Crosby from the burn clinic."

"Oh." Hanna's finger hovered over the HANG UP button

on the steering wheel. She could feel Mike staring at her. "Uh, hi."

"I was just calling to let you know that there's no need for you to come in next week," Kelly went on. "The clinic is closed until further notice because of the . . . murder."

The murder. Hanna swallowed hard.

"I also wanted to let you know that Graham Pratt's funeral will be tomorrow," Kelly went on. "You were such good friends, I thought you might be interested."

"Um, great," Hanna said loudly to Kelly. "Gotta go!"

She hung up and stared straight through the windshield as though nothing were amiss. The only sound was the *clunka-clunka-clunk* of the uneven pavement on the off-ramp. Finally, Mike cleared his throat. "I thought you said Graham was the Unabomber, Hanna."

Hanna gripped the steering wheel hard. Mike had been suspicious about her volunteering stint at the burn clinic, first certain she wanted to reconcile with her ex, Sean Ackard. *That* was ridiculous, but she couldn't exactly tell him the whole truth, either—that would mean explaining about A. She'd finally admitted that Aria and Graham had been in the boiler room of the ship when the bomb went off, and she was spying on Graham to see what he knew. But there were a lot of holes in her story, and Mike knew it.

She shrugged. "I *had* to tell people at the burn clinic that Graham and I were friends. That was the only way they'd let me get close to him."

"And what's this about a murder?"

Hanna stared fixedly at a Delaware license plate on the car in front of her. "No clue."

"Bullshit."

"I don't know!" Hanna protested.

But she did. Yesterday, a girl's body had been found in the woods behind the clinic, and her hospital bracelet read KYLA KENNEDY. The girl had been dead for days, except Hanna had spoken to Kyla—or someone impersonating her—the previous night. Kyla's bed had been outside Graham's room. There was only one girl who didn't want Graham to wake up and say who'd really set off the bomb.

Ali.

Hanna simply hadn't recognized her under those bandages.

Hanna turned up her mom's driveway and parked. She was out of the car and almost to the side door when she realized Mike wasn't with her. He was still standing in the driveway, a strange expression on his face.

"I'm so sick of this," he said in a quiet voice.

Hanna wilted. "Sick of what?"

"I know you're lying."

Hanna cut her gaze to the left. "Mike . . . stop."

"First, you play detective, ditching prom—where you were *queen*—to go to the burn clinic and talk to the potential bomber instead of letting the cops deal with it." Mike listed the items on his fingers. "Then, after you tell me that dude is *dead*, you disappear with Spencer and the others without telling me. When I find you next, you're covered in mud."

Hanna touched her toe to a decorative stone to the right of the welcome mat. The mud on her dress was from when she and her friends had gone to save Aria from Noel at the cemetery.

"And *then*," Mike said, his voice rising, "you tell me you just *happen* to be there when the cops find Noel's body in that shed. I heard you tell a cop this morning that you'd received a threatening note saying to go there."

Hanna's throat felt sandpapery. She'd fudged the story about finding Noel, too—and she *still* didn't know what to do about handing over Kyla's note to the cops.

"You're not just acting crazy with me, either," Mike said. "I talked to Naomi about you. You guys were BFFs on the cruise, and suddenly you're not anymore."

Rage spiraled through Hanna. "You talked to Naomi about me?" She and Naomi Zeigler had been enemies for years, and to make matters worse, Hanna realized Naomi was related to Madison, a girl she'd hurt last summer.

"I was grasping at straws." Mike slapped his arms to his sides. "Naomi said you did some weird shit on that cruise. You looked through her e-mails on her computer. There were times when you ran away from her like you were afraid of her." He set his jaw. "Something tells me that *that* has to do with all of this other crazy stuff that's been going on, too. It's all connected." He looked at her hard. "It's A, isn't it? *Ali*. She's back."

Hanna froze. "I don't know what you're talking about."

Mike stepped closer. "It's the only thing that fits. Just tell me. Don't you trust me?"

Hanna's jaw wobbled. "Maybe I haven't told you for a good reason!" she blurted. "It's because I don't want you to get *hurt*, you idiot! I don't want you to end up like Noel!"

They were face-to-face, Mike's breath minty on her cheeks. He grabbed her hands. "I want to help. I love you. I don't care what the risks are."

She shut her eyes, feeling worn down. There was no way out of this. Mike knew he was right, and the look on her face surely confirmed it. The only thing to do to keep him from knowing more was to break up with him. Not only did Hanna hate the thought of that, it probably wouldn't keep Mike safe, anyway. He already knew too much.

She took a deep, wobbly breath, and suddenly, the whole story spilled out. She told Mike how the new A notes had started coming, how they'd become more and more sinister, and how, on the cruise, the notes had focused on how Hanna had fled the scene of a car crash, leaving Madison Zeigler, Naomi's cousin, for dead. "For a little while, I was afraid that Naomi was A," she said. "That's why I was looking through her computer. I thought I might find something to prove it. But Naomi told me that the crash wasn't even my fault, in the end—someone ran me off the road. I *remember* someone doing it, but I didn't see their face. That's who she and Madison were trying to catch."

Mike winced. "You were in a car crash last summer and you didn't tell me?"

Hanna shrugged. "I couldn't risk telling *anyone*. I'm sorry."

She kept going with the story. When she got to the part where they'd concluded that A was Ali, Mike looked confused. "Are you sure? I thought she didn't survive that fire."

"Emily left the door open for her. She got out." Then she lowered her eyes and explained the Tabitha part of it, too—how they'd feared Ali had followed them to Jamaica and was going to hurt them. "Tabitha followed us to the roof of the resort," she told Mike. "And then she went after Aria. After that, everything happened so fast—Aria shot forward, there was a scuffle, and suddenly Tabitha was tumbling over the railing. She was alive after the fall, though—we're sure of it. But when we ran down there, she was gone. We didn't kill her, but someone is making sure it *looks* like we did."

"Jesus," Mike whispered, his eyes wide. "I was *on* that trip with you. I saw that girl. How could you have kept this from me?"

"I'm sorry," Hanna said quietly. "I was just so scared. I wanted to pretend it had never happened at all. But when we started getting new notes . . ." She trailed off and covered her face with her hands.

Mike sat on the stone wall that surrounded Hanna's house and stared into the distance. After a while, he said, "Let me get this straight. It was Ali—or her helper—who murdered that Gayle woman, too?"

Hanna nodded, thinking of Gayle Riggs, the wealthy woman who had wanted Emily's baby. A had killed her.

"And it was A who set off that bomb in the boiler room of the ship?" Mike's voice squeaked. Hanna nodded again, and Mike made a gurgling sound at the back of his throat. "And it was A who really killed Tabitha?"

"We're almost positive, yes."

"So, basically, Ali has tried to kill you and my sister, like, six times by now, and she's framing you for shit that she did. We need to find this bitch. *Now*."

Hanna glanced worriedly around the yard. "Spencer and Emily seem to think it's a bad idea. The last time we looked for Ali, Noel ended up in the hospital."

Mike kicked at loose gravel in the flower bed. "So we're just supposed to sit around?"

Hanna peeked through the trees, hating how secluded her mother's property was. Anybody could spy on them at close range, and they'd never know. "I'm just afraid that if we get any closer to where they are or who her helper is, someone else is going to get hurt. Maybe you. Maybe *me*."

Mike's icy blue eyes narrowed. "I promise you, Hanna, that she will never, *ever* get you. She'll have to get through me first. I'll stand guard outside your bedroom if I have to. Stay by your side at every class. I'll even come into your dressing room at Otter if you want."

Hanna gave him a playful shove. "You'd *love* coming into my dressing room at Otter."

"Of course I would." Mike leaned in and gave Hanna a gentle kiss on the nose.

Hanna tilted her head up and kissed his lips. Something broke inside her. Salty tears flooded down her cheeks. "I'm so glad you figured it out," she whispered in his ear.

"I'm glad, too," Mike said.

They kissed again, long and deep. Mike moved his hands up and down her back. She took small steps toward the side door, and in seconds, they were inside and lying on her mom's couch in the den, making out furiously. The only thing Hanna wanted to think about was the feel of Mike's lips on hers, the warmth of his hands, the weight of his body. She clung to him like he was a life raft, then found herself pulling her shirt over her head.

Goose bumps rose in her skin. Mike pulled off his shirt, too, revealing his strong chest and toned-from-lacrosse abs. He hesitated above her. Hanna knew, suddenly, what was going to happen next. It was something they'd danced around, teased each other about, plotted for weeks . . . but something they hadn't exactly gotten around to. They would be each other's firsts, after all, and they both seemed to realize how special the moment needed to be. But maybe here, in this empty house, on this terrible day, was exactly the right time.

Hanna undid the button of her jeans. Mike's eyes slid down to watch. "Is this okay?" he whispered, his voice stretched taut.

"Yes," Hanna said, a wave crashing inside her. She grabbed Mike hard and pulled him closer than she ever had before.

4

A MISSING GIRL

The moment Emily Fields burst out of the exit of Rose-wood Day from picking up her assignments later that day, the unwelcome jeers began.

"Miss Fields! It's Alyssa Gaden from the *Philadelphia Sentinel*! Do you have a moment?"

"Emily! Over here!"

Flashbulbs popped. Reporters shoved microphones at her face. Emily tried to scurry past them, but they followed her.

"Is it true you were the ones who found Noel Kahn in the storage shed behind the school?" the *Sentinel* woman shouted.

"Can you tell us what led you there?" a man screamed.

"Do you girls have a suicide pact?" another voice bleated. "Is that why you went out on that lifeboat?"

Emily winced. After the cruise ship had been bombed, everyone had evacuated on lifeboats. Emily and her friends had taken their own boat and sailed away from shore to bury Tabitha's old necklace—A had managed to get it in Aria's hands, and the girls didn't want to be connected to it. But the lifeboat punctured out at sea, trapping them. A crew from the boat had rescued them, and the rumors had begun that they'd sailed out alone to die.

Someone placed a hand on her shoulder, forming a barricade between Emily and the reporters. "No comment, no comment, no comment."

It was Principal Appleton. He draped an arm around Emily and hustled her up the slope to the student parking lot. "I'm so sorry, dear," he said gently.

"Thanks," Emily said gratefully.

Appleton left Emily at her car with a nod and a few encouraging words to hang in there. Emily slumped into the driver's seat of the family's Volvo wagon. For the past few years, she and her friends had been the target of media scrutiny—they even had a movie made about them called *Pretty Little Killer.* She was so, so, *so* sick of it.

If those crows on the telephone pole lift off in the next ten seconds, everything will be fine, Emily thought, staring at the wires by the trees. The birds didn't move. More crows joined them, hunched, black smears against the gray sky.

Sighing, she pulled out her phone and checked her e-mail. The only one was from Hanna: *Will you guys go to Graham's funeral with me tomorrow? I need moral support.*

Aria had agreed. Emily wrote and said she would go, too. She exited out of her e-mail program, then looked longingly at the wallpaper on her home screen. It was a shot of her and her girlfriend, Jordan Richards, on the deck of the cruise ship as it pulled away from San Juan, Puerto Rico.

She shut her eyes, quietly reliving the moment. She and Jordan had connected so quickly and intensely. Emily longed to talk to Jordan now, but Jordan was on the run from the FBI. In fact, they'd made plans to run away together, but A had called the Feds on the Preppy Thief. Now Jordan was hiding out somewhere in the Caribbean to escape arrest. If only Emily could contact her and arrange to meet up with her. What did she have here, after all? It would be the perfect escape from A. But there was no way to get in touch with Jordan.

Or was there?

She tapped the Twitter app. *Need to talk*, she wrote in a direct message to Jordan's secret Twitter alias. *It's important*.

She sent off the message and waited, figuring Jordan probably wouldn't respond—she'd gotten back to Emily a few times, but she'd said over and over that it was really dangerous. But to her surprise, there was a new private message in her inbox within a minute. *Is everything okay?* Jordan wrote. *I just saw that stuff on the news about that boy from Rosewood. He was your friend's boyfriend, right?*

Emily swallowed hard. *He was*, she wrote. *But I'm okay, and so are my friends*.

Good, Jordan said. *I'm glad*.

I miss you, Emily typed fast. *I'm desperate to leave. Things super scary. Where are u?*

A new message popped up after a moment. *I wish I could tell you, but you know I can't right now. It's too risky.*

Emily shifted her weight in the seat, peering through the windshield at a few kids traipsing up the hill to their cars. It had been a long shot, but she'd hoped Jordan would say yes. *I'll wait for you,* she promised.

Good. I'll wait for you, too.

Jordan signed the message with an *XO.* Emily exited out of the Twitter program and tucked her phone back into her backpack. She felt like she did whenever she had a bite of her mom's macaroni and cheese—she could never have just a little. If only she and Jordan could talk for hours instead of seconds. If only she knew where Jordan *was.*

Her phone beeped. It was a Google Alert e-mail for The Preserve at Addison-Stevens, Ali's mental hospital—Emily had set up the alerts a while ago, just in case any pertinent news popped up about escaped patients who could potentially be Ali's secret boyfriend. This e-mail was a press release about a new therapy pool that had been built on the grounds. A picture had been included. Emily stared hard at the patients in the pool, their faces blurred. None of them had white-blond hair like Iris Taylor, the girl she'd busted out of The Preserve last week, chauffeuring her around Rosewood and asking her about Ali, who'd been Iris's old roommate. As far as Emily knew, Iris had returned to The Preserve after the prom. The Preserve didn't allow e-mail, texts, or phone calls, though, so Emily didn't know how she'd settled back in.

Emily paused. Hanna had known Iris during a short stint at The Preserve, and she'd seemed incredibly creepy— maybe even on Ali's team. But Emily had seen a different side of her—she was just a sad, insecure girl who needed someone to pay attention to her. In a world where nearly everyone Emily knew ended up not being what they seemed, it was nice that Iris had turned out to be not so bad. Suddenly, Emily kind of missed her.

A thought took shape in her mind. *Maybe we could go to The Preserve*, Hanna had suggested at the hospital. *Figure out if there was a guy patient whose name started with* N. Maybe Iris knew who that was. Delving back into the investigation scared Emily to death, but what if there was a vital clue sitting right under her nose?

She pulled out of the parking lot, charged with purpose. Instead of turning right, toward her family's development, she took a left that led her down a winding back road, past the farmhouses and the ice-cream stand, and up the long hill. Traffic was light, and she arrived at The Preserve at Addison-Stevens sooner than she'd estimated. As her car climbed the steep hill to the fortlike hospital, all stone and brick and pointy turrets, an ambulance passed, going the other direction. Emily shivered, wondering who was inside—and why.

She parked and strolled into the lobby, glancing at the

familiar planters and fountains. A man standing at the front desk smiled at her. "Good afternoon."

Emily nodded shakily. "I'm here to see Iris Taylor. I'm a friend. Emily Fields."

The man glanced at something on his screen, then frowned. "Iris is no longer a patient here."

Emily cocked her head. "What does that mean?" Had Iris's cruel parents checked her out? Had she been transferred to another hospital?

The man looked back and forth, then leaned toward her. "Since you're a friend, you should know. She's been missing from her bed since yesterday morning."

Emily blinked hard. *Missing?* Iris had been miserable here—maybe she'd escaped, just like she'd escaped with Emily last week. But something on the man's face seemed tense, as if he'd left something out. "I-is she okay?"

Another nurse came through the door just then, and the man clammed up. "It's a private matter," he said, glancing shiftily at the second nurse. "I'm sorry."

Emily hitched forward. "Can you tell me if there was a male patient in the teenage wing a few years ago whose name started with *N*? He was friends with, um, Courtney DiLaurentis."

The man's lips twitched. He glanced at Emily for a split second and then at the nurse who was standing close by. "I'm sorry," he whispered.

"You can't just let me look at a patient list for a second?" Emily pleaded. "It's important."

The second nurse cleared her throat loudly. The man gave her a helpless shrug.

Emily turned away, her mind spinning. Iris had seemed so optimistic about returning to The Preserve to recover for good. Why would she have left so soon?

A horrible thought struck her. Iris had given Emily and the others vital information about Ali. Did Ali *know*?

The automatic doors swished open, and Emily walked into the brick courtyard that led to the parking lot, her head spinning. Just as she passed the bench that bore the IN MEMORY OF TABITHA CLARK plaque, her phone beeped. She pulled it out of her pocket, hoping that somehow it was Iris, letting her know she was okay. But the text was from a jumble of letters and numbers. Emily's heart fell.

Are you done sniffing around, Scooby-Doo? Everyone you involve in this will get hurt. Including YOU. —A

5

A SECRET UNEARTHED

On Tuesday afternoon, Aria walked with her head down to journalism, her last class of the day. A gust of wind whipped bits of freshly mown grass, gum wrappers, and a girl's hair band across the Commons. For a second, when Aria looked up, she swore she saw Noel's loping figure crossing the green.

But of course it wasn't. At lunch today, she'd overheard a few lacrosse players mention that Noel had been released from the hospital and was chilling at home. Was he lonely? What was he watching on TV? Not that Aria would admit it to her friends, but she'd checked his Twitter incessantly. He hadn't posted since prom night.

An ache filled her. She missed Noel like crazy. And she hated herself for it.

She also hated the strange looks people had been giving her all day. Like the way Sean Ackard was staring at her right now: sort of half pity, half fear. After a pause,

Sean rushed up to her. "Here, Aria," he said, pressing something into her hands.

Aria stared down at it. *Rosewood Episcopal Youth Group Counseling for Troubled Teens.*

"I've heard . . . ," Sean began worriedly. "I just thought it might help." He started to say something else, then seemed to think better of it and turned to hurry away.

Aria shut her eyes. The suicide-pact rumors again. They'd circled the school shortly after the Eco Cruise—everyone thought the girls had a death wish for heading out on a lifeboat without a proper captain. And now, for some reason, the rumors had come back with a vengeance.

Aria crumpled the flyer into a ball and turned to the barn. Just as she touched the brass doorknob, someone yanked her from behind and pulled her around the corner. She yelped in protest, only to see that it was her brother.

"I've been looking for you," Mike said gruffly.

Aria lowered her eyes. Last night, when she got home from Wordsmith's Books, where she'd been staring at the same paragraph of *The Breakup Bible* all night, she'd found a note in Mike's handwriting on her bed: *Hanna told me everything. We need to talk.*

She'd called Hanna, furious. How could she have compromised Mike's safety, especially after they'd agreed to keep quiet? But Hanna hadn't answered her phone. A few minutes later, Mike had knocked on Aria's door, but she'd thrown the covers over her head and feigned snoring. This morning, she'd ducked out of the house for an early yoga class before Mike woke up. But not even *om* and downward dog had been able to calm her racing thoughts.

"I get why you didn't tell me anything," Mike said in a low voice. "But I can help. I mean, if Noel hung out with her as much as you guys say he did, maybe I picked up something I don't even realize." He made a face. "I can't believe he did that to you. That guy's dead to me."

Aria flinched, suddenly feeling defensive. She was grateful for her brother's loyalty, but she hadn't thought about Noel's actions impacting his other relationships, too. "Look, you need to stay out of it. If this *is* Ali, we don't know what she's capable of."

Mike furrowed his brow. "I'm not afraid of Ali. Bring it on."

If Aria were in a different mind-set, she might have snickered. Mike's attitude reminded her of when they were little and belonged to the Hollis outdoor pool. Mike, age five, would stand at the edge of the high diving board with his hands on his hips, proclaiming to everyone that nothing scared him. He'd never actually jump *off* the board, though. He'd climb back down the ladder, claiming he didn't want to get wet and ruin his swim trunks.

Aria stared at a far-off riding mower as it made a crisscross pattern on the soccer field. Usually the scent of freshly mowed grass cheered her up, but not today. "You know what I really want? To run away. To be completely anonymous."

"Do you really think Ali would let you do that?"

"No. And besides, everyone in this stupid country knows who I am." Aria glanced up just as, right on cue, the Channel 4 news van pulled into the student lot. There was probably a camera aimed at her that very second.

Mike pushed his hands into his pockets. "People in *other* countries probably don't, though."

"So?"

His blue eyes met hers. "Look, I'm not saying you should go. But when I was in your room last night, I saw the pamphlet on your desk. The one about Amsterdam."

It took Aria a few seconds to recall what he was talking about. It seemed like eons ago when she'd received the letter saying she was a finalist for an artist apprenticeship in Amsterdam. She'd written it off at the time, not wanting to be so far away from Noel.

"I don't know," Aria mumbled. "I probably wouldn't get in, anyway. And traveling seems pretty daunting right now."

Mike sniffed. "Says the girl who's dying to get back to Europe. It sounds awesome, and you know it. And maybe I'm being a little selfish. There's much less chance of Alison flying the whole way to Holland to get you. You'll be safer there."

Oh really? Aria thought. Ali had followed her to Iceland last summer, after all. But she considered it for a moment. It *would* be a great escape—not just from Ali and Helper A, but from the constant reminders of Noel and the relentless press. If Aria remembered correctly, the apprenticeship involved studying with a rotating group of up-and-coming artists. She'd help out in their studios and attend their shows, and there would be time to create her own art. She'd only been to Amsterdam once, for a few days, but she hadn't forgotten the narrow streets, the relaxed attitude, the huge park on the edge of town. Actually, it sort of sounded like heaven.

She pulled Mike into a fierce hug. "Okay. I'll give it a shot."

Mike frowned, looking conflicted. "If you get in, bring me over, too. I bet Amsterdam pot is way better than Colorado's."

Aria ruffled his hair. Ever since Colorado legalized marijuana, Mike had been fascinated with the place. "I promise to at least bring you for a visit," she teased. Then she swept past him into the journalism barn, which had better cell reception. She had an important call to make.

A few hours later, Aria got off SEPTA in Henley, a town ten miles closer to Philadelphia, famous for its liberal arts college and annual film festival. She took a right at the old hardware store on the main street and followed the road past a hospital to the Henley Languages Building. Students swept past her clutching their books and iPads. A bunch of kids congregated under a tree. A long-haired boy strummed a Beatles song near a coffee kiosk.

Aria's excitement swelled. When Aria had called from

school, Ella had given her the number for the apprenticeship's American contact. The contact had answered and
said that today was the second-to-last day for interviews,
and the person she was to speak with, an Agatha Janssen
at Henley's Department of Germanic Languages, had an
opening this afternoon. It seemed like kismet.

The languages building smelled musty and had a serious echo, and the wall tile was exactly like the kind in the
building that housed Aria and Noel's cooking class. She
felt a pang. Should she call him?

Of course not. He lied to you. She set her jaw and swished
the thought out of her mind. She should be thinking
instead about Amsterdam, and her new life. She hadn't
technically gotten the apprenticeship yet, but she wanted
to think positively. She couldn't wait to begin all sorts
of rituals in Holland that Noel would never be into, like
watching the sun rise every morning; seeing long, plotless
foreign films in which people do a lot of smoking and
lovemaking; and going to coffee shops to debate philoso-
phy. There.

Ms. Janssen's office was at the end of the hall. When
Aria knocked, an older woman with frizzy black hair and
wire-rim glasses, wearing what looked like a bunch of silk
scarves sewn together into a sacklike dress, flung open the
door. "Hello, Miss Montgomery!" she said in a Dutch
accent. "Come in, come in!"

The inside of the office smelled like apple pie. On
the wall were drawings of the dykes around Amsterdam

and a photo of a little girl in huge, yellow wooden shoes. "Thanks for seeing me on such short notice," Aria said, shrugging off her plaid spring jacket.

"Not a problem." Ms. Janssen tapped on the keyboard, her wooden bracelets knocking together. "As you know, I have the power to recommend a candidate. I've interviewed students from New York City, Boston, and Baltimore, but your portfolio is quite strong. And you know a little Dutch, so that's helpful."

"I learned when I was in Iceland," Aria boasted. "I lived there for a few years."

Ms. Janssen pushed a lock of hair behind her ears. "Well, the apprenticeship would be for two years. You'll be helping several artists, learning a great deal from each of them. Everyone who has done this apprenticeship has gone on to have a career in the art world in their own right."

"I know. It's a remarkable opportunity." Aria thought of the literature she'd reread this afternoon. The apprentices got to travel all through Europe with their artists.

The professor asked Aria some more questions about her influences, her strengths and weaknesses, and her knowledge of art history. With every question Aria answered, Ms. Janssen seemed more and more pleased, the smile lines at the corners of her eyes deepening. Not once did she bring up how Aria was a Pretty Little Liar. She seemed to know nothing of the stupid movie based on Aria's life, or how Aria had been on a cruise ship that caught fire, or that she'd witnessed Gayle Riggs's murder or found her boyfriend tied up in a storage shed only a few days before. In that little office, Aria was only a budding artist, nothing else. The Aria she *used* to be, before everything went wrong.

"I'll be honest with you," Ms. Janssen said after a while. "You seem quite promising. I'd like to recommend you."

"Really?" Aria squeaked, pressing her hand to her chest. "That's great!"

"I'm glad you think so. Now, let me start your formal application, which is right . . ." She trailed off as she looked out the window. *"Oh."*

Aria followed her gaze. Out the big picture window, she could see three police cars at the curb, their lights flashing. Two uniformed officers got out and marched into the building. Soon enough, footsteps echoed down the hall. Walkie-talkies squealed. As the voices grew closer and closer, Aria swore one of them said, *Montgomery.*

A slithery sensation crept down her back.

The door flung open, and two men walked into the office, eyes narrowed, muscles tensed. Ms. Janssen shrank back against the wall. "Can I help you?"

The man in front pointed at Aria. His jacket said FBI on the breast pocket. He had squinty eyes and a wad of fruity-smelling gum shoved into his mouth. "That's her."

The professor stared at Aria as though she'd morphed into a giant toad. "What's this about?"

"She's wanted for questioning in an international incident," the agent said stiffly.

Aria's throat went dry. "W-what do you mean?"

As if in answer, something made a *ping* inside her bag. Aria reached for her phone, her heart sinking. *One new message*, it said, followed by a jumble of letters and numbers.

Your dirty laundry, Aria? Time to get it dry-cleaned. —A

6

SPENCER GOES DOWNTOWN

At the same time on Tuesday, Spencer had just finished jogging five easy miles on the Marwyn Trail, an old train line turned nature walk. As she walked back to her car, pulling her hair up into a high ponytail, the wind stopped. The trail was clear of runners and bikers, but she swore she could see a human shape in the bushes. *Ali?*

A woman and three dogs appeared around the corner. A Rollerblader skated past, and a squirrel emerged from the bushes. Spencer pinched the inside of her palm. *Ali isn't everywhere.* Only, did she really believe that anymore?

She climbed into the car, drained a bottle of coconut water, and switched on the radio. The first thing she heard was Noel Kahn's name. She twisted the volume knob higher.

". . . Though Mr. Kahn survived his attack, he is among a growing number of victims in Rosewood, along with socialite Gayle Riggs, who was murdered in the driveway of her new Rosewood home, and Kyla Kennedy, a burn patient who was found dead behind the hospital," a deep baritone voice said. "New questions are swirling about a serial criminal on the loose. Authorities are also investigating a possible tie-in to the bombing of the *Splendor of the Seas* cruise ship a few weeks ago—students from Rosewood Day Prep and other surrounding schools were on board."

Spencer shifted jerkily into reverse, nearly taking out a goose. If only they could hand over their texts from A. The texts would clear up this serial-killer thing in no time.

She turned onto her street, drinking in the late spring splendor. Tons of flowers had bloomed, and cherry blossoms floated down from the sky. But when she saw the news vans in front of her house, she hit the brakes. She was about to back out of the street and drive somewhere else—*anywhere* else—when the reporters descended on the car.

"Ms. Hastings, please!" The reporters banged on her window. "Just a few questions! What led you to Noel Kahn's body?"

"Is it all just too much?" another reporter bellowed. "Are you girls thinking about killing yourselves?"

Spencer ducked her head and pulled into the driveway. The reporters had the good sense not to follow her, but they kept shouting. Mr. Pennythistle's Range Rover loomed in front of her. That was odd: It was just past four, and usually Mr. Pennythistle didn't get back from work until after six. And there was Mr. Pennythistle himself, standing on the porch, staring at Spencer as she drove in. Spencer's mother, who wore knee-length khaki shorts and an old polo shirt from the Four Seasons Hotel in St. Barts, stood next to him, her expression grave. Spencer's quasi stepsister, Amelia, sat on the steps, still in her St. Agnes school vest and plaid skirt—she was the only girl Spencer knew who wore her uniform after dismissal. There was a satisfied smirk on her face.

Spencer shifted into park and glanced at all three of them, feeling like something was up. "Uh, hi?" she asked cautiously as she walked up.

Mrs. Hastings guided her toward the door. "Good, you're home," she said through gritted teeth.

Spencer's heart did a somersault. "W-what's going on?"

Mrs. Hastings pulled her into the house. The family's two Labradoodles, Rufus and Beatrice, lumbered up to greet them, but Mrs. Hastings paid them no mind—which meant something *really* must be wrong. She looked at her fiancé. "*You* tell her."

Mr. Pennythistle, still in his business suit, sighed deeply and showed Spencer a picture on his phone. It was of a trashed living room. After a moment, Spencer recognized the heavy, copper-colored curtains and the marble-topped coffee table. "Your model home?" she squeaked. The model home had the panic room where she and her friends talked about A.

"A neighbor called last night," Mr. Pennythistle said gravely. "They walked by with their dog and saw smears all over the window and broken glass on the floors. And Amelia said she saw you stealing the model's keys from my office last week. Did you do this?"

Spencer shot a look at Amelia, who was now practically jumping up and down with glee. *Narc.* "Of course not. I mean—yes. I went into the model a few times. But I didn't trash it last night. I was *home* last night." She looked pleadingly at all of them, but then she realized—she'd been the *only* one home. Her mom and Mr. Pennythistle had gone to Amelia's orchestra performance.

Mr. Pennythistle cleared his throat, then flipped to the next photo. In this one, a tall blond girl stood in the corner of the living room, her gaze on the front door. It was *Spencer.*

"This is impossible," Spencer squeaked. "Someone Photoshopped me in."

Mr. Pennythistle cocked his head. "Who would have done that?"

"The real person who did it, I guess." Spencer sank onto the ottoman in the living room. And that, of course, was Ali or Helper A. But why? To send a message, loud and clear, that they'd always known what the girls were talking about in the panic room? To get her in trouble? She thought again of the presence she felt at the housing complex she and Chase had investigated. Maybe Ali *had* known they were there.

She handed the phone back to Mr. Pennythistle. "I know what this looks like. But it wasn't me. Honest. Call the police. Have them dust for prints on all the stuff that was trashed."

"That won't be necessary," Mr. Pennythistle said gruffly.

"Please?" Spencer begged. She *needed* him to do it—maybe Ali's prints would turn up.

Mrs. Hastings pressed the back of her hand to her forehead. "Spencer, do we need to get you another appointment with Dr. Evans?"

"No!" Spencer gasped. She and Melissa had visited Dr. Evans, a psychologist, last year, and though Spencer would love some headshrinking right now, going there and being forced to lie about most of her life seemed stressful. "I didn't trash the model, but I'll clean it up if that'll make you happy," she said wearily.

"Cleaning up the model is a good start," Mr. Pennythistle said stiffly.

Knock.

Everyone's head whipped up. Two shapes shifted behind the curtained windows. Mrs. Hastings lunged toward the door, her face a twist of fury. "I'm going to strangle those reporters."

"Is anyone there?" a stern, deep voice shouted. "It's the police."

Mrs. Hastings froze. Spencer stared at Mr. Pennythistle. "I thought you said you weren't going to call the cops," she whispered.

Mr. Pennythistle blinked. "I didn't."

He angled past Spencer's mom and gingerly opened the door. Two uniformed police officers stood on the porch. "I'm Officer Gates," the taller of the cops said, flashing his badge. Spencer recognized him: He was the same person who'd asked her questions about Noel at the hospital. Her stomach swirled.

Officer Gates gestured to the man next to him. "This is my partner, Officer Mulvaney. We need to take Spencer to the station to ask her a few questions about a crime we're investigating."

They glared at Spencer. She shrank back on the ottoman. Had they come here because they knew she'd *lied*?

"What crime?" Mrs. Hastings was now standing by the side table of the couch, clutching the large, jade bear statue she and Spencer's father had bought years ago in Japan.

Officer Mulvaney, who had steely gray eyes and thin lips, tucked his badge into his pocket. "We received an anonymous tip that Miss Hastings framed another girl for drug possession last summer."

Spencer's ears began to ring. *What?*

Mrs. Hastings burst out laughing. "My daughter doesn't do drugs. And she was at the University of Pennsylvania doing a very intensive pre-college program last summer."

The taller cop smirked. "The crime happened on the Penn campus."

Mrs. Hastings's cheek twitched. She looked at Spencer, whose head was spinning. *Anonymous tip. Drug charge.*

Ali.

Something in her face must have given her away, because Mrs. Hastings's expression drooped. "Spencer?"

It felt like a hockey-puck-sized lump had grown in Spencer's throat. All she pictured, suddenly, was a study session a few weeks into the pre-college program. Spencer and her friend Kelsey Pierce had sat on their beds in their dorm room, trying to cram too much information in their minds at once, and there had been a knock at the door. "Oh, thank *God*," Spencer had said, leaping up from the bed.

It was Phineas O'Connell, another student in the pre-college program—and their dealer. She threw her arms around Phineas's skinny frame, mussing his layered, emo-rock hair, and playfully poked fun at his vintage-looking Def Leppard T-shirt that had probably cost eighty bucks at Saks. And then she'd said in a serious voice, "Okay, hand 'em over."

Phineas had dropped two Easy As into her palm—one for her, one for Kelsey. Spencer had paid him, and then he'd waltzed out the door. Kelsey kowtowed. Spencer blew him kisses. Then they popped the pills, studied like mad, and aced the exams the next day.

No wonder Spencer sought a dealer off-campus after Phineas left, though that was what had led to her and Kelsey's arrest. Surely Phineas hadn't told the cops, though—he was just as guilty. Had Kelsey? Would the cops really believe someone from a mental hospital?

"I'm sure it's a mistake," she said shakily as she walked toward the cops. "But, um, I'll just answer their questions, okay?" She was eighteen, which meant she could go to the police station alone. There was no way she was having the discussion with her family right now. The longer she could hold off her mom from finding out the truth, the better.

As the cops walked her to the squad car, reporters outside the gate snapped photos and begged for comments. Over the din, Spencer heard her phone chime. She reached for it in her pocket and peered at the screen. As soon as she saw that the new text was anonymous, she wanted to smack herself. *Of course.*

This one was an easy A for me, Spence. You didn't think I was going to keep your secret to myself forever, did you?
—A

7

NO RESPECT FOR THE DEAD

Hanna had never been to the St. Bonaventure Church in Old City, Philadelphia, but it reminded her strongly of the Rosewood Abbey, where Ali's memorial service had been held. The air also smelled like incense, dried flowers, and musty, wet Bibles. The same pointy-faced icons leered at her from their high windows. An organ stood at the front of the church, phallic-looking pipes protruded from the back wall, and there were even the same song books in the little slots on the backs of the pews. Graham's closed casket stood at the front of the room. Hanna bit her lip and avoided looking at it.

Countless funeral goers filed wordlessly through the imposing doors and down the aisles. Hanna peered out the window again, taking in the police officers, reporters, and ogling pedestrians that clogged the busy city street. Beyond them, a crowd of middle-aged men and women marched up and down the front sidewalk, holding signs.

Hanna squinted before she stepped into the lobby. Were those . . . *protesters*? Their signs had pictures of cruise ships and bombs.

"Mr. Clark. Mr. Clark?"

Hanna swiveled around. A long-haired brunette holding a microphone chased a man across the lobby. When she caught up to him, he raised his face, and Hanna almost gasped.

It was Mr. Clark, Tabitha's father and Gayle Riggs's husband. There were bags under his eyes. His jowls were pronounced and sagging, and his gray hair was unkempt. It made sense why he was here: Graham and Tabitha had once dated.

Hanna sucked in her stomach, wanting to melt into the walls. Instantly, images of Aria shoving Tabitha off the roof of the hotel in Jamaica flashed in her mind. They might not have killed her, but they'd still hurt her badly.

"Mr. Clark, can you comment on your daughter's murder case?" the brunette asked, shoving a microphone at him.

Mr. Clark shook his head. "There is no case right now. No leads."

"The authorities are checking with other hotels nearby for footage from that night, yes?" the reporter pressed. "They've really found *nothing*?"

Mr. Clark shook his head.

"And what about Mr. Pratt's death?" the woman asked. "Do you have a comment on that?"

Mr. Clark shrugged. "It's open-and-shut medical malpractice. They found excess Roxanol in Graham's system. End of story."

"But . . ." The reporter fumbled with her microphone just as two muscled guys in suits appeared out of nowhere, grabbed her, and edged her out of the lobby. She was still screaming questions as she went. Mr. Clark wiped his brow, looking like he was going to burst into tears.

Roxanol? Hanna pulled out her phone and did a quick Google search. Apparently Roxanol was another name for morphine. It would have been easy for Ali to up his dosage and make it look like malpractice.

She felt a hand on her arm. "Hey."

Emily was dressed in rumpled black wool pants and a black V-neck sweater, and her red-gold hair was pulled off her makeup-free face, making her look scrubbed and young. She peered around the lobby. "Where are Aria and Spencer?"

"I don't know." Hanna slipped her phone back in her pocket. "I haven't heard from them."

Organ music began to play, and two clergymen lit candles at the front. Hanna and Emily shrugged at each other, then walked into the church and slid into seats halfway down the aisle. After she took off her jacket, Emily turned to Hanna. "Have you heard from A?"

Hanna shook her head. "But I told Mike."

Emily widened her eyes. "What? *Why?*"

An old woman in front of them turned around and gave them a sharp look. "Because he guessed, okay?" Hanna whispered. "And honestly, I think doing nothing is ridiculous."

"Do you think that, or does Mike?"

"Well, we both do. We talked about it a lot." Which wasn't exactly true—Hanna and Mike had done very *little* talking the day he'd guessed about A. Hanna allowed herself a moment to savor the delicious memory.

Then she turned back to Emily. "We might as well put targets on our backs to make it even easier for Ali and Helper A to kill us. I wish we could investigate this."

Emily crossed her arms over her chest. "Be careful what you wish for."

"What does that mean?"

The funeral goers mumbled a group-prayer response. Emily slid closer to Hanna. "I went to The Preserve yesterday."

Hanna's eyes lit up. "You asked about N?"

"I tried. They wouldn't tell me anything. I tried to see Iris, too, but she's disappeared."

Hanna frowned. "She escaped?"

Emily shrugged. "It didn't sound like it. I'm worried that Ali found out Iris helped us and did something to her. Especially after I got this."

She passed over her phone. Hanna read the text. *Everyone you involve in this will get hurt. Including YOU.*

"Shit," Hanna whispered.

"We have to stop digging," Emily said. "No more asking questions—for real."

"But what if it's too late? Ali knows how much we know. We had that suspect list. And I had to hand over Kyla's note to the cops." Hanna had done it yesterday, although she doubted they'd connect it to Ali.

"Well, we don't say anything else. We give up."

Hanna set her jaw. "I don't want to live in fear for the rest of my life! We can't let Ali control us forever!"

Emily curled her fist. "Didn't you see this text? Ali's going to come for us next!"

"Girls!" The old woman turned around and faced them. Her eyes were a rheumy blue, and she wore a bedazzled pin of a cat on the lapel of her black dress. "Have some respect!"

Hanna ducked her head and rolled her eyes.

The organist began to loudly play "Ave Maria," and Emily looked at Hanna again. "I really don't think we should be talking about this right now." She glanced around nervously. "What if Ali is *here*?"

When a hand touched her shoulder, Hanna jumped. A familiar police officer stood above her. It was Gates, the officer to whom she'd given Kyla's note. For a moment, she thought he was here as a mourner, but he was staring at her so intensely. "Hanna." He said it like a statement, not a question.

"Y-yes?" Hanna whispered.

Gates offered his arm. "You need to come with me."

At the exact same time, a skinny, dark-haired man in an FBI jacket appeared behind him. He was looking at Emily. "And you, Miss Fields."

People up and down the aisles stared. Emily nudged Hanna, and she staggered to her feet. Whispers swirled as she and Emily walked toward the nave. *Pretty Little Liar. Noel Kahn. Alison DiLaurentis. Suicide pact.*

Once the church doors shut, Hanna stared at Gates. "What's going on? Does this have to do with the note about Noel?"

Gates led Hanna out the door. "No, Hanna. It's not about that." He sounded almost sad.

They stepped out onto the sidewalk. Cars on Market Street slowed to a crawl. The reporters looked surprised, then sprinted toward the girls. "What's going on?" they shouted. "Is this because of Graham's death?" "Are you girls the serial killers?" "Officer, what did these girls do?"

"No comment," Gates growled, holding tightly to Hanna's arm.

They stopped at a black sedan parked at the curb. It had a removable siren on the front, and the blue lights were whirling. The Rosewood Police vehicle was parked farther down the curb, the engine still running.

The FBI agent opened the door for Emily and pushed her inside. Gates was about to do the same when he realized that a pickup truck had blocked him in. "Damn it," he cursed, looking around for the driver. No one came forward.

"Ride with us." The FBI agent walked hurriedly to the front seat of the sedan. "We're going to the same place, anyway."

Gates nodded, then gestured for Hanna to get into the back with Emily. She slid onto the leather seat. Gates slumped in the passenger seat and slammed the door as the car pulled onto Broad. The reporters followed them for almost a block, hurling questions. Hanna stared straight ahead, afraid she might burst into tears.

Beep.

Hanna fumbled for her bag. She lifted her phone out and looked at the screen. *One new e-mail.*

Take this, bitch! —A

The attached file contained a series of images. The first was a picture of a BMW crumpled against a tree. Though blurred by the rain, Hanna could easily make out her face in the driver's seat. The second image was of that same night, only Hanna was out of the car and talking on the phone. In the third image, Hanna was moving Madison Zeigler's body into the driver's seat where she'd just been. Somehow, the other girls weren't in the picture—it looked like Hanna was doing it alone. And of course the picture didn't show the car that had swerved into her lane, pushing her off the road.

Hanna placed her hand against her mouth.

Next to her, Emily quietly gasped. She was staring at

something on her phone, too. Hanna looked over, raising an eyebrow.

Emily showed Hanna the screen. On it was a picture of Emily and a pretty, dark-haired girl kissing on the deck of the cruise ship.

"Jordan?" Hanna whispered. Emily nodded miserably.

The FBI officer glanced at her in the rearview mirror. "We know you've been in touch with Katherine DeLong. Aiding and abetting is a crime."

"But I didn't do anything!" Emily cried.

Their phones beeped once more. Hanna looked down at the screens, both of them cheerfully flashing ONE NEW TEXT MESSAGE.

They both opened the message at the same time. Emily let out a small whimper. Hanna read it and winced.

Time to pay for your sins. —A

8

COMING CLEAN

Spencer had been sitting in a holding cell at the Philadelphia FBI branch office for more than an hour now. The room was small and dim, with a splintery table and absolutely nothing for her to do—they'd taken her phone and purse—except to pace back and forth. The only object in here was a plastic cup that had once been full of water. A heater rattled in the ceiling. The whole place smelled vaguely of grape Popsicles.

She made another lap around the room, her mind spinning. She didn't get why Officer Gates had brought her to the FBI. Shouldn't her crime be handled by local police? Or was drug possession a bigger thing? What if she was headed to federal prison? She shut her eyes, seeing her future at Princeton float down the drain. Of *course* this was Ali's next move. She'd been an idiot not to anticipate it.

The door swung open, and Spencer leapt to attention. Aria appeared. Officer Gates and a man with FBI emblazoned on his jacket in blue thread pushed Hanna and Emily inside as well.

A had gotten them, too.

Gates looked at Emily and Hanna. "Empty your pockets and give me your purses. I want your keys, phones, and any other personal items."

Hanna and Emily did as they were told. Aria just shrugged, seemingly already stripped of her belongings. Then the agents handed them cups of water and backed out of the room. The metal door closed with a *clunk*.

Everyone slumped down at the table. Spencer touched Emily's hand. "Jordan? Or Gayle?" she asked in a low voice.

Emily hung her head. "The FBI knows I was in touch with . . ." She trailed off. "What if they ask me where she is?"

"Do you *know* where Jordan is?" Spencer whispered.

Emily was about to answer, but then Spencer caught her arm and glanced around. *They might be listening*, she mouthed. A mirror hung on a far wall. For all she knew, the agents were observing them on the other side.

Emily shifted her chair closer and whispered into Spencer's ear. "I don't know where she is."

Aria cupped her hands around her mouth and spoke softly, too. "Well, at least you won't be extradited. I might spend the next twenty years in an Icelandic prison for breaking and entering and helping—even though the painting was a fake."

Hanna pushed her hair around her face and said in a low voice, "Guys, what if the press realizes why we're here?" Her eyes glinted with tears. "It's going to ruin my dad's campaign."

"My mom was there when the cops came for me." Spencer thought about the horrific scene at the house. "You should have seen the look on her face."

Emily looked shiftily back and forth. "Why now?"

Aria laid her head on the table. "Maybe I'm being punished for trying to get answers out of Noel."

"No, it's because I went to The Preserve," Emily insisted. Spencer looked at her, surprised. Emily filled her in.

"Maybe it's because I told Mike," Hanna murmured.

Spencer felt a lump in her throat. "I'm to blame, too. I tracked down the building from that surveillance photo. The one that had Ali in it."

Hanna's head whipped up. "You *did*? What happened?" Her voice rose in volume, and she clapped her mouth shut.

"Why didn't you say anything?" Aria said under her breath.

Spencer hunched her shoulders and looked at the others. "Ali wasn't there. I don't think she'd ever *been* there. I guess it was a trap all along."

"We never should have pursued any of this," Emily hissed. "Noel wasn't punishment enough—Ali needed to make *us* pay. And she had all the ammo she needed."

"I guess we just lost sight of everything A knew about us," Aria said softly.

Spencer looked around. "But why are we *here*, at the FBI? I mean, yes, Emily and Aria, it makes sense for you guys. But why did they bring *all* of us here? Why are we in the same room?"

Emily picked at her fingernail. "Well, you know who works for the FBI. Fuji."

Spencer pressed her tongue hard against the roof of her mouth. Jasmine Fuji was an FBI agent who'd been asking the girls questions about Tabitha Clark's death. *Jamaica?* she mouthed.

Aria looked around nervously. "Maybe they found out about . . . you know." She drew a *T* on the table with her finger. *T* for Tabitha.

"Maybe *Ali* told them," Emily said.

"But we have proof that we didn't do it," Hanna said. "Ali texted us and said *she* killed her. We'll just show them that."

"How can we?" Emily said, her eyes full of fear. She drew something on the table with her finger, too. The letter *A*.

Spencer knew what she meant. If they told about A, A might hurt someone else.

Aria sat back in the chair, making it creak. "I wish there was a way to talk but to remain protected. *Besides* the witness protection program."

Spencer licked her lips. "We could request immunity,"

she whispered. "Make them promise to protect us if we come forward about A."

Emily looked nervous. "But what if they say no . . . and then manipulate it out of us anyway?"

"Or what if they *say* they'll protect us but don't follow through with it?" Aria asked.

"Yeah, I don't think that sounds like a good plan," Hanna said, biting a nail.

"It *is* a good plan," Spencer insisted. "I see it on *Law and Order* all the time."

Footsteps rang out in the hall, growing closer. Then the door opened, and a woman walked through. Everyone jumped. "Hello, girls," a familiar brisk voice said.

It was Agent Fuji. She shut the door behind her. Spencer swallowed hard. This *was* about Tabitha.

Fuji's black hair was sleekly styled as usual, but there was something tired-looking about her face. When she pulled out a chair to sit, one of her nails broke. "Let's talk," she said. Fuji glanced at each of them as she sat down.

No one said a word. Hanna's hair hung in her face. Aria wiped tears with her sleeve. Spencer had picked away all the skin on the side of her thumbnail. She wondered if Fuji had heard everything.

Agent Fuji settled back in her chair and jingled her keys. Her keychain held a picture of a West Highland terrier with pink bows in its hair. Spencer hadn't pinned Fuji as the type who liked dogs.

Outside, another door slammed. A phone rang. A heater clicked on with a rattle. "Okay," Fuji said finally. "Hit and run. Aiding and abetting. Dating a fugitive. And international art theft. And it all comes out at once? It seems like an awful coincidence. You girls could face serious prison time. This will ruin your father's campaign, Hanna. If you've gotten accepted to colleges, they'll probably renege the offers. You're ruining your lives. Did you even think about that?"

No one dared to look at Fuji. Spencer's heart banged in her chest.

"I've been working with the state and local police forces on this Clark case, and I think there's stuff you're hiding from me about that, too." Fuji folded her hands. "You'd better start talking—about *something*."

Hanna shifted. Aria wiped another tear from her cheek. Spencer cleared her throat and glanced around the table. "Anderson Cooper," she said in a calm, even voice. Their secret code for Ali.

"Spence, I don't know." Aria looked pained.

Hanna gulped. "Yeah, maybe we should—"

"We *have* to," Spencer interrupted. "It's the only way. Just trust me on this."

Everyone clammed up. Fuji stared at them, waiting. Then Aria sighed. "Fine. Let's do it."

After a moment, Hanna ever-so-faintly nodded. Emily did, too. Spencer glanced around the room, seeing things for the very last time before they finally came clean about

Tabitha. Before their lives, possibly, changed forever. But she knew it was the right thing to do. They were drowning by themselves. They needed help.

She leaned forward and gazed at Fuji. "Look. We're not saying that what we did was right, but we messed up, and we're sorry about what we did. But there are reasons why we haven't come clean. And we *do* have more information on Tabitha, but we haven't been able to tell you."

"Why not?" Fuji asked sharply.

"Because it hasn't been safe," Spencer explained. "We're being threatened. What we know is really, really dangerous. So if we say something, we want something in return."

"Go on." Fuji folded her hands. "I'm listening."

"We need to make sure you'll keep us safe," Spencer said firmly. "We don't want anything to happen to us or our families."

Fuji nodded. "All right. We can arrange that."

"And we also want our charges dropped. Everything we did—the drugs, the theft, the secret communication with the fugitive, and the accident—it needs to be wiped clean from our records."

"Spencer!" Emily cried.

Aria covered her eyes.

But Spencer didn't apologize or renege the demand. She adopted the tactic she used when she used to play forward in field hockey: stare down your opponent during face-off. Don't let them see you sweat. Don't back down. "That's what we want. Can you do that for us?"

Fuji was the first to blink. "Okay. But whatever you have, it had better be good."

Spencer took a breath. She hadn't thought Fuji would actually go for it.

Then she explained what they knew, including how they'd accidentally pushed Tabitha off the balcony but didn't kill her. They couldn't tell anyone the truth, though, because of how it looked. *And* because someone was threatening them.

Agent Fuji tented her fingers. "So there's another A?"

Emily glanced at the others. "More than one, we think."

Fuji folded her hands. "And who do you think your stalker might be?"

Again, everyone exchanged a glance. Aria cleared her throat. "Alison," she said loudly.

Fuji widened her eyes. "I *see*."

Spencer launched into an explanation of exactly why they thought A was Ali and how all the pieces fit. "Wait a minute," Agent Fuji interrupted, when they got to that part about Emily's baby. "You think Alison killed Gayle Riggs?"

Spencer nodded.

Fuji squinted hard. "But in the police notes, you girls said it sounded like A spoke to the person who shot her."

"That's right," Emily said. "We heard Gayle talking to

someone. Kind of like, *What are* you *doing here?* And then there was the shot."

Fuji's brow furrowed. "So perhaps Gayle knew Alison?"

"Maybe," Spencer said. "Or maybe she knew her helper."

"Do you have any idea who her helper might be?"

The girls looked at one another. "We had a lot of theories," Spencer said. "Graham Pratt for a while. And then Noel Kahn."

"Noel?" Fuji cocked her head. "What does he have to do with this?"

Spencer opened her mouth to explain, but Aria caught her arm. "It was a false lead," she said quickly. A look flashed across her face that said, *Let's not rat out Noel right now.* Spencer just shrugged.

"This is really, *really* serious, girls," Fuji said. "We're talking about a serial killer. I'm glad you finally came to me about this—there's no way you can handle this on your own, and you shouldn't have to."

No one spoke. Spencer held her breath.

"With your permission, I'd like to keep your phones. I want to look at all of these texts A has sent. There are ways to track which phone they're being sent from, even from what part of the Philadelphia area. Give me any other evidence you can think of, too. Things these people might have touched. Places they might have been. We need every tip you can get."

Spencer brightened. "I think Ali and her helper trashed my stepfather's model home."

Fuji nodded. "Maybe there are fingerprints."

"I'm also worried that Ali might have done something to a girl named Iris Taylor," Emily added, explaining how Ali had known Iris and that Iris had gone missing after Emily asked her questions.

Fuji wrote Iris's name on a notepad. "We'll look into her."

Hanna tentatively raised a hand. "We have a lot more texts, but we'll have to get them off our old phones from home. We switched phones when we figured out A was tracking us."

"A lot of notes aren't on our phones at all," Spencer added, thinking of the very first missive they'd received from this A. It had been a postcard inside Ali's mailbox—*Jamaica is beautiful this time of year! Too bad you can't ever go back.*

"That's fine," Fuji said. "Collect everything and bring it back to me as soon as you can. And as far as security goes, you have my personal promise for a twenty-four-seven security team on all of you—*and* your families—until we crack the case. A won't be able to get to you anymore."

Aria blinked hard. "So you're really letting us *go*?"

Fuji nodded. "I'll talk to my partners and the state police and let them know that your charges are dropped."

"So my dad won't know about this?" Hanna bleated.

Emily's hands trembled. "I'm not in trouble with the FBI?"

"What you gave me is very important. I need to hold up

my end of the bargain," Fuji said as she stood. "However, if you receive another A note, I want you to forward it to me immediately. But I ask that you tell no one about what we're doing *or* why you have a security detail. The less people know, the better. Is that clear?"

"Yes," everyone said at the same time, though Hanna then raised a hand.

"My boyfriend knows," she admitted. "He kind of guessed."

Fuji winced. "Well, he'll be under watch because he's Aria's brother." She glanced around. "A, Alison, whoever it is, this is Tabitha's killer. Gayle's killer. Graham's and Kyla's killer. Obviously she's dangerous. I'm going to personally lead this team—and believe me, there will be a *team* on this. We're going to work day and night to find out what's going on. Whoever this is, they're not smarter than all of us. We'll get them."

Everyone exchanged another glance. "Oh my God," Hanna bleated. "That sounds . . ."

"*Awesome,*" Emily breathed.

They stared at one another in disbelief. Spencer glanced at Fuji, and the agent gave her a small, genuine smile, the first smile Spencer had ever seen from her. A delicious feeling washed down Spencer's back. Could it finally, *finally* be over? Was someone actually going to help them?

The girls stood up and hugged one another tight. They didn't have to handle this on their own anymore. They didn't have to look over their shoulders or freeze when they heard a footstep or a twig crack or cringe when their cell phones chimed. They wouldn't have to skulk around having secret conversations in dark places, fearing all the while that Ali was listening in.

Spencer threw back her head and laughed. It felt amazing, suddenly, to have power. If only Spencer knew how to reach Ali now, she'd send an anonymous note of her own: *Take that, bitch.*

9

WELCOME HOME

About an hour later, an FBI officer drove Emily back to the Philadelphia church where she'd parked her car for Graham's funeral, leaving Emily to drive the fifteen miles back to Rosewood alone.

Only, she *wasn't* alone. As she pulled onto the expressway toward the suburbs, she peeked in her rear-view mirror. A large, black Escalade switched lanes when she did. Fuji had instated the security detail immediately, instructing the bodyguards that they should watch the girls at all times, twenty-four hours a day. Emily's guard had introduced himself as Clarence, taking her hand in his meaty palms and giving it a good shake, then giving her a business card with his phone number on it. "Me or my partner will be outside day and night," he said in a New Jersey accent. "But if you get scared, you can always call us, too."

A huge smile spread across Emily's face, and she

drummed happily on the steering wheel. *If you get scared.* How many times had she been terrified and had no idea how to rectify it? She might be able to sleep through a whole night now. She might be able to go for a jog around her neighborhood without fearing an attack by a mysterious assailant.

Of course, she did feel a twinge of apprehension about everything that had happened. The cat was definitely out of the bag, and Ali would probably know soon. Her potential rage was terrifying—especially given her track record. Rehashing the past brought back memories about seeing Gayle's dead body in her driveway. And what if Ali *had* done something to Iris? At least the FBI was looking into it now . . . but what if Iris turned up dead?

Emily took the Rosewood exit off 76 and sped up the hill toward home. When she pulled into her driveway ten minutes later, her stomach flipped a few times. What if her parents somehow found out that the FBI had escorted her out of the funeral? Fuji insisted that they would keep everything very quiet, but there were all those reporters outside the church—could they have leaked the story? She really didn't feel like going through the third degree.

Nervously, she turned on KYW, the area's news channel. Over the sound of clacking typewriters, the reporter read out the hour's top story. A robbery on the north side. The mayor arguing over budget cuts. An accident on the Blue Route. Nothing about police activity. She breathed out.

She got out of the car and crept up the front walk, careful not to tread on her mom's freshly planted azaleas. The inside of the house was quiet. There were marks on the carpet that indicated it had just been vacuumed, and the dining room table was free of dust. When Emily sniffed, she smelled baked ziti. It was her sister Carolyn's favorite dish, but they hadn't had it since she'd left for college.

"Emily, look who's here!"

Her mother stepped into the hall. Next to her, in a Stanford long-sleeved T-shirt and black jeans, was Carolyn herself.

Emily blinked. The last time she'd seen her older sister was the day before she'd gone into the hospital for her C-section. Emily had been hunched over the toilet in Carolyn's dorm room—her morning sickness had lasted all nine months—and her sister had stood in the doorway, glaring at her with disdain. Emily had come clean to her parents about the baby not long ago, and her parents had forgiven her. Although they said Carolyn was going to call and apologize, too, her sister never had. Judging by the ambivalent look on her face, it didn't seem like she wanted to now, either.

Mrs. Fields pushed Carolyn closer. "Carolyn came home to see you."

Emily carefully dropped her backpack to the wood floor. "Really?"

Carolyn shrugged, a lock of red-gold hair falling in her face. "Well, all my exams were over. And I had a ticket voucher, so . . ."

"So, surprise!" Mrs. Fields said hurriedly. "Family needs to stick together, don't you agree, Carolyn?" She nudged her again. "Give Emily what you brought."

Carolyn's mouth twitched. She grabbed a plastic bag and pushed it in Emily's direction. Emily's hand closed on something cotton. It was the same Stanford T-shirt Carolyn was wearing.

"Thank you," Emily murmured as she held the shirt up to her chest.

Carolyn nodded stiffly. "It's a good color on you. And I figured it would fit now that . . ." She trailed off, but Emily knew what she was going to say. *Now that you're not pregnant.*

"Well!" Mrs. Fields clapped her hands. "I'll leave you two alone to catch up." She shot Carolyn an encouraging, hopeful smile, then disappeared into the kitchen. Emily sank into a chair in the living room, her nerves snappy.

Carolyn remained standing, her mouth twisted. She stared blankly at a picture of a barn that hung in the foyer like she'd never seen it before, even though it had probably hung in that spot for fifteen years. "I like my shirt," Emily said, patting the Stanford T-shirt in her lap. "Thanks again."

Carolyn shot her a look. "You're welcome."

She looked absolutely tortured. Emily crossed and uncrossed her legs. This felt like a disaster. What were they going to talk about? Why had her mom forced this? And seriously, Carolyn was *still* pissed? She needed to get over it.

"You can go upstairs if you want," Emily said. The words came out more bitterly than she intended. "You don't have to hang out with me."

Carolyn's mouth tightened. "I'm trying to make an effort, Emily. You don't have to be so mad."

"*I'm* mad?" Emily squeezed the chair's arms. Then she sighed. "Okay. Maybe I am kind of mad at you. For the millionth time, I'm sorry I forced my secret on you—I shouldn't have. But I wish you'd handled it differently."

Carolyn's eyes flashed. "I took you in," she said in a hushed voice. "I slipped you passes to the dining hall. I didn't tell Mom. What more did you want?"

Emily's heart beat faster and faster. "I hated coming home to your room. And I was *pregnant*—that AeroBed was so uncomfortable."

"You never complained," Carolyn said exasperatedly.

"I didn't feel like I *could*!" Emily exclaimed. "You made me feel so unwelcome!" Suddenly, she felt exhausted. She stood and turned toward the stairs. "Forget it. *I'll* go."

She curled her hand on the railing, fighting back tears. Just as she stomped on the first riser, Carolyn caught her arm. "Don't, okay? You're being silly."

Emily's spine stiffened. She didn't *feel* silly. *Five more minutes*, Emily decided. If her sister continued to be bitchy, she was definitely, definitely shutting herself in her room.

She sat back down in the same chair. Carolyn sat opposite her. A few seconds passed. Pots clanked in the kitchen. Silverware banged together.

"You're right. I just didn't know how to handle last summer," Carolyn finally said. "I was scared for you and the baby. I didn't want to think of it *as* a baby, either. I couldn't get attached—it just seemed too hard."

Emily bit her lip. "Yeah, well." It didn't sound like that great of an excuse.

Carolyn lowered her chin. "I heard you crying in the middle of the night so many times. . . ."

Emily stared absently at the Hummel figurines her mother collected in the large curio cabinet in the corner. She remembered crying all too well. At least she'd had Derrick, her friend who worked with her at the seafood restaurant on Penn's Landing. He'd served as sort of a substitute Carolyn.

"She's supposed to be family," she'd moaned to him once. "But she can't even *look* at me. The other night, she was on the phone well past one thirty, with me on the floor next to her. I was so tired, and she knew it, but she didn't hang up."

"Why don't you stay with me?" Derrick had offered. "I'll crash on the couch. It's fine."

Emily had looked at him. Derrick was so tall that when he sat on the bench, his long limbs folded up in an awkward, insectlike way. He was looking at her intently and kindly from behind his wire-rimmed glasses.

She'd considered taking him up on his offer, but then she'd shrugged. "No. I'm probably already making your life miserable by dumping all this on you." She'd kissed him on the cheek. "You're sweet, though."

Now Carolyn sighed. "The things you were dealing with were over my head."

Emily nodded. There was no arguing that. "So why are you here now? Why didn't you just stay away?"

Carolyn looked away. "I got a letter. I was afraid if I didn't come home this time, it might be too late."

A shiver danced up Emily's spine. "What are you talking about? Who wrote you a letter?"

"I don't know. It was just signed *A Concerned Friend*." Carolyn's throat bobbed. "It said you seemed really upset and might do something . . . irrational." Her eyelashes fluttered fast. "I was afraid I'd never see you again."

Emily's skin prickled. It wasn't the first time she'd heard the suicide rumors, but a letter seemed pretty extreme. "A lot of upsetting things have happened to me, but I'm really okay," she assured Carolyn.

Her sister looked unconvinced. "Are you sure?"

"Of course I'm sure." Emily's throat caught, knowing

she had to choose the next words very carefully. "I'd like to see the note, though. Do you still have it?"

Carolyn's brow crinkled. "I threw it away. I couldn't stand it being in my room."

"Was it handwritten? Did it have a postmark?"

"No, it was typed. I don't remember where it was mailed from." Carolyn gazed at her curiously. "Do you know who might have written it?"

Emily ran her tongue over her teeth. *A Concerned Friend.* Ali? Her helper? Who else could it be?

Mrs. Fields popped her head into the hall. "Dinner's ready!" she crowed.

Emily and Carolyn turned toward the kitchen. Emily's heart was still banging from the argument, but at least it was all finally out in the open. She snuck a look at Carolyn as they walked into the hall. Carolyn shot her a small, tentative smile. When Emily moved toward her and spread out her arms for a hug, Carolyn didn't dart away. The hug was kind of stiff and awkward, but it felt like a step in the right direction.

Mrs. Fields passed around plates. Then, something out the window caught Emily's eye. The black SUV was parked alongside the curb. Clarence sat in the front seat, reading the newspaper. A car drove past, and he lowered the paper and stared hard at it until it rounded the bend.

None of Emily's family noticed it there. They would, eventually—Emily would have to tell Clarence to park in a more secluded location. But for now, she appreciated his close range. *Stay out*, Clarence was telling Ali, who was surely watching. *From now on, she's off-limits.*

That felt like a step in the right direction, too.

10

A BRAND-NEW DAY

When the squad car pulled up to Aria's mother's house, the mowing service was just finishing up. Two brawny, college-age boys loaded the lawn mowers onto the trailer behind their truck. The boys waved to Aria like it was completely normal that she was getting out of a police car on a Tuesday evening.

"Do you want an escort to your door, Miss Montgomery?" the cop who had driven her asked, looking right and left cautiously.

"That's okay," Aria answered.

"Well, if you need anything at all, just signal Buzz." The cop gestured to a minivan parked on the street. Though it had a bumper sticker that read MY CHILD IS A ROSEWOOD ELEMENTARY HONOR STUDENT and a pair of Mickey ears on the antenna, a brawny guy in sunglasses who looked like The Rock's stunt double sat in the driver's seat.

"Got it." Aria smiled. She felt almost airy as she walked across the front lawn.

"Aria?"

Ella stood on the porch. She was wearing the yellow, zigzagged tunic she'd owned since her days in art school, and her silvery-black hair was tied up on top of her head in a bun. There was a horrified expression on her face. "Why did the police just drop you off?" she asked, staring at the cruiser that disappeared down the street.

"Oh, that." Aria waved her hand. "It's nothing. I'm not in trouble."

Ella blinked hard. "You had your interview today, right? Did something happen at the college?"

"Hey, it smells really good in here!" Aria said loudly as she walked into the foyer, hoping to change the subject. "Did you just bake some bread?"

Ella pushed the door closed. "Aria, tell me what's going on. *Now.*"

Aria let out a long sigh. "It's a long story, but I'm not in trouble. Really. And I did have the interview . . . but I blew it."

Ella cocked her head. "What happened?"

Aria shrugged. "I wasn't the right fit." She slumped down on the couch. "I really wanted to go, too."

Ella sat down next to her and gathered Polo, the family's cat, into her arms. "*Why* did you want to go, exactly?"

Aria gave her mom an *uh-duh* look. "Because art is the field I want to go into. Because I'd get to meet amazing people and help out with cool projects. Because . . ."

Ella placed her hand on Aria's knee. "But couldn't you do those things in New York? Philly? Rosewood, even? Why did you have to go all the way to Holland?"

Aria studied Ella's piercing blue eyes and questioning expression. "Does this have anything to do with Noel?" Ella went on. "Mike told me you two broke up. That Noel lied to you."

Aria's jaw twitched. Said like that, it sounded so . . . harsh. Awful. But then, maybe it was kind of the truth. Even if Noel hadn't done anything with Ali, he'd still lied.

She shut her eyes, thinking yet again of Noel. Sometime between when she'd gone to the police station and when she'd been released, he'd sent her a message that said, *How are you?* She doubted he had any idea what was happening to her; it was just a coincidence. On the ride home, she'd composed a text back.

But she hadn't sent it. She needed to move on, right?

She stared across the room at a table that held framed family photos. Long ago, Ella had removed the ones that had Byron in them, so now they were mostly of Aria and Mike, with a random one of Aria's ancient great-grandma Hilda. "How did you feel when you found out about Dad's thing with Meredith?" she asked.

Ella groaned and sat back against the pillows. "Awful. I wanted to run away, too. But I didn't."

"Of course you didn't. You had me and Mike."

"*You* have me and Mike, too," Ella said firmly. "And your dad and Lola. We still need you." She cleared her throat. "I've heard some other things, too, honey." She took Aria's hands. "You're not thinking of . . . *hurting* yourself, are you?"

There were tears in her eyes. Her voice was so tender. Aria lowered her shoulders, hating those stupid suicide rumors. "Of course not," she said softly. "I'm stronger than that."

"I thought so," Ella said, her voice trembling a little. "I just wanted to make sure."

Aria snuggled into her shoulder. Ella's gauzy blouse smelled like patchouli oil. She stroked Aria's hair, the same way she used to do when Aria was younger and afraid to go to sleep because she thought a giant eel lived in her closet.

"I'm sorry about Noel, honey," her mom said softly. "And I know not going to Holland seems like a setback. But you're resilient. *And* you don't need to go to some faraway country to be happy. You can find an amazing art scene here in Rosewood."

Aria sniffed. "Yeah, *right*." Rosewood's idea of cutting-edge art was painting the apples in a still life *slightly* off-red, the pears a marginally unnatural shade of green.

"I think I know of something that might cheer you up.

There's an opening for a part-time assistant at the gallery. If you want the job, it's yours."

Aria resisted the urge to snicker. Her mother worked at an art gallery in Hollis that sold tame, tepid landscapes of old Pennsylvania barns and detailed paintings of local birds. Aria got a headache every time she went in there because the place smelled overwhelmingly like the Yankee Candle store that was next door.

"It'll be good for you to be around people," Ella urged. "And bring your portfolio—maybe Jim will frame one of your pieces and give you a mini-show."

Maybe Ella had a point. A job would give her something to do in the afternoons—she had so many hours to fill now that she and Noel weren't together. And though Aria hated the idea of someone buying one of her paintings and hanging it next to a hokey Amish hex sign, she *did* like the idea of selling her work.

"Okay, I guess I could do that," she said.

"Great." Ella went to stand, then paused and looked at Aria again. "And you're positive I don't have to worry about the cop car?"

Aria pretended to be interested in the psychedelic swirls on the couch. "Of course not," she mumbled.

"Good!" Ella pretended to wipe her brow. "I've got enough gray hairs as it is!"

Aria managed a chuckle. Ella was using that gray-hair line on the kids long before Aria was ever getting tormented by A. But this time, she was pretty sure she could hold up her side of the bargain. From now on, there would be no drama. No trouble. No lies.

And maybe, now that A was out of her hands, Ella would get her wish.

11

ONE MAN'S TRASH . . .

On Wednesday afternoon, Spencer and Chase stood on the lawn of Mr. Pennythistle's model home. It had carefully trimmed hedges and a weed-free front walk. Daffodils exploded out of ceramic pots by the door. Birds chirped from the branches of the big oak on the front lawn. The only eyesore was the yellow police tape across the front door.

Spencer walked up to it and moved it aside. Then she looked at Chase. "Are you sure you want to help? It's a huge mess in there."

"Of course," Chase insisted, walking up to the house and gingerly stepping over the police tape. "That's why I'm *here*, Spencer." Chase had called her this morning, asking what she'd been up to, and the whole story of her arrest had spilled out of Spencer before she could stop herself. He had insisted on driving out to Rosewood to comfort her, which Spencer had to admit felt . . . well, comforting.

Spencer reached for the keys Mr. Pennythistle had left for her earlier that day, but as she was about to push them into the lock, the door swung open. She froze, listening for whoever might be inside. Then she glanced over her shoulder at the tough-looking security guy behind the wheel of the SUV. He was staring straight ahead, impassive behind his dark sunglasses.

"Hello?" Spencer called into the house, her heart pounding.

"Hello?" a voice called back.

There were footsteps, and Officer Gates stepped into the living room, navigating around the four couch cushions that lay on the floor and the tipped-over furniture. He blinked at Spencer. "What are you doing here?"

"I'm supposed to clean up," Spencer answered. "What are *you* doing here?"

"Dusting for prints." Gates held up his palms; he was wearing plastic gloves. "The forensic team just left. I'm heading out, too."

Spencer's heart lifted. Fuji was taking her seriously. Gates was searching for Ali.

"Did you find anything?" she asked eagerly.

Gates ran his hand over his bristly red hair. "A few prints here and there, but nothing conclusive." His cell phone bleated out a calypso ringtone, and he held up a finger to Spencer. "Hello?" he said into the speaker. After a moment, he added, "I'm on my way."

He turned back to Spencer. "Family emergency, sorry.

I bagged a couple of things as evidence, but I'm not sure it's going to give us much." He cast an uncertain look at Chase. "Anyway, we're done here. You can start cleaning up the place." He nodded at Spencer and strode out of the house.

Spencer shut the door behind him, leaned against the wall, and heaved a huge sigh. "Well, that's disappointing." She looked around the room. Though she'd come and gone from this place several times while the girls were investigating Ali, it looked so different now. Desk drawers hung open, and there were crayon slashes all over the walls. There was a big crack in the glass on the grandfather clock. A ceiling light had been pulled out of the plaster, the wires dangling. "How is it that there's no trace of Ali *anywhere*?"

Chase poked his head into the kitchen, which had broken glass on the floors and trash strewn everywhere. It smelled like rotten milk. "Ali's wickedly smart. I'm sure she thought everything through before trashing this place." He cleared his throat. "That cop was looking at me as though he thought *I* did it."

"No, he just didn't want to say anything about Ali," Spencer assured him, picking up a flattened Coke can and dropping it into the trash. "They don't want us to tell anyone else." She paused, peering at him. "Are *you* okay with knowing? It could be dangerous."

Chase shrugged. "It's not like you told me anything I didn't already know. I'll be fine."

Spencer turned back toward the door to get the cleaning supplies from the car. "I guess we should get this over with, huh?"

"Wait a sec," Chase called from the kitchen. "C'mere."

He was standing in the middle of the kitchen, gesturing at the ceramic tile floor. Nestled between broken pieces of plates and glass was something shiny.

Spencer knelt to pick it up and frowned, holding it up to the light. It was a silver keychain, minus the key. An Acura emblem was etched into the metal. "I can't believe Gates missed this," she murmured. "Do you think it's Ali's?"

"Maybe," Chase said. "Or maybe it's her helper's."

Spencer pulled out her phone. Her finger hesitated on Fuji's number, but she dialed Hanna instead.

"Do we know anyone who drives an Acura?" she asked when Hanna answered.

Hanna didn't miss a beat. "Scott Chin. Mason Byers. My mom's divorce lawyer. One of my neighbors. That lady who—"

"Whoa," Spencer interrupted. "I didn't realize you knew every Acura driver in Rosewood."

"They're nice cars," Hanna answered matter-of-factly. "Why do you want to know?"

Spencer explained what she'd just found. "Could her helper be one of those people? Scott Chin doesn't make sense as Ali's secret boyfriend—he's gay. I'm not sure Mason does, either—he moved here in sixth grade, remember? And he and Ali never seemed to get along."

"Spence, weren't we *just* at the police station turning over the case to a team of professionals? Hand the keychain over to Fuji and forget about it."

Spencer knew Hanna was right, but it was more difficult to relinquish control than she realized. At school, when they had to do group projects, Spencer always insisted on doing most of the work. *The others will just screw it up*, she always thought. *They won't do it as well as I can.*

Still, she dutifully stuffed the keychain into her bag, making a mental note to call Fuji when she and Chase were finished cleaning. Hanna was right. She didn't have to worry about this anymore. It was off her plate—and that was a *good* thing.

She canvassed the rest of the model home, sifting among the stuffing fluff and shredded newspaper and yards of toilet paper wound around the chandelier, but found no other clues.

There was a knock at the door, and Spencer froze again. "Yoo-hoo?" Spencer's mother's voice called into the living room. "Spencer? Are you there?"

Frowning, Spencer padded toward the front door. Her mother, Mr. Pennythistle, and Amelia stood in the foyer, all dressed in jeans and T-shirts. They were all holding brooms, mops, and the cleaning supplies from Spencer's backseat.

"What's going on?" Spencer asked. Had they come over to urge her to clean faster?

Mrs. Hastings tied her short blond hair back with

a stretchy headband. "We're going to help you clean, honey."

"R-really?" Spencer stammered.

Mrs. Hastings ran her finger along the crayon marks on the walls. Some of it came off on her skin. "It's not fair for you to have to do it yourself. I'm not saying it was right that you took Nicholas's keys without his permission, but it was unfair of us to assume that you were the one who did this to the place."

Mr. Pennythistle clapped her on the shoulder. "You *were* home the night this place was trashed—I checked the security video in the house. I'm sorry I doubted you."

Maybe Spencer should have been more bothered that he didn't take her at her word, but it felt like too much emotional effort. She kind of liked the stern way he was looking at Amelia right now, too. "I'm sorry for telling on you," Amelia muttered, after he nudged her.

"And the police explained that your drug arrest was a mistake," Mrs. Hastings added as she scrubbed the wall with a Mr. Clean Magic Eraser. "Thank *God*."

"Oh," Spencer said. "Well, good."

"Anyway, let's get to work!" Mrs. Hastings handed Amelia a broom. Then she stopped and noticed Chase in the kitchen. "Oh. Hello."

"This is my friend Chase," Spencer said. "*Another* Chase," she added, realizing that her mom was introduced to Curtis as Chase when he'd picked her up for the prom. "He's helping me clean."

"How nice!" Mrs. Hastings trilled, shooting him a kind smile. "Well. Any friend of Spencer's is a friend of ours."

Spencer almost snickered. *Someone* certainly felt guilty for assuming false blame. Spencer was just happy that her mom was here, helping, and that she didn't hate her.

Mr. Pennythistle plugged in the vacuum and turned it on. Amelia begrudgingly picked up the couch cushions and crammed the salvageable stuffing back inside. Spencer shot Chase a secret smile as she began to sweep up the broken glass with the broom. She was glad he was here, too. All of a sudden, everything felt—well, not perfect, but better than it had in a long time.

Just the way she liked it.

12

DADDY'S LITTLE HANNA

Hanna was heading back from Wawa, where she'd gotten a loaded-with-sugar, totally-adding-inches-to-her-thighs, irresistibly delicious cappuccino. Between sips, she glanced in her rearview mirror at the black Suburban behind her. She waved to Bo, the driver, and he waved back. Though Bo had a broken nose, ripped muscles, and flame tattoos peeking over his collar, earlier, when Hanna had sauntered over to the car to ask if he wanted anything to drink, he'd been listening to Selena Gomez. He also had a picture of his little girl, Gracie, hanging from his rearview mirror.

Her phone beeped. At a stoplight, she pulled it out. GOOGLE ALERT FOR TABITHA CLARK, read the screen. Her heart jumped.

But it was only an article about how the authorities were trying to get video footage from other hotels near The Cliffs—apparently, some of the hotels were having trouble locating footage from that long ago.

Her phone rang. MIKE, said the caller ID. She pressed the button on the steering wheel to activate Bluetooth. "Is your dude on your tail?" he asked without saying hello.

"Yep," Hanna answered in a chipper voice.

"Mine, too!" Mike sang. "It totally rocks. Do you think he's carrying a flamethrower?"

Hanna snorted. "This isn't a superhero movie."

Mike made a disappointed sound, which Hanna found totally adorable. She was thrilled that Fuji had put security on him, too. With Noel almost dying and Iris going missing, Mike would have probably been next on Ali's list.

"So I drove by the burn clinic, and it was swarming with cops," Mike said. "That means they're probably looking for Ali clues, don't you think?"

"Probably," Hanna said. The cops would surely find traces of Ali in no time. There was lots of DNA evidence—hairs, skin follicles, drawn blood—from her time as Kyla. "Are there tons of news vans?"

"Yeah, but I heard a report. The cops gave a statement that Kyla's killer was an escaped mental patient. They aren't breathing a word about Ali."

"That's good," Hanna said, relieved.

Then Mike cleared his throat awkwardly. The phone line crackled. "So . . . are you feeling okay?"

Hanna giggled. "You mean, like, am I *sore*?" She and Mike had been able to steal some time last night together when her mom wasn't home. They hadn't left Hanna's bed for two hours.

"No . . ." Mike cleared his throat. "I was worried after your text."

"What text?" Hanna hadn't texted all day.

"Uh, the one that said you were having a really bad morning and you wanted to kill yourself?"

"What?" Hanna hit the brakes hard, and the Prius made a squealing sound. Her bodyguard almost rammed her bumper. "You got a note that said that from *my* phone?"

"Uh, yeah. At about eight forty-five."

Hanna's mind spun. She was in English then. *Not* thinking about killing herself.

She pulled over and yanked up the clutch. The Suburban pulled over, too. "Mike, I didn't write that. Someone must have gotten hold of my phone and sent you a text just to mess with us."

Static crackled on the other end. "The thing is, Hanna, it's not the first time I've heard about you guys wanting to kill yourselves. The rumors are everywhere. And you *do* have a lot going on. You'd tell me if something was bothering you that much, right?"

Hanna rested her forehead against the steering wheel. The interior of the car suddenly smelled overwhelmingly like coffee. "I'm not even dignifying that with a response. You need to forward that note to Agent Fuji."

She gave him Fuji's information, then hung up. As she pulled back into traffic, her head was pounding like it had the time she and Mona Vanderwaal, her old-best-friend-turned-lunatic, had drank too much Patrón Silver. Why would A send Mike a fake suicide note?

But when she pulled into the driveway of her father's new house, her worries took a sharp turn. Something had occurred to her last night, after everything at the police station went down. Ali and Helper A weren't going to sit idly by once they found out the girls had involved the cops. Even if all their charges had been dropped, police could do nothing to prevent the A-team from spilling their secrets to the public. And if A released Hanna's car-crash photos, her dad's future would be over.

Hanna had to do damage control, and fast. She parked under the weeping willow and stared at her dad's new house, mustering up the courage.

Legs shaking, she pushed through the door into the house. She glanced at herself in the big mirror in the powder room just off the pantry. Her auburn hair was bouncy and full, her eyes were bright, and her makeup was perfect. At least she *looked* fabulous.

Her dad and Isabel, his new wife, were in the kitchen. Isabel, whose skin had paled considerably in the past few months—she used to fake-tan nonstop, but Hanna suspected campaign advisers had told her she looked too orange on camera—was loading dishes into the dishwasher. Mr. Marin was at the island, flipping through pictures. He looked up at her and smiled broadly. "Hanna!" he cried, as if he hadn't seen her in months. "How *are* you?"

Hanna gave him a suspicious look. It wasn't every day

that her dad was so happy to see her. *Don't tell him*, a voice in her head goaded.

But she *had* to . . . before A did.

She walked over to him. "Dad, I need to talk to you."

He sat back on the stool, looking suddenly scared. Isabel paused at the sink. "What's going on?" she asked.

Hanna glared at her. "I said I wanted to talk to my dad, not you."

Mr. Marin glanced at Isabel uncertainly, then back at Hanna. "Whatever you have to tell me you can say in front of Isabel."

Hanna squeezed her eyes shut. Seconds later, there were footsteps in the hall, and Hanna's stepsister, Kate, appeared, her hair wet from the shower. *Perfect.* The whole family was here to listen to her latest screwup.

"Hanna?" Mr. Marin encouraged gently. "What's up?"

Hanna bit the inside of her cheek. *Say it.* "I've been keeping something from you," she said quietly. "Something I did last June."

She couldn't look at her dad as the words spilled out of her mouth. She could literally feel his confusion leading to shock leading to disappointment. Isabel made little gasps. At one point, she even grabbed her chest like she was having a heart attack.

"And you're telling me this . . . *why*?" her father said, when Hanna was finished.

Hanna paused. She couldn't tell him about A. "Well, a few people know about it. And if they wanted to ruin your campaign, they could tell on me." She swallowed hard. "I thought I was doing the right thing at the time—Madison was *so* drunk. If she drove herself home, she would have definitely gotten hurt—and hurt someone else, too. And, I mean, someone swerved into my lane—I didn't know what to do. But when I crashed, I freaked. And I didn't stand and take the rap because I wanted to protect you and your campaign. I know now that was wrong, though."

Isabel slapped her sides. "Wrong?" she squealed. "Hanna, it's beyond wrong. You've been nothing but a burden for this campaign. Do you realize that every step of the way, we've had to do damage control for the trouble you've gotten yourself into? Do you know how much money we've spent to clean up your messes?"

"I'm sorry," Hanna squeaked, tears coming to her eyes.

Isabel turned to Hanna's father. "I told you this would happen. I told you it was a bad idea to bring Hanna back into your life."

"Isabel . . ." Mr. Marin looked torn.

Isabel's eyes widened. "I know you think it, too! I know you wish you were rid of her as much as I do!"

Hanna gasped.

"Mom!" Kate's voice rang out through the room. "Hanna is his *daughter*!"

"Kate's right," Mr. Marin said.

Hanna sucked in her stomach. Isabel looked like she'd been slapped.

Mr. Marin ran a hand over his forehead. "Hanna, I'd

be lying if I told you what you did is not upsetting on a lot of levels. But it doesn't matter. It's done. I just want you to be okay."

Isabel marched over him. "Tom, what are you talking about? You can't let her get away with this."

Even Hanna was amazed. She thought her dad would yell at her, kick her out, something.

Her father peeked at her from behind the hand that covered his face. "I thought you were going to tell me something else." He looked guilty. "I received a letter this morning. My head is still spinning. It said you wanted to commit suicide."

"Oh my God," Kate gasped. "Hanna!"

Hanna opened and closed her mouth. First Mike, now her dad? This was getting ridiculous.

"I called your mom, but she said you weren't home. I called your cell phone—twice—but you didn't pick up."

Hanna twisted her mouth. She'd seen those calls from her dad. She hadn't answered because she wasn't prepared quite yet to talk to him.

"I was so worried you were going to . . ." He trailed off, pressing his lips together. His chin wobbled, and his throat bobbed as he swallowed.

Isabel shifted in the corner. There was a disgruntled look on her face, but she didn't say anything.

"Dad, I'm okay," Hanna said softly, walking toward him and wrapping her arms around his shoulders.

Mr. Marin squeezed her tight. "I just want you to be

happy," he said in a thick voice. "And if this accident was part of why you wrote that note, if you were afraid about telling me or how I'd react, don't worry about it." He sniffed hard. "I've probably been too focused on the campaign. Maybe I should withdraw."

"Tom, have you lost your mind?" Isabel screeched.

Hanna pulled back from her father. The right thing to do was to come clean that she'd never intended on killing herself, but his attention felt so good. Besides, she *did* feel overwhelmed. She *did* need his help.

And though she was dying to ask her dad to see the note, she didn't want to raise his suspicion that there could be a new A.

"Don't pull out of the campaign," she told him instead. "I'm fine, I promise. And I'm sorry, again. Whatever I can do to make this right, I'll do it."

Mr. Marin patted Hanna on the back. Isabel's face got redder and redder, and finally she let out a closemouthed groan and stormed out of the room. Kate fidgeted in the doorway. Hanna locked eyes with her and shot her a grateful smile. What she really wanted to do was to give her stepsister a hug, but she was still afraid to leave her father's grasp.

Mr. Marin's eyes were red and watery; Hanna hadn't seen him cry in a long, long time. "I think it would be good if you made amends with the girl. What was her name, Madison?"

Hanna nodded. "I didn't know how to find her until a

few weeks ago. Her cousin is Naomi Zeigler, though, from school." She figured her father would remember Naomi—Hanna used to complain about her when she and her dad talked. "She could tell me how to get in touch with Madison."

"Okay. I want you to reach out to Madison's family and go to see her. After that, I'm thinking you and I do a public service announcement about drinking and driving. If you're amenable, that is."

Hanna squinted. "What do you mean?"

"You admit what you did on TV. We do the media circuit talking about it."

"You want to call *attention* to this?" Maybe her father *had* lost his mind.

"We'll be drawing attention in the right way. Remember, one of my issues is underage drinking. If you're comfortable with it, you can tell your story and support the stricter underage-drinking penalties I want to enforce."

Hanna twisted her mouth. Only losers wanted drinking laws to be *stricter.* But she couldn't very well say that right now. "Okay. I guess I can do that."

"Then we have a plan." Mr. Marin's gray eyes canvassed her face. "Oh, Hanna. I almost lost you."

There was a huge lump in Hanna's throat. *You* did *lose me*, she wanted to remind him. He lost her when he up and left Hanna and her mom, found Isabel, and started a new life. But whatever. Maybe that didn't matter anymore.

Mr. Marin opened his arms. "Come here."

Hanna hugged him and laid her chin on his chest, inhaling the smell of detergent and soap. She smiled into his scratchy sweater. *Here* was the release she'd been waiting for after they confessed to the police. Nothing felt snagged in her brain anymore. No troubles poked her like splinters, stopping her in her tracks.

But then something caught her eye out the window. She turned just as a shadow slipped out of sight. Had it been Ali, listening? Helper A, monitoring? Then she remembered it didn't matter if they were. She stood up straighter and stared through the glass, then stuck out her tongue and rolled her eyes. *Take that*, she mouthed.

It felt so frickin' good.

13

THE WINGED HORSE

That Wednesday night, Emily changed into a Marple Newtown Relay Carnival T-shirt and a pair of Victoria's Secret Pink sweats, her favorite pajama combo. Just as she was pulling back the covers of her twin bed, she felt a presence in the doorway. She yelped and whirled around, half certain it was A. Carolyn backed away.

"God, it's just me," her sister said, sounding offended.

"Sorry," Emily said quickly. "I guess I was off in another world."

They stood silently for a few beats. Emily expected Carolyn to move on down the hall—Carolyn was sleeping in the guest room while she was here, so they were no longer sharing the space—but she remained where she was. Emily shifted. Should she invite her in? They weren't exactly fighting now . . . but were they friends? Last night after dinner, Emily had retreated to the den and turned on a snowboard competition on NBC Extreme,

Carolyn's favorite channel. Carolyn had sat down next to her, but they hadn't said a single word through the entire competition, not even when one of the contestants took a scary-looking tumble off the ramp. *That* was their big sisterly bonding time?

Now Carolyn leaned against the doorjamb. "So I was thinking about going to a bar."

Emily was so surprised that she sat down on the bed. *"Now?"*

Carolyn set her mouth in a line. "Don't sound so excited. I thought we could hang, but forget it."

"Carolyn!" Emily whined, springing up from the bed. "Wait! A bar . . . with *alcohol*?" At the Rosewood Day French Festival last year, which was held during lunch, the school had allowed the students to sample a glass of wine each, provided no one drove anywhere. Carolyn had abstained even from *that*, opting for Dr Pepper.

She caught her sister's arm. "I'll go to a bar with you. Which one?"

Carolyn stepped into the bathroom. "It's a surprise. Meet me in ten minutes. We'll go out the back door and take the minivan. It's in the driveway."

Emily raised an eyebrow. The back door was farther from their parents' bedroom—they wouldn't hear. Same with taking the car in the driveway: They always heard a car start in the garage. Was goody-goody, rule-abiding Carolyn sneaking out?

Her sister shut the bathroom door before Emily could

ask. She smiled to herself, wondering what she was in for. Then again, did she really care? She was just happy her sister was making the effort after so, so long.

"Pegasus?" Emily blurted thirty minutes later as Carolyn steered the minivan into a parking lot. In front of them was a long, squat building with floor-to-ceiling windows and a large, neon winged horse hanging over the front door. Three women in matching plaid shirts sashayed toward the entrance. Two skinny girls in miniskirts held hands in the window.

Emily and Carolyn were in a wooded neighborhood in West Hollis nicknamed The Purple Triangle . . . for obvious reasons. Emily had never dared go into Lilith's Tomes, the lesbian bookshop; Closer to Fine, the lesbian teahouse; or Pegasus, the only lesbian bar in the area, but she'd always been curious. She didn't think Carolyn even *knew* about this neighborhood, though.

Carolyn shifted into park. "There's a cool singer tonight." She started across the gravel lot toward the front door.

Emily scampered after her sister and grabbed her arm. "We can go to a regular bar in Hollis. We don't have to go here."

Carolyn's eyebrows made a V. "My roommate at Stanford is gay. I've been to a lesbian bar in Palo Alto with her a bunch of times."

Again, Carolyn had that defensive, I'm-pretending-

I'm-not-mad-at-you-but-I'm-still-furious tone, almost like she expected Emily to apologize to her for assuming she was being narrow-minded. Emily raised her palms to the sky in surrender. "Okay. Let's go."

They were halfway across the parking lot when Emily heard a giggle. The cars cast long shadows onto the ground. There was a rustling sound behind a picnic table. *Even if it's Ali, I'm safe*, she thought, glancing at the black town car that had parked discreetly in the back of the lot.

Still, there was something spooky about the fact that it really *could* be Ali. If Ali walked up to Emily right now, would Emily be vengeful and punishing, or would she smile weakly and accept her apology? In the days since they'd told the cops, Emily had felt guilty twinges. She'd told them everything. The cops would be looking for Ali now. Emily didn't love Ali anymore, though—the guilt was more a knee-jerk reaction. She wondered how long it would take to go away.

Inside were sounds of a female singing voice and an acoustic guitar. Emily followed Carolyn inside, noting the silvery streamers hanging from the ceiling, the fruity-smelling candles on the bar, the giant tropical fish tank, and the plushy armchairs—which were all filled with girls. There was a stage set up at the back with a dance floor in front of it. Several couples were waltzing. Two girls were making out on the windowsill. But other than that, the bar didn't seem that different from anywhere else in Hollis—the same beers were on tap, and the same dart boards and pool tables stood at the side. There was even a hockey game on a small screen over the bar.

Carolyn hovered at the edge of the bar. Emily stood next to her, not knowing what to say. A pretty black girl caught Emily's eye. She raised her hand and waved. Emily looked down, feeling shy. Carolyn still didn't say a word. Were they just going to stand here all night?

The singer played a Beatles cover, then something by Bob Marley. Suddenly, Carolyn whirled around. "We need to lighten the mood. Want to dance?"

Emily almost burst out laughing. Carolyn totally wasn't the dancing type. But her sister looked serious, her arms outstretched, her hips rocking back and forth. "Okay," Emily said, following.

They walked onto the dance floor and started to move to the beat of the reggae song. The pretty black girl who'd waved at Emily sidled up to her and took her hand, but Emily gave her a demure smile. "I have a girlfriend."

"Don't we all?" The black girl smiled, showing off the straightest teeth Emily had ever seen. "It's just a dance, honey. No strings." Then she handed Emily a champagne flute full of bubbling liquid. "I'm River. And this is on me."

Emily glanced at her sister, who was grinning at her. Suddenly, amid the hand-holding, cheek-kissing, slow-dancing couples, Emily could almost feel Jordan's soft skin in her palm, smell the jasmine perfume on her neck. She missed Jordan times a million, but it *was* only a dance and a glass of champagne. Whatever.

The song morphed into something fast, with a techno beat, and River took Emily's hands and spun her around. Emily sipped her drink, the fizzy bubbles making her feel lighter and free. A tall girl who had her hair in pigtails coaxed Carolyn into a conga line, and they shuffled around the dance floor, their cheeks shiny and their eyes bright. Emily and her new friend grabbed on and followed them. Someone held up her phone and snapped a picture. The bartender, a muscled girl with arms full of tattoos, tipped back her head and laughed.

Suddenly, Emily noticed a familiar skinny, white-blonde in the crowd. *Iris?*

She pushed away from Carolyn and wove through the group. The white-blond girl stood in front of an ATM, her back to Emily. Emily touched her bony shoulder, her heart pounding. The girl turned. She had a pointier face, brown eyes instead of green. "Yes?" she said in a friendly enough voice. But it wasn't Iris's voice.

Emily's heart sank. "Sorry. I thought you were someone else." Despair fluttered through her. *Please let Iris turn up*, she prayed to the universe. *Please let her be okay.*

She went back to Carolyn, trying not to think about it. They danced for three more songs, to the point of sweatiness. Finally, Carolyn careened to the sidelines, breathing hard. River kissed Emily on the cheek and disappeared into the crowd. Emily plopped down on a couch with her sister again, daring to lean into Carolyn's shoulder.

Carolyn didn't pull away.

"Thanks," Emily said. "That was a good idea."

Carolyn's eyes softened. "So . . . truce?"

"Truce," Emily said. "Definitely."

Carolyn held up a drink and clinked it to Emily's drained champagne glass. Emily peered at Carolyn's tall glass of dark liquid. It had a familiar smell, and she burst out laughing. "Is that straight-up Dr Pepper?"

Carolyn raised her glass. "Heck yeah, it is."

Emily clinked her glass to her sister's, hiding a smile. It seemed like Carolyn was still the same girl from the Rosewood Day French Festival, after all.

And you know what? Emily was kind of glad.

14

COFFEE TALK

That same Wednesday evening, Spencer lay on her bed, looking at the picture of the Acura keychain she'd taken with her phone just before dropping it off at Fuji's office. Had Ali meant to drop it? Also, if Ali or Helper A were driving around in an Acura, it meant they had some cash. Clearly that wasn't coming from Ali—her family was in financial trouble from keeping her in The Preserve for so many years. Did that mean Helper A had money? Maybe Spencer should call Fuji and suggest they get a list of every Acura driver on the Main Line. Maybe it would turn up a rich boy whose first name started with *N*.

"Spence?"

Spencer shot up. Her sister, Melissa, stood in the hall. She still had on a gray business suit and heels, which meant she'd come from her job at an investment firm in Philly. Only, Melissa didn't live at home anymore—she'd moved into her city town house last year.

"What are you doing here?" Spencer asked.

"I came to talk to you," Melissa said softly. She shut the door and walked into the room. "Look, I know what's going on."

"What are you talking about?"

"It's her, isn't it?" she said in an almost inaudible voice. "She survived the fire. She's torturing you again. And now the cops are after her."

There was a wide quality to Melissa's eyes that made her look a bit possessed. "How did you know?" Spencer demanded.

"Don't be mad. I heard about the cops coming after you but you being let go. Wilden still has a lot of connections in law enforcement. I made him ask around, and he found out about . . . *you* know." She sat back. "I deserved to know, Spencer. She's my half sister, too."

Spencer got up and faced the window, which had a view of Ali's old house. She hated thinking about how Ali was her half sister. "Don't ask any more questions. You don't want to end up in a closet with a dead body again."

"But I don't want *you* to end up dead, either." Melissa walked up behind her and squeezed her shoulder. "If you need something, *anything*, I want to help. I hate that bitch as much as you do."

She gave Spencer a hug, then rose and patted her shoulder. *Call me*, she mouthed before closing the door.

Spencer sat back against her headboard, blanket in her lap. Had that just happened? Her sister, now her ally? It was about time . . . but it was also the *wrong* time. Though Fuji had put security on Spencer's family, too, it didn't comfort her entirely. Melissa needed to stay as far away from Ali as she could.

A few minutes later, the doorbell downstairs rang. Spencer sprang up again, her heart thudding hard for a different reason. *Chase.*

She checked her reflection in the mirror, fluffing her blown-out hair. Did an above-knee-length Tory Burch wrap dress scream too formal? Chase was just taking her for coffee, after all. She glanced at her jeans, stacked neatly on a shelf in the closet. She didn't even know why she was making such a big deal out of this, anyway—Chase was just a friend. A helpful friend, of course—a *cute* friend—and a friend she felt a bit indebted to, since he knew about Ali. But she had no idea why it had taken her so long to do her makeup or why, whenever she thought about Chase nosing around Mr. Pennythistle's model home the other day, a small smile came over her face.

The doorbell rang again. Spencer groaned, shoved on a pair of low heels, and clomped down the stairs just as Mrs. Hastings was answering the door. "Well hello, Chase."

Chase walked into the foyer. He smiled when he saw Spencer, then looked her outfit up and down. "Whoa. You look awesome."

Spencer blushed. Chase was in cargo pants and a T-shirt. But before she could ask to change, Chase offered his arm. "Come on," he said. "Let's get out of here."

He opened the door to his Honda, then pulled away from the curb. He took the exit toward the city, then turned right into a neighborhood Spencer didn't recognize. "Where are we?" she asked, looking around. Judging by the red, white, and green flags hanging from the porches of the quaint brownstones that lined the streets, half of Italy must have pulled up stakes and relocated here.

"You'll see," Chase said as he parallel parked in front of an unassuming-looking coffee shop. Once again, he opened the door for Spencer to get out and took her hand but dropped it fast. Then he pushed open a jingling door to the café. It smelled strongly of espresso beans inside. The room had marble floors, bronzed countertops, and wrought-iron tables and chairs. Opera played over the speakers.

"Look who's here!" a voice called, and then a silver-haired man in a pinstriped, three-piece suit emerged from behind the counter. He gave Chase a huge hug, giving off a strong scent of cigars. Spencer shifted from one foot to the other. He looked like someone out of *The Sopranos*.

"Spencer, this is Nico," Chase said, when the hug ended. "Nico, Spencer."

Nico looked Spencer up and down, then cuffed Chase on the arm. "Quite a catch, buddy."

"Oh, we're just friends," Chase said quickly, glancing at Spencer. She smiled.

Nico winked like he didn't believe them, then made a sweeping gesture around the room. A few couples were at the tables. An old man was doing a crossword in the corner. "Sit anywhere you like."

Spencer settled on one of the chairs and looked around. Metal pots hung from the ceiling. Zillions of black-and-white photographs of serious-looking women holding babies or cooking in kitchens were on the walls. There were also old ads in Italian and posters for operas she'd never heard of. It reminded her of Paris or Rome.

She leaned across the table to Chase. "And you know this place *how*?"

Chase smiled. "I found this when I was working on one of the cases for the blog. Nico provided me with a lot of insider information—plus he gets me tickets to the opera."

Spencer crossed her arms. "I thought opera was only for old ladies."

"Absolutely not." Chase apprised her. "I can't believe you've never been. I'll take you sometime."

Spencer smiled. "I'd like that." Not long ago, whenever she conceived of the future, she imagined A finally catching up with and punishing them. It was like a huge bucket of dirty water that had taken up way too much space in her brain had finally emptied.

"What are you thinking about?" Chase asked.

Spencer took a deep breath. "The way things have suddenly changed," she admitted. "I mean, there's this enormous weight off my shoulders."

"I can imagine," Chase said.

"I mean, I know I shouldn't get too comfortable. They could still be watching me." With that, Spencer cast a glance out the stained-glass windows. Pigeons shuffled on the street. A Parking Authority worker strolled past, ticket meter in hand.

"Do you know what's happening with the investigation?" Chase whispered.

"Well, I handed over the Acura keychain," Spencer said. "It's up to them to figure out the rest." Suddenly, the hair on the back of her neck rose. She looked up just as a back door creaked open, half expecting Ali to emerge. It was just an old woman, though, scuttling past them to wipe down a table.

Spencer looked at Chase. "I don't think we should talk about Ali in public."

Chase nodded. "Got it."

Nico appeared again and delivered their drinks in delicate little china cups. "*Grazie*," Spencer said, trying to get in the spirit of things, and lifted hers from its saucer. It was the most smooth, buttery, heavenly tasting coffee she'd ever had. "Wow," she said, when she'd swallowed.

"Told you it was good." Chase pulled a napkin from the silver holder on the middle of the table and handed it to her. They were quiet for a while. Nico whistled as he cleaned the insides of the tiny espresso cups behind the counter. "I invited Nico to Sunday dinner once," Chase admitted in a low voice, watching him, too. "My parents looked at me like I was out of my mind. They were sure there was going to be a police raid on the house."

"My mom would've probably done the same thing," Spencer said. She placed her chin in her hand. "Does your family have big Sunday dinners?"

Chase settled back in his chair. "I have a huge extended family, so it can get pretty insane. I'd miss it if we didn't do it anymore, though."

He described the comfort food his mom made, the same old jokes his grandfather always told, and the plays his younger cousins put on during dessert. "It sounds fun," Spencer said. "I've always wanted a family who actually likes one another."

Chase smiled. "You can come sometime if you want."

There was a flutter in Spencer's chest. "First you invite me to the opera, then to dinner . . . what next?"

"I'd say prom . . . but been there, done that," Chase blurted. "*Kind* of."

Spencer giggled. She liked his flirtatious side. And suddenly, when she looked at him again, he had a twitchy, excited look on his face, almost like he might kiss her. Spencer thought about it for a moment, then inched forward.

Beep.

Her cell phone chimed loudly through the room. "Ugh," Spencer said, peeking inside her bag.

The texter's number was a jumble of letters and

numbers. Spencer's stomach sank. Quickly, she opened the text.

Do you really want another innocent life on your hands, Spence? Then give up your boy toy. —A

The blood drained from her face. "Spencer?" Chase touched her arm. "What is it?"

Spencer glanced around the little coffee shop. Nico turned on the espresso grinder. One of the couples fed each other bites of cannoli. All at once, the air cleared. She knew exactly what to do.

"It's nothing," she said. She straightened up, gripped her phone, and typed in Agent Fuji's number. *Just got another text*, she wrote, forwarding the message. *Go to it.*

15

GALLERY GIRL

Thursday afternoon, Aria pulled into Old Hollis and found a space on the street. Then she got out, retrieved her portfolio from the backseat, and stood in front of her mother's gallery. It was in a large Victorian with bay windows and a big front porch. There was a sun catcher in the front window, and bronze wind chimes hung from the eaves. Tulips sprung from the flower beds in the front lawn. Today was her first day of work, and she was trying to feel excited, but she just felt numb. Her portfolio felt heavy in her hands. She doubted that Jim, the gallery owner, would actually sell her stuff, but her mother had insisted she bring everything she was working on.

Squaring her shoulders, she started up the front walk, careful not to trip in her brand-new, hot-pink kitten heels. As she passed a large maple with a tire swing and a bird's nest in one of the low branches, her phone bleated in her bag. She reached for it. AGENT FUJI, said the caller ID.

Aria's heart flipped. Had there been a break in the case?

"Hi, Aria, it's Jasmine Fuji," came the agent's smooth, professional tone. "I have Spencer on the line, too. Do you have a sec?"

"Sure." A shifting shadow across the street caught her eye, but when Aria looked over, whatever it was had disappeared. She didn't see her security guy anywhere.

Fuji cleared her throat. "First of all, I appreciate you girls forwarding your notes from A to me. It's been very helpful."

"I got one last night, Aria," Spencer's gravelly voice broke in. "Have you gotten any?"

"Nope," Aria said. "What did yours say?"

"It was threatening a friend of mine, Chase—the guy who runs the conspiracy website. I'm afraid he might be in danger. You may want to look into security for him, too."

"I'll see what I can do," Fuji said. "But actually, I was calling because I want to clarify something with you girls about Graham Pratt. Aria, you sought out Graham, correct?"

Aria leaned her portfolio against the lamppost. "Not at all. We ended up in the same group on the cruise."

"Hmm," Fuji said. "So you didn't realize until later that Graham was Tabitha Clark's ex?"

"That's right," Aria said, turning away as a girl on a bike passed on the street. "Then I got a text from A almost the moment I found out, like A was watching."

"Okay." Fuji sighed. "I wish we could have spoken to

Graham before he died."

"Before he was *killed*," Spencer corrected her. "By the way, have you looked into the *N* clue he gave Hanna at the burn clinic?"

Fuji chuckled softly. "We're following up on everything, don't worry."

"What about a Preserve patient list from the time Ali was there?" Spencer goaded. "That would go a long way."

"We're on it." Fuji sounded a little impatient. There was another muffled voice in the background on Fuji's end. "Okay, girls, I gotta go," she said. "Thanks for your time."

"Wait!" Spencer said, but Fuji had already hung up.

Aria hung up, too, rolling her eyes. Spencer was type A to a fault.

"Aria! Thank goodness you're here."

The door to the Victorian had opened, and Ella stood just inside. Her mother was in her "gallery uniform"—a long patchwork skirt, a white peasant blouse, and a pair of blue suede Birkenstocks. She ushered Aria inside the house, which had been gutted into one large room that displayed countless paintings of Pennsylvania barns and wildlife on the walls. "A new artist is coming in a few minutes. We're going to debut his work in a private show. It's very exciting."

Aria touched the top of an old spinning wheel that had sat in the corner of the gallery as long as she could remember—kind of like a lot of the artwork here. "What's his name?" she asked.

Ella peeked out the front window. "Asher Trethewey."

Asher Trethewey. Aria couldn't have made up a more appropriate name for a retired lawyer-turned-artist if she tried. She could just picture him with a box of pastels, dithering over a pastoral scene of the Brandywine Water Gap. "Do you need my help?" she asked.

"Actually, I do." Ella checked her watch. "I'm scheduled to meet another artist for lunch in fifteen minutes—so I have to go. I'm wondering if you'll talk to Mr. Trethewey in my place."

"Me?" Aria thumbed her chest. It seemed like a big responsibility.

"He just needs to pick up some paperwork." Ella gestured to a stack of papers on the desk. "All you need to do is make sure he gets it, okay?" She checked her watch again, then grabbed her keys and purse from her desk. "I've got to run. I'm sure you'll be fine!"

She flew out the door. Aria walked to the window and watched her scurry down the front steps and climb into her car. The motor growled to life, and her mother was gone. The street was eerily quiet in her absence. A squirrel paused on a branch, its head cocked. Wind chimes on the front porch swayed but didn't touch. An airplane soared overhead, too high up to hear.

Aria spun around the big room, first staring blankly at a wall of watercolor still lifes, then looking down at the paperwork for the artist. It was full of legal mumbo-jumbo she didn't understand. What if the artist had questions? This was *so* her mother. When they were living in Iceland, Ella had broken her leg while trying to catch a lost baby puffin up a tree, and while she was laid up, she'd asked Aria to drive their Saab to the grocery store. Never mind that Aria was only fourteen and had never driven in her life. "You'll be great!" Ella had insisted. "Just stay on the left side of the road and stop at red lights!"

There was a knock at the door, and Aria turned. Rolling back her shoulders, she crossed the room and tried to prepare what she'd say—only, she had no idea what *to* say. When she opened the door, a young man in a black T-shirt and skinny gray pants, carrying a large black portfolio, stood on the porch. He had broad shoulders, smoldering ice-blue eyes, a perfect nose, a strong chin, and sensuous lips. He looked like a cross between a sexy British soccer player and a guy from a Polo cologne ad.

Aria raised an eyebrow. "Um, hello?"

He thrust out a hand. "Hi. I'm Asher Trethewey. Are you Ella Montgomery?"

"O-oh," Aria stammered. She backed up, almost stumbling over her kitten heels. "Um, no, I'm her daughter, Aria. But I can help you. Come on in." Her voice rose on that last part, making it sound like a question. "I have the papers right here," she said, walking toward the desk.

Asher walked into the room and placed his hands on his hips. "Actually, I was going to show your mom my work—see what she thought would be best for the exhibit."

"Oh." Aria gritted her teeth. See? She *knew* something like this would come up. "Well, she'll be back soon, I think . . ."

Asher cocked his head and smiled at Aria. "Or *you* can take a look, if you like."

He set the portfolio on the desk and opened it up. Inside were a bunch of photographic images. All of them had an ethereal, out-of-focus quality to them, and most featured people caught in movement—jumping, spinning, flipping on a trampoline. Aria leaned down and inspected one picture of a little girl running through a sprinkler more closely. It wasn't a photo at all but made of tiny pixels, like a mosaic.

"Whoa," Aria said. "You're a digital Chuck Close."

A corner of Asher's bow-shaped mouth rose. "A few reviewers have said that, too."

"He's one of my favorites," Aria admitted. "I've tried to do pieces in his style, but I'm not talented enough." She'd been inspired after going to a Chuck Close retrospective at the Philadelphia Museum of Art last summer. Noel had gone with her, spending hours there while she intently studied each work, not saying even once that he was bored.

She stiffened. *Don't think about Noel,* Aria chided silently, giving herself a mental slap. She cleared her throat. "Don't take this the wrong way, but why are you in Rosewood?"

Asher raised his head and chuckled. "I'm in Hollis

because I have a fellowship gig I have to fulfill. Before that, I was in San Francisco."

"Really?" Aria picked up a coaster that featured a fly trapped in a blob of amber, kind of feeling sorry for the poor bug. "I've always wanted to go there."

"It's chill." He stretched his long, sinewy arms over his head. "Tell the truth. You thought I was going to be one of those artists who painted Amish buggies and cow pastures, huh?"

"Well, maybe," Aria admitted. Her gaze returned to Asher's work again. "Have you had a lot of shows?"

"I have an agent in New York, so I've been lucky." He lowered his long lashes. "A couple of celebs have been interested in my work, so that's kind of cool."

Aria raised an eyebrow. "Anyone I'd know?"

Asher closed the portfolio. "A lot of indie musicians, old players in the art-gallery scene. The biggest name was probably Madonna."

"*The* Madonna?" Aria couldn't control her shriek. "Did you actually *meet* her?"

Asher looked embarrassed. "Oh no. I've talked to her on the phone. She's so stuck-up with that fake British accent."

"Oh, right," Aria said, trying to regain her cool.

Asher closed the portfolio lid. "So you're an artist, too?"

Aria fiddled with a stray lock of hair that had fallen out of her ponytail. "Oh, not *really*. Not seriously." Her gaze darted to her own cardboard portfolio in the corner. It looked so shabby compared to Asher's leather one. "There's some stuff I'm still fiddling with."

Asher's blue eyes lit up. "Can I check it out?"

Before Aria could give permission, Asher strode over to the folder, lifted it up, and laid it next to his own on the desk. When he opened to the first piece, Aria's face felt hot. It was a colorful, surreal painting of Noel. His skin was purplish. His hair was green. His body melted into a puddle. But it was Noel all the same—his eyes, his smile, his tufty hair. There was a hum inside her chest.

Asher flipped to another image of Noel. Then another. Aria glanced away, suddenly unable to endure them. Noel used to tease her about painting him over and over; he'd asked if he could have her work after the end-of-the-year art show at Rosewood Day. "Will you bring them to college with you?" Aria had joked. "*Duh*," Noel had answered. "I'll hang them in my room, next to my roommate's porn pinups." She supposed that wouldn't be happening now.

"Are you okay?"

Aria blinked hard. To her horror, tears had filled her eyes. She tried to smile. "Sorry. All those paintings are of an ex. I'm still getting over him. I actually hate all this stuff. I should burn it."

Asher peered at Noel's face for a beat, then shut the folder. "I incorporate people I'm in love with in my paintings as well. It's only human, you know?" He rolled toward her. "Don't burn these. They could be worth something someday."

Aria looked at him crazily. "Yeah, right."

"I'm serious. These are amazingly deep. You're really talented."

The sun emerged from a cloud and streamed in through the window. Aria swallowed hard, not knowing whether she should smile or burst into tears. "Thank you," she said softly.

Asher laced his fingers together. "You should keep at it. Show me stuff as you finish it. I could put you in touch with my agent."

"*What?*" Aria blurted.

But Asher just smiled confidently. "I know talent when I see it." Then he grabbed the stack of papers from the desk, slipped them into his portfolio, and tucked the whole thing under his arm. "Anyway, I'll be in touch. Have your mom call me."

"I will," Aria said.

A warm, pleasant feeling enveloped her as she watched him step off the porch and lope down the street. She wanted to call someone right now and tell them a famous artist had encouraged *her* to paint more—imagine if he really hooked her up with his agent! Then she realized who it was she wanted to call: Noel.

But as Asher turned the corner, her mood shifted. The street was so dark and shadowless, suddenly. A car swished past a side street and didn't slow. A cat meowed in an unseen alley.

Ping.

Her phone vibrated in her palm. Aria flinched and stared at the screen. ONE NEW MESSAGE FROM ANONYMOUS. She opened the text.

Don't get too close to your new little artist friend, Aria. Or I'll just hurt him, too. —A

Aria's stomach clenched. How did Ali know? Was she listening? Was she just going to take down *everyone* Aria knew?

There was a way to solve this. She hit FORWARD and sent the note to Fuji. Then she stuffed her phone into her bag and willed herself to walk back into the gallery with her head held high. *You're safe*, she repeated over and over in her mind. *It's all over. You're finally going to move on.*

At least she hoped so.

16

HANNA MARIN, POSTER CHILD

That afternoon, Hanna stared into the impassive eye of a TV camera lens. When the red light that indicated they were filming began to blink, she smiled brightly. "And that's why I stand behind Tom Marin's Zero-Tolerance Plan," she said clearly and slowly. She was six takes into the Tom and Hanna Marin Families Against Drunk Driving PSA, and this one was going to be a keeper.

Her father, who sat on the stool next to her, recited his lines in a presidential voice. The cameras did a close-up on him, and Hanna peeked at her reflection in the mirror that was set up on the other side of her father's campaign head-quarters-turned-studio. She wore a navy-blue sheath dress and a pearl necklace she'd borrowed from her mom. Her auburn hair had been professionally blown out, cascading in a smooth waterfall down her back. Her green eyes sparkled, and her skin glowed, thanks to an expensive cream in the makeup artist's tool bag. Hanna *definitely* had to get its name.

The camera turned back to Hanna. "We need to keep teens of Pennsylvania safe," she said emphatically. "I know this not only as a teen of Pennsylvania . . . but also as a victim of stalking *and* drunk driving."

Pause. Smile bright. Look earnest and patriotic. "And . . . cut!" said the director, who was perched on a stool behind the camera. "I think that one's a winner!"

Everyone in the room applauded. Mr. Marin patted Hanna's shoulder. "Good work."

"That really was amazing," Kate agreed, appearing by Hanna's side. "You're a natural in front of the camera, Han. I'm so impressed."

"She gets that from me," boasted Hanna's mom. Hanna was pretty sure her mom and Kate had never been together in such a small room, but they seemed to be getting along okay. *Isabel*, however, was standing in the opposite corner gripping a clipboard so tightly, Hanna was surprised she hadn't bent it in half by now.

Sidney, Mr. Marin's top aide, approached. "I've been thinking. Let's spin this so that the bar that served Hanna and Madison is to blame. It will test well with our voters, Tom," he said. "People will think, *If they would have been tougher about carding, this accident never would have happened.*"

"Exactly." Then Mr. Marin's expression grew serious. "What was the name of that bar that served you? We should shut them down. Make an example of them."

"The Cabana." Hanna had thought a lot about the

South Street dive she'd ducked into that fateful day. The smell of smoke and the twangy country song washed back to her. So did Madison's boozy breath and the way the soles of Hanna's shoes were sticky after walking across the bathroom floor.

"Got it." Mr. Marin tapped something into his iPhone. "Okay, Han. Ready for Phase Two?"

Hanna shifted uneasily. Phase Two was apologizing to Madison at Immaculata University, where she'd transferred after the accident. Madison had agreed to speak to Hanna, but it still made Hanna feel uneasy. If only they could skip it.

Sensing Hanna's apprehension, Mr. Marin wrapped his arm around her. "I'll be with you the whole time, honey, I promise. We'll do it together."

Isabel rushed forward. "But Tom, we've got that meeting with your new donors today at four."

Mr. Marin set his jaw. "Reschedule it."

Isabel's face clouded. "You lost a huge donation when Gayle Riggs died—we need the cash." She cleared her throat. "Speaking of Gayle, did you hear the news? There was a break in the case. The police are looking through her house again for new evidence."

Hanna shifted her weight. Of course there was a break in the case. It was from *them*.

Mr. Marin started for the door. "I'm sure the donors can wait a day, Iz. I told Hanna I'd do this with her, and I want to honor that."

"Good for you, Tom," Hanna's mom gushed. She shot Isabel a snarky smile. A deep wrinkle appeared between Isabel's eyes. Hanna had a feeling that if they didn't get out of here soon, it would devolve into an episode of *Real Housewives: Rosewood, P.A.*

"I'll be ready in a second," Hanna said quickly to her father. "I just want to call Mike." She hadn't heard from him all day, and she wanted to make sure he was okay. Usually, Mike texted her nonstop, even during school.

She stepped out of her father's office, stood on the walkway that overlooked a large atrium with a burbling fountain, and dialed Mike's number. Once again, it went to voicemail. Hanna hung up without leaving a message. Where *was* he?

When a door slammed shut, Hanna jumped. It echoed so loudly, like it was right behind her. Just being in this building gave her the creeps; a few months ago, A— *Ali*—trapped Hanna in the elevator. The lights had gone out, the power had died, and when Hanna had gotten free and on solid ground again, she'd found the elevator control box wide open, its levers and switches tampered with. Ali's telltale vanilla perfume had wafted through the air, taunting her nostrils. If only Hanna had called the cops *then*.

Hanna peered out the front windows for Bo, her security guy, but she didn't see his car in the lot. She dialed Agent Fuji. "Do you know where Bo is?" Hanna asked, when she answered. "I don't see him anywhere."

The sound of typing echoed in the background. "Just because you can't see him doesn't mean he's not there," Fuji answered.

"But I haven't seen him all day."

"Hanna, I don't have time to monitor your security detail's comings and goings. I'm sure it's nothing to worry about."

"It's just I heard that the cops are looking into Gayle's murder," Hanna said in a small voice. "And I know that probably will make Ali nervous. And I have my boyfriend to worry about, too. I'm afraid Ali might hurt him because he knows so much."

All at once, just talking about Mike, she remembered a dream she'd had last night. Her phone had buzzed, and a note from A said that Mike was in danger and Hanna had to find him. Hanna had darted into the street and looked around. Incongruously, the DiLaurentis house was next door—and the old hole the workers had dug to build the gazebo was back. Hanna had run to it and peered inside . . . and there was Mike at the bottom, curled up in a fetal position. It was obvious he was dead.

"What if something happens to him?" Hanna said now, horrified she was only just remembering the dream. "Are we sure everyone is safe?"

"Hanna, calm down," Fuji interrupted. "Everyone is safe. Every time you girls call, it takes me away from solving this case. I'm sure you understand."

CALL ENDED flashed across the screen. Hanna recoiled,

not sure whether to feel dissed or reassured. But Fuji was doing her job—she had to trust that. Soon enough, this would all be over.

Thirty minutes later, Mr. Marin's SUV pulled through the gates of Immaculata University, a liberal arts school not far from Rosewood. Girls in rugby sweaters and plaid kilts crossed the quad. Boys carrying lacrosse sticks over their shoulders climbed the steps to a dorm. Nearly everyone was wearing Sperry Top-Siders.

They parked at Madison's dorm and got out. "Come on." Mr. Marin took Hanna's hand and led her to the path toward the dorm entrance. The inside of the building smelled like a jumble of perfumes and bustled with girls.

"This is it," Mr. Marin said when they got to a door marked 113. There was a white board filled with messages for Madison. Hanna paused to read a few. *Dinner, 6?* And, *Are you going to that meeting tomorrow?* And, *Did you do the chem homework?* Did that mean Madison had a relatively normal life?

Hanna hesitated before knocking, dread squeezing her chest corset-tight. "You can do this," Mr. Marin said as if reading her mind. "I won't leave your side."

Hanna was so grateful, she almost burst into tears. Mustering up the courage, she reached out and knocked. The door flung open immediately, and a blond girl with an oval face and overplucked eyebrows stood on the other side.

"Hanna?" she said.

"That's right." Hanna looked at her dad. "And this is my dad."

Madison's brow crinkled, her focus still on Hanna. "Huh. I thought you were the blond Pretty Little Liar."

"That's Spencer."

Madison leaned against the jamb. "Wow. I really don't remember that night at all."

She stepped aside and let Hanna and her dad into her room. A neatly made twin bed with a downy, white comforter stood near the window. There was a desk filled with books, papers, and a Dell computer pushed against another wall. A pile of laundry was near the bathroom, and shoes lay in a heap by the closet.

"You have a single," Hanna commented, only noticing one bed. "Lucky."

"It's on account of my leg." Madison pulled up her jeans to reveal a brace around her calf. "They took pity on me, I guess."

A heavy weight settled on Hanna's chest. Naomi had told her that Madison's leg had been shattered in the accident. She wouldn't be able to play field hockey ever again. "Does it hurt?" Hanna said in a small voice.

Madison shrugged. "Sometimes. I'm having surgery to reset the bone this summer. The doctors say I'll be good as new after that."

Surgery. Hanna glanced at the door, tempted to run out and never come back. But then she peeked at her father.

He nodded at her encouragingly.

She took a deep breath. "Look, Madison, I'm sure you know by now what went down that night, right? I drove you home . . . and then someone swerved into my lane and we crashed and I left the scene. I never should have left you."

Madison sat down in her desk chair. "It's okay, Hanna. I forgive you."

Hanna's eyebrows shot up. Well, *that* was easy. "Okay, then," she said, starting to stand. Done and done!

But then she paused. Maybe that was *too* easy. "Wait. Are you just saying that? If you're really pissed, you can tell me. It's okay. *I* would be pissed."

Madison twirled a pen between her fingers. "It sucks that we got in an accident. It sucks that you felt you had to leave. But as far as I'm concerned, I would have been in way worse shape if I would've driven myself."

"I should have been more forceful about getting you a cab." Hanna perched on the edge of Madison's neatly made bed. "*They* wouldn't have crashed."

Madison spun around in the chair. "We don't really know that for sure. The same person might have crashed into them." She paused, her eyes lighting up. "Did you know we found video footage?"

"Of the other driver?" Hanna leaned forward. "Did you see who it was? Was it *Ali*?"

"They had part of a license plate, and for a while I thought they were on to something, but they couldn't figure out who the driver was," Madison answered. "The only thing the cops figured out was that the car was an Acura."

Spots formed in front of Hanna's eyes. An Acura? Hadn't Spencer found an Acura keychain in her stepfather's trashed model house?

Madison pinched the bridge of her nose. "I wish I could remember who the driver was. I wish I could remember *anything* from that night." She grabbed her phone from her desk. "I barely remember going into that bar. I'd had a couple drinks at this other place that never cards down the street before I even went there, but I kind of remember this hot bartender really, *really* wanting me to come inside."

Hanna straightened up. "Yeah, Jackson. He did that to me, too."

She thought about passing the bar that day, Jackson eyeing her from the entrance. *Drinks are half off right now*, he'd said in a flirty voice, flashing her an ultrawhite smile. He had the look of a guy who had played lacrosse and rowed crew in high school, though there was something predatory in his eyes, too. Much later, after Hanna and Madison bonded, Hanna had leaned over to catch Madison before she fell off the bar stool. As she looked up, she caught Jackson sneaking a look down her blouse, a smirk on his face.

"I wish I could get my hands on him," Hanna's father said gruffly.

Madison looked conflicted. "Maybe he didn't know I was underage."

Hanna opened her mouth but didn't say anything. Jackson might not have known Madison was under twenty-one, but he *had* been pouring drinks for Madison faster than she could drink them. And when Hanna suggested he call Madison a cab, he just laughed.

Mr. Marin tapped his lip. "Could you describe what he looked like?"

Madison smiled sheepishly, then tapped her phone. "I do have a picture. I took it secretly because I thought he was hot."

Hanna peered at the photo. It was a dark shot of the profile of a handsome guy with short hair. Madison had caught him while he was mixing up a margarita. "Yeah, that's him."

Then Madison checked her watch. "Actually, I have to get to orchestra practice." She awkwardly stood and held out her hand. "It was very nice to meet you, Mr. Marin. And to see you again, Hanna."

"It was nice to see you, too," Hanna said, shaking her hand. "Good luck with . . . everything."

"Good luck with your PSAs," Madison snorted. "Better you than me."

Hanna and her father were silent as they headed down the hall, but suddenly, Mr. Marin put his arm around her. "I'm so proud of you," he said. "It's hard to face your demons and come clean."

Hanna felt tears well in her eyes again. "Thanks for coming with me."

Then her phone pinged. Her heart lifted. It was Mike, finally getting back to her. *Sorry, busy day*, he'd written, and she let out a sigh of relief. He was fine.

Then she noticed a second text had come in as well. She looked at the screen, and her heart dropped. This one was from an unknown sender.

Just when you make peace with Daddy, I'm going to have to take it all away. Don't say I didn't warn you. —A

"Hanna?" Mr. Marin turned. "Are you okay?"

Hanna's hands trembled. Was that a threat against her father?

Squaring her shoulders, she forwarded it to Fuji. Then she looked at her father, who was peering at her worriedly from the end of the hall. "I'm great," she said with certainty. And she was. If Fuji was working so hard on the case that she couldn't even take Hanna's calls, then she would keep everyone safe.

She'd *better*.

17

THE WALLS COME CRASHING DOWN

Friday morning, Spencer and Chase sat at Wordsmith's Books. The place smelled like fresh-brewed coffee and sugary crullers, jazz played faintly through the stereo speakers, and a free-verse poet was reciting his latest work on a makeshift stage. The store was holding a performance series called "Morning Muses" in which local authors read their works to caffeine-starved patrons.

"That was awesome, wasn't it?" Chase asked when the poet finished his zillion-line free verse and they stood to leave. "That guy has such an amazing sense of imagery. I wish *I* could write poems like that."

Spencer raised an eyebrow. "Does that mean you write poems?"

"Sometimes." Chase looked bashful. "They mostly end up really lame."

"I'd love to read them," Spencer said softly.

He met her gaze. "I'd love to write one for you."

Spencer's stomach flipped over, but she cut her gaze away, suddenly overwhelmed with guilt. A's threat against Chase. Should she warn him?

"You okay?" Chase asked.

"Of course." Spencer cleared her throat. "So . . . nothing else has happened lately?"

Chase's brow furrowed. "What do you mean?"

"Nothing . . . weird?" Spencer didn't know how to phrase it. Saying something like *Have you felt like someone's been watching you?* would just get Chase riled up.

Chase shrugged. "The only weird thing going on right now is that *you're* paying attention to me." He lowered his head. "I really like it, by the way."

"I really like it, too," Spencer said, her cheeks turning red. She *should* just tell him. But Fuji was handling it, right? Maybe Chase had a security detail so secret that they didn't even know they were there.

"I'd better get to school," she mumbled, standing up and tossing her coffee cup into the chrome trash can near their seat.

Chase followed her onto the street, and they parted with a demure hug. "Call you later?" Chase asked eagerly.

"Definitely." Spencer shot him a shy smile.

She kept the innocent look plastered on her face until he rounded the corner to the back parking lot. Then she pulled out her phone, scrolled to find Fuji's number, and dialed. Annoyingly, it went to voicemail. Just like her six other calls to Fuji in the past twenty-four hours had.

"It's Spencer Hastings again," Spencer said after the beep. "I'm just checking about that extra security detail on my friend Chase—I'm really worried about him. Also, I think my sister might need one, too. And you got the Acura keychain, right? And my letter?"

Yesterday, because e-mailing was far too risky, she'd hand-delivered to Fuji a letter of connections and leads. Like how Ali and/or Helper A had been in New York a few months ago when Spencer, her mom, Mr. Pennythistle, and his son and daughter visited—Spencer had gotten an A note practically the second Mr. Pennythistle walked in on Spencer and his son, Zach, in bed together. Maybe Team A was staying in the Hudson Hotel, too. Perhaps it would be useful to search Amtrak passenger manifests from around that time. There were *tons* of avenues to investigate.

"Anyway, give me a call back when you can," Spencer chirped. Then she hung up and turned into Rosewood Day. After parking the car, she trudged through the wet grass to the elementary-school swings, where she and her friends always met to talk—they hadn't spoken about A in a while, and maybe it was time. Emily dangled languidly from a low swing, her long legs dragging on the ground. Aria pulled the strings on the hood of her bright-green jacket. Hanna checked her reflection in a round Chanel compact. It was one of those beautiful spring mornings where practically the whole senior class was lingering outside before the bell.

"So what's the news?" Spencer asked her friends when she approached.

"Well, Sean Ackard's now officially a stalker," Aria mumbled. She gestured to a clump of kids on the stairs. Both Sean and Klaudia Huusko, the Kahns' exchange student, were staring at them. When they noticed the girls looking back, they turned away fast.

"Maybe Sean likes you again, Hanna," Emily teased.

"Or maybe it's about those suicide rumors." Aria looked at Hanna. "Sean gave me a pamphlet the other day for a support group at his church. He was looking at me like I was going to slit my wrists right there."

Hanna rolled her eyes. "I'm getting sick of those rumors."

Spencer cocked her head. "I wonder if the cops questioned Sean about Kyla."

Hanna shrugged. "There were cops all over the burn clinic. They probably did."

Aria scratched her chin. "Maybe Fuji slipped and admitted that Kyla was secretly Ali."

Spencer twisted her mouth. "I thought Fuji wanted to keep that a secret. Not freak out anyone until they were close to tracking her down."

"Well, maybe this means they *have* tracked her down," Hanna said excitedly.

A dreamy smile spread across Aria's lips. "Guys, can you imagine it? Ali behind bars. For *real* this time."

Everyone paused, the fantasy sinking in. Spencer

pictured Ali in a prison jumpsuit, stamping out license plates, guarded twenty-four hours a day. That bitch totally deserved it.

"Once they catch her, we're going to have to do a lot more interviews," Aria pointed out.

"Yeah, but *cool* interviews," Hanna said. "Like on *Oprah*. Jimmy Fallon. Not the six-o'clock local crap where they don't even spring for a makeup artist."

Emily stopped swinging. "Speaking of the suicide rumors, has anyone told you they've gotten anonymous notes about us wanting to hurt ourselves?"

Hanna's eyes widened, and then she nodded. "Mike did. And so did my dad." She rolled her eyes. "I don't know if it was from Team A, though, or someone just messing with him."

Emily suddenly looked worried. "My sister got one like that, too. Saying something like we're all really upset and we might go off the rails. What do you think *that's* about?"

Spencer waved her hand dismissively. "It's all over school that we have some sort of suicide pact going. It's such a stupid rumor."

"So you don't think they're from A?" Emily asked.

"Even if they are, does it matter?" Spencer asked.

Behind them, sirens blared. Four black SUVs raced up the drive, swerving around the buses.

Everyone on the sidewalk and in the Commons stopped and stared. Elementary-age kids dropped from the climbing domes and gawked. Teachers stepped out of their classrooms, their faces sheet-white. The cars screeched to a stop by the curb.

Spencer reached over and grabbed Aria's hand. "Guys, maybe this is it. Maybe they found Ali *today*."

The first cruiser door opened, and a tall agent who could have been Will Smith's *Men in Black* body double stepped out. Spencer leaned forward, expecting to see Ali slumped in the backseat, handcuffs around her wrists, but the seat was empty. A second SUV door opened, and a shorter, chubbier agent, still intimidating in his mirrored sunglasses, got out and slammed it shut.

The agents strode across the lawn toward the girls, their faces grave. Spencer's heart hammered fast. Whatever news they had, it was big. *Serious.*

Will Smith Look-alike stared hard at the four of them. "Spencer Hastings? Aria Montgomery? Emily Fields? Hanna Marin?"

"Yes?" Spencer's voice cracked.

Aria squeezed her hand tight. Hanna's lips parted. Spencer could feel the stares of her classmates. And at the curb, another figure stood by the SUVs. Agent Fuji. She had her arms crossed over her chest, and there was a proud, satisfied look on her face.

This is it, Spencer thought. *They really* did *find her.*

The second agent stepped forward. At first, Spencer thought it was to take her hand, but then he revealed a pair of shiny handcuffs. He quickly and deftly secured them to her wrists with a snap. Then he did the same to Aria. Will Smith cuffed Hanna and Emily.

"W-what the hell?" Aria wailed, jolting away.

"Don't try to run, girls," the second agent said in a low voice. "You're under arrest for the murder of Tabitha Clark."

"*What?*" Spencer shrieked.

"Us?" Emily screamed.

The first agent spoke over them. "You have the right to remain silent. Anything you say can be used against you in a court of law . . ."

The men pushed Spencer and the others toward the cars. Spencer's feet tumbled over each other across the grass and the sidewalk. Fuji's face loomed before her, her satisfied smile still there. "What are you doing?" Spencer wailed at her. "This is a mistake!"

Fuji sank into one hip. "Is it, Spencer?"

"What about the notes we gave you?" Hanna called out. "Everything we told you? What about *A*?"

Fuji removed her Ray-Bans. The expression in her eyes was derisive, absolute. "We retrieved IP information on every single text and e-mail sent from A. We dusted every postcard and handwritten note for prints. And you know what we found?"

Spencer blinked. Next to her, Aria shifted. "What?" Emily whispered.

Fuji stepped forward, drawing the girls into a circle.

"Every one of those texts came from one of your phones," she hissed. "Every note, every picture had only your fingerprints on it, no one else's. The only A in your lives, girls, is the four of you."

18

PRISON BLUES

Aria sat up like a shot and looked around. She was sprawled out on the floor of a dingy cinder-block cell. The fetid scent of urine and sweat wafted through the air, and she could hear angry shouts and swears through the walls. She was locked up.

"Aria?" It was Spencer, who was in the next cell over.

"Y-yeah?" Aria turned toward the wall.

"You were mumbling really loudly," Spencer whispered. "Were you *sleeping*?"

Aria ran her hand through her gnarled hair. She must have passed out from fear and shock. She doubted she'd been out for long, though—light still streamed through the small window at the ceiling.

The past few hours twisted in her head like a tornado. After the bombshell at Rosewood Day, the police had shoved the four of them into separate cars and driven them to holding cells at the Rosewood jail.

It *couldn't* be true. A had orchestrated this. Only . . . *how*? Once again, Aria relived the moment Fuji had told them that every single A note they'd received had been from *their phones*. It was like those dreams she sometimes had where she tried to dial an emergency phone number again and again, but the buttons kept disintegrating. She felt trapped. Helpless. Voiceless.

Aria glanced at the window near the ceiling of her cell. The light was dimmer; maybe a few hours had passed. Did her parents know about their arrest? Had the news picked up the story; was Aria's face plastered all over CNN? She pictured Noel watching from his couch, slack-jawed. She imagined Asher the artist paling as he read a Google Alert, and she pictured her artistic future as a drawing on a chalkboard slowly being erased. She envisioned her parents and Mike getting a phone call and sinking to their knees, inconsolable.

Someone rapped at the bars, and Aria shot up. A familiar man in a well-fitting suit stood outside her cell. "Dad?" Spencer's voice rang out from down the hall.

"Hello, Spencer." Mr. Hastings sounded very serious.

"What are you doing here?" Spencer called out.

"My firm is going to represent you. *All* of you." He looked up and down the cells. "My associate is with me, and he's working on posting bail for all four of you. You'll be out of here soon, don't worry."

Aria ran her tongue over her teeth. She'd never known Mr. Hastings well—even on weekends, he was always out doing something, whether it was going on marathon bike rides or taking care of the lawn or playing a round of golf—but he'd always seemed friendly and caring. He'd look out for them, right?

Mr. Hastings glanced down the hall, then leaned forward. "But we'd like to speak to you about a few things while we're here. My associate Mr. Goddard is going to question you—criminal cases are more his area of expertise. But you're in good hands."

Criminal cases. Aria almost threw up.

"Anyway, they've allowed us a conference room," Mr. Hastings said, clapping his hands. "We have twenty minutes."

The door slammed, and there were footsteps and the jingling of keys. The bristly-haired police officer, Gates, appeared, unlocking the girls' cells one by one. "Conference room's that way," he said, jutting a finger to the end of the hall.

Aria struggled to stand. Her legs felt cramped and weak, as though she'd been a prisoner for years instead of hours.

She followed Mr. Hastings into the small, square, cinder-block room she and the others had sat in more than a year ago, not long before Jenna Cavanaugh's body was found in her backyard. It was very cold inside. A pitcher of water sat in the center of the table, a stack of plastic cups next to it. The room smelled vaguely of vomit.

Spencer walked into the room next, and Emily and

Hanna followed. Each looked dazed, terrified, and exhausted. Everyone sat down without looking at one another. Mr. Hastings spoke to someone in the hall, and then a tall man with receding dark hair walked in. "Hello, girls," he said, extending his hand to each of them. "I'm George Goddard."

Mr. Hastings shut the door behind him. Goddard pulled out a chair and sat down. A few pregnant seconds passed. "So," he finally said. "Let's figure out what's going on here."

"How many times can we tell you that those A notes weren't from us?" Spencer blurted. "They were from Ali and her helper. They set us up."

Mr. Goddard looked conflicted. "The FBI—and the rest of the world—is pretty sure Alison is dead, girls."

"But how do they *know*?" Spencer pressed.

"That I'm not sure," Goddard said. "They just seem very certain that she's no longer alive." He looked back and forth at them as he undid the snap of his briefcase and pulled out some files. "Have you actually *seen* her? Have you been in touch with her?"

Aria exchanged a glance with the others. "We have her on a surveillance video," Spencer admitted. "Or someone who *looks* like her, anyway."

"Any other evidence she's alive?" Goddard asked.

Everyone shook their heads. "But what about the note Hanna gave to the cops from the girl pretending to be Kyla?" Aria asked, assuming that Goddard had done his homework and knew who Kyla was. "Didn't it have Ali's fingerprints on it? And what about Kyla's blood samples—didn't they match Ali's? Didn't you find hair, skin, something?"

"Or how about Gayle's house?" Emily pushed her matted hair off her face.

"Or that Acura key I dropped off?" Spencer pitched in.

Goddard looked through his notes. "According to the information the FBI has released, the only samples at the burn clinic were from the *real* Kyla, the girl who'd been murdered. As for the Acura key, the only prints on it were yours, Spencer."

"It just makes no sense," Aria said shakily. "Why would we send messages about our secrets to ourselves?"

Goddard shrugged. "It doesn't make any sense to me, either. But their take on it is that you wanted to pretend you were bullied to garner sympathy."

"Sympathy for *what*?" Hanna squinted.

"You wanted to make it look like someone was setting you up. Like someone was framing you for killing Tabitha."

"Someone *was* framing us!" Emily cried.

Aria nodded fiercely. "We would never do something like that."

Goddard pressed his lips together. "They have evidence that proves that perhaps you *might* be someone who would do that. Something about pushing another girl off a ski lift?"

Aria jolted up. The incident with Klaudia rushed back to her. How could Fuji have found out about that? But then it hit her: It had been in an A note. And Aria had handed over every single one of her texts.

She covered her mouth with her hand.

"They have eyewitness reports of how you attacked a girl named Kelsey Pierce at a school party a few months ago, too, Spencer," Mr. Goddard said glumly, looking at his notes. "Beau Braswell is willing to corroborate this. And now Ms. Pierce is in a mental hospital."

"Not because of *me*," Spencer blurted. Her chin started to wobble.

Then Goddard looked apologetically at Emily. "Someone named Margaret Colbert can attest to your criminal behavior, too."

Emily blinked. "Isaac's mother? S-she hates me!"

"She said you tried to sell off your baby." His voice rose at the end of that last sentence, like a question.

Emily wilted. Her face turned ghost-white.

Again Goddard glanced at his notes. "I'm sure they're digging up people who think you girls are emotionally unstable." Then he turned to Hanna. "They found out you stole from your own father's political campaign to pay someone off."

Hanna made an *eep*. "Did my father tell them that?"

"He didn't need to." Goddard pinched the bridge of his nose. "It was right there on your phone. That isn't all they have on you, either. The police did a thorough investigation of the burn clinic after the deaths, including eyewitness reports about who was in and out of Graham Pratt's room. According to quite a few people, you were the last one in there before he had his fatal seizure."

Hanna backed up. "*I* didn't kill him!"

Goddard nodded. "They think Graham might have seen Aria set off the bomb in the bottom of the ship. You had a lot to lose by keeping him alive."

"I didn't bomb that ship!" Aria cried.

"You already admitted you were down there." Goddard looked tormented. "They're even trying to connect you to Noel Kahn's attack. Mr. Kahn was apparently working with Fuji on the Tabitha case. You needed him out of the way."

Aria pressed her hands to the sides of her head. "Noel didn't send those e-mails to Fuji about the case—someone hacked into his e-mail account. Did Fuji even talk to Noel, or is she just making all of this up?"

Goddard shrugged. "Probably a little bit of both. And look, this is just the evidence they've shared with me. Who knows what else they're holding closer to the vest, stuff they *don't* want me to know."

Hanna let out a breath. "But it still doesn't make any sense. We didn't kill Tabitha. Someone else did."

"How are they so certain we did it?" Aria asked in what she hoped was a calmer voice. "We worried that A would have methods of making us look more culpable than we were. And yes, we *did* push her—Fuji knows that. But by the time we got down to the beach to save Tabitha, she was gone. A dragged her somewhere."

Goddard laid his hands on the table. "That's what I really want to talk to you about, girls. A new piece of evidence came to light."

There was a long pause. Hanna squinted. "*What* else?"

Goddard pulled a laptop from his briefcase. He lifted the lid and moved the mouse around to wake up the screen. A shaky, black-and-white surveillance image appeared. Waves crashed on a pristine, white beach. A large building with balconies at every window stood in the distance. The angle was different, but it was clear where this was: The Cliffs in Jamaica.

Spencer breathed in sharply. "Where did you get this?"

"This is official video footage from the Lychee Nut, the resort next to The Cliffs. The FBI received it late last night."

Aria stared at the screen. After a moment, something fell from the sky, hitting the sand with an eerily silent *thunk*. Aria saw a limp head, a hand.

"Is that . . . ?" she asked, her voice quivering.

"Tabitha," Goddard answered for her. "This is footage from that night."

Tabitha's hand twitched. She raised her head. Her jaw moved up and down, and it looked like she was calling out. "Look!" Emily cried. "See, she survived!"

Tabitha's mouth opened and closed again, like a fish out of water. Then, four figures appeared from stage right.

One was tall with dirty-blond hair and wearing a blue beach dress. Another had strong swimmer's shoulders and had on a T-shirt that said MERCI BEAUCOUP across the front. The third girl wore a sarong and a white halter. And the fourth girl . . . well, Aria would recognize her own dark hair and tie-dyed maxi anywhere.

Only, it couldn't be. Because as these four girls gathered around Tabitha, they began to kick her hard. Spencer beat her abdomen with her fists. Emily pummeled her legs. And then Aria raised a piece of driftwood and brought it down over Tabitha's head.

Aria twisted away, too horrified to look. Emily let out a stifled scream. Hanna dry-heaved. Aria peeked through her fingers to look at the video again. It sure as hell looked like all of them.

"A—*Ali*—created this," Aria said. "This is her revenge on us because we got the police involved. She knew she had to step it up, and this was the only ammo she had."

"It's a pretty convincing video, ladies." Goddard sounded grim. "Now look, I honestly think the best course of action is a plea bargain. You've been psychologically traumatized from various bullies last year. You clearly didn't know what you were doing. You could get a drastic reduction in sentence if we go that route. Plus all of you were under eighteen at the time, which means you might not be tried as adults."

Spencer widened her eyes. "Does my father agree with this strategy?"

"I haven't spoken with him about it yet, but I have a feeling he will."

Spencer shook her head. "No plea bargain. No sentence, *period*. We're innocent."

"You believe us, don't you?" Hanna asked, tears in her eyes. "Will you fight for us?"

Goddard hesitated for a long time, spinning and spinning his wedding ring on his finger. "I believe you," he said in a defeated voice. "But I'm going to tell you right now—it's going to be tough." He stood. "I'm sorry. Bail will be posted soon—you can wait here until they come for you. We'll talk tomorrow."

And then, just like that, he was gone.

19

NO LOVE

Everyone stared at one another around the conference table after the lawyer left the room. Hanna was trembling so hard, she was making the chair she was sitting on shake. Aria looked like she was going to pass out.

"How can this be happening?" Spencer whispered, looking around helplessly. "I mean, okay, I can buy that Team A routed every note back to our phones. They're smart. Maybe it's possible."

"And we should have taken better precautions about the people in the A notes," Emily added. "Isaac's mom has had it out for me from the beginning. Of course Kelsey is going to rat out Spencer."

Hanna tentatively touched her face. She could feel that her eyes were puffy, her hair was sticking out in a million directions, and she'd sprouted several zits on her chin. When she shifted in the chair, her abdomen pulsed with pain. She hadn't peed since they'd arrived, too horrified that the police officers could be watching her on a hidden camera.

"But still," Spencer said. "*How* did they make that surveillance video?"

There was a pause.

"Do you think Ali roofied us and made us do it?" Aria's voice rang out.

"Guys, I remember every second of that day," Hanna said. "We ran downstairs the moment Tabitha fell. I didn't wake up in a daze a few hours later. Did you?"

"No," Spencer's voice called from far away.

"Maybe Helper A hired four girls who looked like us," Emily suggested. "And then, I don't know, dug up a Tabitha look-alike blow-up doll, and just . . ."

". . . *staged* the whole thing?" Hanna finished. "How would she have gotten girls to do that?"

"Maybe he told them it was for a movie he was making," Aria said. "Maybe he paid them tons of money, and that was it."

Hanna sniffed. "So, what, we should look for an old ad on Craigslist that says *Wanted: Four Girls to Reenact a Murder in Jamaica*?" It didn't sound very realistic, but who knew? Perhaps Team A killed the Hanna, Aria, Spencer, and Emily clones after the video had been made so they'd never talk. It was hard to tell the extent of their madness.

A door slammed somewhere down the hall. The air

conditioner kicked back on, and the sharp smell of stale coffee suddenly wafted through the air.

"We should get someone to check out this Lychee Nut hotel," Emily suggested. "Was this really their video footage? Why would they have had a murder on tape the whole time and not come forward with it?"

"It's obvious the tape was planted," Hanna said. "But who do we have on the outside to actually investigate this for us?" *On the outside.* She wasn't even in prison yet and she was already using the lingo.

"Excuse me?"

Hanna jumped. Spencer's father poked his head inside. "Your bail has been posted. You're all free to go."

"We *are*?" Emily didn't get up.

"Your arraignment is in one month." Mr. Hastings held the door open for them.

"And then what?" Aria asked nervously. "We come back here?"

Mr. Hastings gritted his teeth. "Don't freak out, but we just found out that they want to extradite you to Jamaica."

"*What?*" Spencer exploded.

Hanna pressed a hand to her chest. "Why?"

"That's where you committed your crime. Your trial will be there, and you'll serve your sentence there, too, if you're convicted. That's what they're pushing for, anyway." Mr. Hastings looked furious. "We're doing everything we can to change it, though. It's bullshit. They're just trying to make an example of you."

A bomb went off in Hanna's brain. The prospect of spending the rest of her life in an American prison was bad enough, but spending it in a Jamaican one?

She followed the lawyer out of the conference room, her heart hammering. They walked down a long hallway. Mr. Hastings opened the door that led into the lobby. Hanna blinked in the brightness of the front room, then looked around at everyone waiting. When Mrs. Hastings saw Spencer in handcuffs, she burst into tears. To her left were Mr. and Mrs. Fields, looking shocked and pale. Next to them were Aria's parents, though no Mike. Hanna's mom was next to them. Hanna looked around for her dad but didn't see him.

Hanna's mother ran up to her. "Let's get you out of here, honey."

But Hanna was still looking around. "Dad's here, too, right?"

Ms. Marin held Hanna's hand and steered her through a sliding door. They came to a desk, and a guard asked her to sign some papers. The guards gave Hanna back her belongings, including her phone. Hanna checked the messages and texts. Lots of worried texts from Mike but nothing from her father.

"Mom." She placed her hands on her hips. "Where is Dad?"

Ms. Marin handed the papers back and took Hanna's

arm. "I brought a scarf for you to put over your head when we go outside. There's a lot of press out there."

Hanna's heart banged faster. "He knows about this, doesn't he? Why isn't he here?"

Finally, Ms. Marin stopped halfway down the hall. She looked positively heartbroken. "Honey, he couldn't risk the bad publicity."

Hanna blinked. "D-did you talk to him? Is he worried about me?"

Her mother swallowed hard, then slung an arm around Hanna's shoulders. "Let's get you in the car, okay?"

She handed Hanna a scarf, then pushed through the exit door. At least twenty reporters and cameramen swarmed toward them, flashbulbs popping, video cameras pointed, microphones poised.

The questions came fast and furious. "Ms. Marin, did you know your daughter did it?" "Hanna, how do you feel about being extradited to Jamaica?" "Ms. Marin, is your ex-husband going to withdraw from the Senate race?"

Hanna knew that if her father were here, the press would be asking him these questions instead. But not-so-deep-down, she didn't care. He *should* be here. Who cared about his campaign at a time like this?

She blinked through tears and clung even tighter to her mother's arm, suddenly more grateful for her mom than she'd been in years. Ashley Marin bulldozed through the press, not letting them take even one decent picture of her daughter, not uttering a word except for "No comment" to the leechlike reporters. She didn't ask Hanna if she did it or not. She didn't give Hanna shit or think of ways to spin this so it benefited her. That, Hanna realized, was how a parent was *supposed* to act.

And that was what she needed.

20

SHE'S DEAD TO US

Emily had returned to her house after a fair share of trouble—Ali's death, A outing her at a swim meet, her banishment to Iowa, her secret baby coming to light. Each of those homecomings had been stilted and strange, but nothing, *nothing* was like returning to the Fields abode after being arrested for murder.

Her family was silent the whole ride home. Her mother stared straight ahead, unblinking, and her father gripped the steering wheel so hard, his knuckles were white. Only once did Emily dare to protest her innocence, but her parents hadn't responded. Her phone buzzed, and she looked at it. To her astonishment, Jordan had sent her a private message. *I'm so disappointed in you, Em.*

Emily recoiled. Had Jordan heard? Did she actually believe the news?

There was an Instagram attached to the message. Emily thought it would be a still shot of the fake video, but instead a shadowy photo of her on a dance floor appeared. Emily held a champagne flute in her hand. A pretty black girl spun her around.

Pegasus? Emily dropped the phone to her lap. The night with Carolyn at the bar. The dance with River. Who had snapped and posted this? *Ali?*

Her fingers hovered over the keyboard. *It's not what it looks like!* she wrote. *We were just dancing. I still love you, I promise.*

But Jordan didn't write back.

The Fields house was cold, and most of the lights were off. Emily followed her parents inside the kitchen and clapped eyes on Carolyn, who was bustling around gathering silverware and plates from drawers and cupboards. Her heart lifted.

But Carolyn didn't even meet Emily's gaze. "I have Chinese," she announced in a brisk voice, plopping a large paper bag on the table.

Mrs. Fields's brow furrowed. "How much did that—"

"It's fine, Mom," Carolyn cut her off, then slammed a bunch of forks down.

Emily took a few more forks from the pile and placed them at the rest of the seats. She glanced at her sister. "You know this is a huge mix-up, right? Someone framed us for killing that girl."

Carolyn turned away. Emily's heart slowly began to sink.

She waited until everyone else had served themselves

lo mein and kung pao chicken, then took a paltry amount of fried rice and sat in her normal chair. The only sounds were chewing and the scraping of knives and forks.

She shut her eyes. How could Fuji think they killed not only Tabitha but Gayle and Graham, too? And why was Fuji so convinced, suddenly, that Ali was dead? Emily wished she could talk to the agent, but Mr. Hastings had forbade them from saying a word to anyone except for the legal team.

She decided to try again, turning back to Carolyn. "We think it was Ali, actually. She's alive. We were afraid that Tabitha Clark *was* Ali, in fact . . . but she wasn't, and . . ."

Carolyn looked desperately at their father. "Dad, tell her to stop."

"Carolyn, I'm telling the truth." Emily knew she should shut up, but she couldn't control her mouth. "Ali survived. It's really her."

She looked around at her family, wishing *someone* would say they understood. But everyone was staring at their plates.

The doorbell rang. Everyone's heads swiveled toward the hall, and Mr. Fields stood to answer it. There were low murmurs, and then the front door slammed.

Emily got up from the table and peered through the front window. Two tow trucks sat in the driveway. A man in a blue jumpsuit hitched the Volvo wagon to the tow, and a balding guy in a black jacket did the same with the family's minivan. Mr. Fields just stood there on the lawn, hands in his pockets, a forlorn expression on his face.

"Why are our cars being taken away?" Emily called to her mom in the kitchen.

No answer. She walked back into the room. Mrs. Fields and Carolyn picked at their meals. Emily's heart started to pound. "Mom. What's going on?"

"Why is she asking that?" Carolyn's voice rose in pitch. "How could she not know?"

Emily looked back and forth at them. "Know *what*?"

Mrs. Fields's jaw was clenched tight. "We had to sell both cars and use the money we got to pay your bail," she said calmly. "Among other things."

Emily blinked hard. "You did?"

Carolyn leapt up from the table and walked over to Emily. "What did you expect? You killed someone."

Something exploded in Emily's brain. "N-no, I didn't!"

Carolyn's nostrils flared. "We saw you on that video. You looked like a monster."

"That wasn't me!" Emily glanced desperately at her mother. "Mom? You believe it wasn't me, right?"

Mrs. Fields lowered her eyes. "That video. It was so *violent*."

Emily looked at her imploringly. Did that mean her mom believed her . . . or she thought she'd done it?

Carolyn sniffed. "All your lies have finally caught up to you. But *we're* paying the consequences. We might even lose the house."

Emily walked back to the window and stared at her

father, who was standing with his back to her, facing the tow truck.

"I'm going to have to get a job—that is, if anyone will even hire me," Carolyn said from the kitchen. "All because of *you*, Emily. It's always about you, isn't it? You're always ruining everything."

Mrs. Fields kneaded her temples. "Carolyn, please. Not now."

Carolyn slapped the table hard. "Why not now? She needs to understand. She doesn't live in the real world, and I'm really sick of it." She faced Emily. "It's always an excuse with you. Your best friend was murdered. You were getting text messages from Mona Vanderwaal, who I *personally* saw you guys make fun of when Ali was alive. But hey, it's different when *you're* bullied, huh? Everyone's just supposed to drop everything and treat you like some sort of delicate flower."

Emily walked back to the table. Her jaw dropped. "Are you kidding me? She tried to *kill us*."

Carolyn rolled her eyes. "And when you get pregnant, you don't actually face up to it. Nope, you hide in Philly. You use me all summer, make my life hell, and then, afterward, it's all about *you*, how I hurt you, how I should have just accepted what you were going through without being upset or afraid or *anything*."

Emily pressed a hand to her chest. "I thought you forgave me for that!"

Carolyn shrugged. "I might have forgiven you if I

hadn't known you were *still doing it*, Emily. Now you've *killed* someone, and you're still blaming everyone but yourself, basically. But you can't make excuses anymore. I'm sorry Ali tried to kill you in the Poconos last year. I'm sorry you loved her, and she rejected you. But get *over it*. Take some responsibility."

"Get over it?" Emily screamed, anger she'd never experienced before rising up her throat. "How can I get over it if she's *still doing it*?"

"She's not still doing anything!" Carolyn screeched back. "She's dead! Face it! She's gone, and what you did is nobody's fault but yours."

Emily let out a primal roar, ran for her sister, and grabbed her shoulders. "Why can't you believe me?" she screamed. How did Carolyn not understand? How could her family believe she'd made all of this up, done something so awful?

Carolyn pushed Emily away, and Emily slammed against the back wall. Emily lunged for her sister again, and suddenly, they were on the ground. Carolyn's strong body pressed into Emily's. Her nails scratched Emily's face. Emily shrieked and nudged Carolyn's abdomen with her knees, then wrapped an arm around Carolyn and flipped her on her side. Carolyn's eyes flashed. She bared her teeth and then bit down on Emily's arm. Emily screamed and pulled away, staring at the marks where Carolyn's teeth had broken the skin.

"Girls!" Mrs. Fields wailed. "Girls, *stop*!"

Two hands grabbed Emily around her waist and lifted her to stand. Emily felt her father's hot breath on her neck, but she was so angry that she elbowed him off. She reached out and grabbed a chunk of Carolyn's hair. Carolyn screamed and wrenched away, but not before Emily pulled several strands of hair from her sister's head. Carolyn rammed her body into Emily hard, sending her careening across the room and knocking into a cabinet that held her mother's Hummel knickknacks.

There was a creaking sound as the cabinet tipped on its side and slowly, slowly, slowly started to fall. Mrs. Fields leapt forward, trying to grab it, but it was too heavy and too late—the cabinet was already too far gone.

The floor shook. There was the sound of breaking glass, and all of the figurines spilled out. Suddenly, the room was silent. Emily and Carolyn stopped and stared. Mrs. Fields dropped to her knees, gaping at everything that had broken. At least that was what Emily thought she was doing until she turned around. Her mother's face had turned a ghostly white. Her mouth was an O, and she sucked for air. She clutched at her chest, a look of terror frozen on her face.

"Mom?" Carolyn ran to her. "What's going on?"

"It's . . . my . . ." It was all Mrs. Fields could get out. She grabbed her left arm and hunched over.

Carolyn yanked the cordless phone from its cradle on the desk. Her fingers shook as she dialed 911. "Help!" she said, when someone answered. "My mother is having a heart attack!"

Emily knelt by her mother helplessly. She took her mom's pulse. It was racing fast. "Mom, I'm so sorry," she said tearfully, staring into her mother's widened, desperate eyes.

Mr. Fields appeared from behind, pushed a baby aspirin into his wife's mouth, and made her swallow. Seconds later, sirens blared from up the street. EMTs burst through the front door in a swirl of boots and reflective jackets. They elbowed Emily and the others out of the way and started to attach Mrs. Fields to monitors and an oxygen tank. Two strong men lifted her onto a stretcher, and before Emily knew it, they were carrying her out the door.

Everyone ran outside to where the ambulance was parked. A couple of neighbors stood on the adjacent lawns to gawk. "Only two can ride with us," the head EMT was saying to Mr. Fields. "The other can follow along behind."

Mr. Fields looked at Emily. "Stay here," he growled at her. "Come on, Carolyn."

Emily shrank back into the house like he'd kicked her. Her father had never spoken to her like that in her life.

She pushed the door shut and leaned against the back of it, breathing hard. In the kitchen, everything was still as they'd left it. Forks protruded out of bowls. The coffeemaker beeped loudly, indicating that the pot had finished brewing. In the living room, the Hummel cabinet lay ruined on the floor, broken Hummels scattered across the carpet. Emily walked over to them and knelt down. Her mom's favorite milkmaid had a severed head. There was a single arm holding a water bucket by the vent. The little ballerinas were now legless, the tranquil-looking cows were hornless and without tails.

She wanted to find Ali and strangle her with all her might. But all she could do now was look at the shattered remains of her mother's prized possessions and cry.

21

CLOSED DOORS

A week later, Spencer crept through the woods behind her house to meet Aria, Hanna, and Emily. It was almost too dark to see anything, so she used her cell-phone light to guide the way. Thick roots jutted up from the earth. A fallen log lay across her path. Before long, she came upon the old wishing well, a stone relic left behind from farmers in the 1700s. Moss grew over the sides. Some of the rock had crumbled away. Spencer peered over the edge and threw a pebble down the hole. There was an empty-sounding echo as it plopped into shallow water.

Then she turned and gazed down the hill at her house. Most of the lights were off. The basement window she'd snuck out of was ajar. The spot where her family's barn apartment had been before Ali burned it down still had no grass. She counted seven news vehicles at the curb, staking out the house. They'd been parked there around the clock since their arrest.

"Hey." Emily's head appeared over the other side of the hill. It was a chilly night, and she had on a black hoodie and jeans. She glanced at the well and made a small whimper. "Do you think she really used to come here?"

"I guess." Spencer dared touch the slimy curved stones. The frame was half-rotted, there was a fuzz of moss on the top and sides, and a rusted metal bucket lay a few feet away. "The top of this hill gave her the perfect vantage of my house."

Emily clucked her tongue. A twig snapped, and they turned. Aria and Hanna trudged up the hill. When they got to the top, the girls just stood under the moon, staring at one another.

"Well?" Spencer finally blurted. "We'd better start talking. There will be a witch hunt for me soon." There had been too much turmoil for the four of them to meet after they'd returned home, but finally, tonight, Hanna had sent a text that they needed to talk. But it was true about the witch hunt: The reporters camped outside Spencer's house were so nosy and clever that they'd figure out she was missing before Spencer's family did. In the week since the arrest, her mother had barely gotten out of bed, and Mr. Pennythistle had tiptoed around her nervously, as if afraid she was going to freak out and do something crazy. "I'm not *actually* a murderer!" Spencer had cried out to him once, but it hadn't done any good.

"Yeah, I shouldn't stay out long, either," Aria mumbled. "But it is good to see you guys."

"Seriously." Emily looked at them, her eyes wet. "It's awful, though, isn't it?"

Hanna nodded despondently. "I'm going to lose my mind if I have to sit in my house another day." That was part of their punishment: Until they were extradited to Jamaica, they were to remain in their homes full-time. Rosewood Day hadn't expelled them, but the school didn't allow the girls to come back, either.

"Everyone ready for finals?" Aria said in a not-so-joking voice. They were allowed to take their exams at home.

"I don't see the point," Spencer said sadly. She looked at the others. "I got a letter from Princeton this week. They don't want an alleged murderer in their freshman class."

Emily winced. "I heard from NC State, too." She made a thumbs-down sign.

"Yep, I'm out of FIT," Hanna mumbled. She squeezed her eyes shut and lowered her shoulders. "This isn't *fair*, guys. That's what I keep thinking. This. Just. Isn't. *Fair*."

"Tell me about it," Aria murmured, shuffling her feet through the dry leaves. "But it's not like we can do anything."

Hanna pounded a fist into an open palm. "Yes, we can. I say we look for Ali again ourselves."

"Are you crazy?" Spencer leaned against the well's rickety frame. "A could still hurt a lot of people we love. Besides, we should just lie low and not do anything else to stir up the press."

"So we just wait for them to send us away?" Hanna

shrieked. "Have you *seen* the prisons in Jamaica? They're filled with snakes. And they, like, *force* you to do gravity bongs there. It's one of their torture methods."

Spencer's eyebrows knitted together. "I'm sure they don't do *that*, Han."

"I bet they do." Hanna placed her hands on her hips. "Mike made me smoke out of one once, and I broke out into hives and hallucinated. I was in hell."

"My dad promised that our legal team will figure out a way to keep us from going there," Spencer said weakly.

Aria sighed. "No offense to your dad or our legal team, but all the papers are saying the FBI wants to make an example of us. It's almost guaranteed we're going to Jamaica."

Spencer gritted her teeth. "Well, maybe Fuji will realize the truth. Or maybe Ali will screw up."

"That's not going to happen," Emily said despondently. "Ali has us exactly where she wants us. And when has she *ever* screwed up?"

"I really don't think we should start digging again, guys," Spencer warned.

"But we have clues," Aria said. "That doctored video. Whoever N is."

Spencer paced in circles. "I know, but . . ."

"Your friend Chase is good with computers, right, Spence?" Hanna begged. "Maybe he can zoom into that video file and show the girls' faces, prove to the cops it isn't us."

Spencer twisted her mouth. "But I can't put him at risk."

"He already *is* at risk," Aria reminded her.

There was a long pause. A truck shifted gears far off on the turnpike.

"I'm not going to Jamaica," Hanna said firmly. "I want to stay in Rosewood."

Aria swallowed hard. "I do, too."

Spencer stared into the dark sky. Aria was right. If Ali was going to get Chase, the plan was already in motion. Spencer hadn't heard from Chase since before their arrest, but she knew he would do anything for her.

A light snapped on in her house, and she lowered her shoulders, half expecting her mom to appear on the back porch any second. "I'd better go back. But I'll do it, Han. I'll reach out to Chase."

"Good." Hanna sounded relieved.

Spencer started back down the hill, her heart pounding. Mercifully, the light snapped off shortly after it turned on, and no one appeared on the back deck. She walked around to the front of the house, eyeing the car in the driveway, then the vehicles parked at the curb. They'd see her if she backed out—she'd have to take the bus. There was a SEPTA stop only a mile from here, on Lancaster Avenue.

She looked down at her shoes, thankful she was wearing sneakers. *Here goes nothing*, she thought, taking off jogging. It was the only way.

* * *

A half hour later, Spencer boarded a brightly lit, cigarette-stinky Rosewood bus toward Philadelphia and sank into a seat. Across the aisle, a woman was reading a copy of the *Philadelphia Sentinel.* On the front page was Spencer's picture.

One Lie Too Many, read the headline. Spencer turned toward the window and scrunched up her body to make herself seem smaller. She'd avoided the news all week, knowing she'd only see stories like that. *Please don't see me, please don't see me*, she willed. The woman folded over the page. Spencer's picture vanished. No one said a word.

Chase lived in Merion, a suburb closer to the city. Spencer pulled the chain at her stop and rushed off the bus. Though she had never been to Chase's house before, she found the apartment building easily and walked up the uneven sidewalk to the front door. There was a *swish* behind her, and she turned. A car slowly drifted by, a MERION PD logo blazing across the side.

Spencer ducked behind a tree. The cruiser rolled past at a steady clip, the cop staring straight ahead. After a moment, the car rounded the corner. *Safe.*

She scurried inside the first door and examined the list of names of residents. Chase lived in apartment 4D; she pressed the buzzer. A few seconds passed. Nothing happened. Spencer cocked her head, listening. It was only a little after ten thirty, and Chase had once admitted that he often stayed up until one or two in the morning. Maybe he wasn't home?

A woman carrying a green purse appeared on the stairs inside the building. She gave Spencer a cursory glance, then pushed out the door and into the street. Spencer caught the door and slipped inside the building, her heart hammering hard. Maybe Chase's buzzer didn't work. She would knock on his door herself.

She climbed four flights, huffing a little as she finally reached Chase's door. She had to stop breathing to listen for sounds inside the apartment. Music thumped in a back room. And then, a cough. *Yes.* He *was* home.

The doorbell was broken when she tried it, so she knocked—first quietly and then louder. "Chase?" she called out. "It's me. Spencer. I need to talk to you."

The music went silent. Footsteps sounded near the door, and Chase opened it a crack, the chain unlatched. "Spencer." His eyes met hers. "You can't be here."

Spencer's jaw dropped. "B-but we're being framed. There's a video I need you to look at—one of us in Jamaica. Alison obviously doctored it."

Chase's Adam's apple bobbed as he swallowed. "Why didn't you tell me I was on the hit list, too?"

"*What?*" She thought of the A note threatening him. How had Chase found out? "D-did you get a note from A? Has someone tried to hurt you?"

Chase's eyes darted back and forth. "No," he said, after too long a beat, but it was the most pitiful lie Spencer had ever heard.

Spencer's head buzzed. All she could focus on, for a

moment, was the bumpy texture of the hallway walls. "I-I thought the police would keep you safe," she said helplessly. "I thought they'd keep *all* of us safe." She tried to pull open the door. "Please let me in. We can crack this video—I know we can. I need you."

Chase pressed his lips together as if he were trying to keep from crying. "You have to go, Spencer. I'm sorry. I've just been through too much, okay? This is too intense, even for me."

"But—"

"And I can't believe you didn't warn me." Chase's eyes were sad. "I thought I meant more to you than that."

Then the door slammed. There were clicking sounds as Chase twisted the locks on the inside. Footsteps receded. The music came on again, louder now. A fast, angry song drowning out everything.

Spencer felt like he'd slapped her across the face. She stepped away from the door, surprised tears coming to her eyes. All at once, she felt completely abandoned. No one would help her anymore.

The magnitude of what was happening hit her hard. There *was* no way out of this. Ali had really and truly won.

Spencer reached for her phone and stared at it hard. *Text me, bitch*, she thought fiercely, desperately. If only Ali would write to her right now and rub this in her face. *Boohoo*, maybe. *Poor widdle Spencer lost her boyfriend.* She was probably *dying* to.

She stared hard at the screen, willing something to

happen. She walked to the front of the apartment building and stood on the porch so Ali could see her, so that she'd *know* her pain. "Come get me," she even said out loud into the still darkness. "Stop hiding and actually show your face, you coward."

No one moved behind the bushes. No giggles echoed in the treetops. Spencer's phone remained silent. She shut her eyes and drew back her hand, ready to hurl the phone to the sidewalk.

But instead she let her arm wilt at her side and walked the three blocks to catch the bus home.

22

SLOWLY SINKING

Two weeks after her arrest, Hanna staggered down the stairs of her mom's house with her mini Doberman, Dot, following on her heels. All the lights were still on in the kitchen, but the room was empty. A note on the table said, *I made coffee. Muffins in fridge.*

Hanna listened, but there were no sounds of her mom anywhere—she must have already gone to work. Ms. Marin had been weirdly attentive in the past few days, bringing home sushi from the store, watching *Teen Mom* marathons with Hanna and Mike, even offering to give Hanna a mani-pedi, although Ms. Marin had a very well-known aversion to feet. On the one hand, Hanna thought it was sweet that her mom was trying to make an effort and stand by her. But it was too late. Her fate was sealed.

She fell into a kitchen chair, flipped on the TV, and absently stroked Dot's smooth, flat head. Her blinking phone on the table caught her eye. TEN NEW MESSAGES. Her heart lifted, thinking one might be from her dad, who she hadn't heard from since before her arrest. But then she scrolled through each of the messages. They were all from her classmates.

You're disgusting, wrote Mason Byers. *I bet you hurt Noel, too, right?*

And from Naomi Zeigler: *I hope you rot in Jamaica forever, bitch.* And Colleen Bebris, Mike's ex: *I knew you were capable of this sort of thing.*

Even Madison had written: *Maybe I forgave you too soon. Now I don't know what to think about the crash.*

More of the same. Hanna had been getting these non-stop since she had been released from jail. She deleted them without reading more. Maybe it was good she'd been suspended: If she returned to Rosewood Day, she'd be the most-hated girl at school.

She held her phone in her palms for a few moments, then clicked over to a saved video link. An image of a waving American flag appeared. Then came her father's voice-over: *I'm Tom Marin, and I approve this message.*

Hanna watched the whole PSA from start to finish. She would be the only person in Pennsylvania who actually saw it, as it had been pulled from the networks before it even aired. "And that's why I stand behind Tom Marin's Zero-Tolerance Plan," TV Hanna said brightly at the end, offering a huge smile.

The camera zoomed in on her father's supportive

expression. He turned to Hanna at the end of the commercial, his essence oozing love and pride and loyalty.

What a farce.

As if on cue, a news broadcast appeared on the TV in the kitchen. Hanna looked up. The anchor was talking about Hanna's dad's run for Senate. "Since Mr. Marin's daughter's arrest, there has been a sharp downturn of Tom Marin supporters," the woman said. A line graph appeared on the screen. A bold red line, representing the number of Tom Marin devotees, made a roller-coaster-like plunge. "Protesters demand that he withdraw," the reporter added.

There was a shot of an angry mob holding picket signs. They'd been on the news nonstop, too—they were the same people who had protested outside Graham's funeral, and the news had spent a good deal of time with them the day Hanna was released from jail, when they'd picketed her father's office. It looked like they were in front of the office again today. Some of them bore the same STOP THE ROSEWOOD SERIAL KILLER message, but there were new signs now of Mr. Marin's face with a red slash across it and Hanna, Spencer, Emily, and Aria wearing devil horns.

Hanna flicked off the TV fast, experiencing the dizzy feeling she got when she knew she was going to puke. She fled to the bathroom and leaned over the bowl until the queasiness passed. Then she felt for her phone in her pocket. She had to fix this for her dad. His voters needed to understand that this wasn't her fault. *He* needed to understand it, too.

The doorbell rang. Dot scampered toward it, barking hysterically. Hanna stood up and trudged down the hall. A shape moved through the opaque sidelight, and she worried for a moment it might be the cops coming to take her to Jamaica *now*. Maybe her dad had arranged to get her out of the country early.

But it was just Mike. "Your final exam, madam," he offered, pushing an envelope into her hands.

Hanna stared at it. *Honors Calculus* it said at the top.

"You have two hours," Mike said, glancing at his watch. "And they're even letting me be your proctor. Do you want to start now?"

Hanna suddenly felt exhausted. When was she ever going to use calculus—especially if she was in prison? "Let's do it later," she said, placing the envelope on the side table in the foyer. "I need a favor."

"Anything," Mike said automatically.

"I need to go to my father's campaign office. Now."

Mike's eyes darted back and forth. "Are you sure that's a good idea? I thought you weren't allowed to leave the house."

Hanna glared at him. "You said anything."

Mike pressed his lips together. "But I don't want to see you upset."

Hanna crossed her arms over her chest. She'd told Mike how her dad hadn't shown up at the police station or contacted her in the week since. And then, because she'd been extra upset, she'd also told him every other shitty thing her father had ever done to her.

"It's something I need to do," she said firmly.

Mike walked up to Hanna and took her hand. "Okay," he said, opening the front door again. "Then let's go."

When Hanna and Mike pulled up to Mr. Marin's office building, at least fifty protesters clogged the sidewalks. Even though Hanna had anticipated them from the news, it was intense to actually see them in person.

"It's okay," Mike said, then handed Hanna a hoodie from the backseat. "Put this on so they don't recognize you. I can handle them."

He grabbed her wrist and led her through the picketers. Hanna kept her head down, her heart pounding the whole time. She was terrified one of the picketers would notice her. They surrounded Mike, screaming, "Are you going to see Tom Marin?" And, "Make him withdraw!" And, "We don't want your kind in Washington!" someone else bellowed.

Mike wrapped his arms tightly around her and ushered her through the doors. The protesters' voices were muffled once they were in the atrium, but they were still chanting the same things. Her heart beat fast as she padded toward the elevator and removed the hoodie, wishing she were still home in bed.

"Come on," Mike said, heading to the elevator and pushing the CALL button. He held her hand the whole way up, squeezing it every so often. When they reached the fourth floor, Hanna peered out the long windows in the hallway to center herself. One of them didn't face the protesters but the thick, untended forest to the left of the property. Trees jutted every which way. Poking above them was what looked like the crumbled remains of a stone chimney. The Main Line was full of old wrecks—the historical commission protected them if a famous general ever slept there or if it was the site of an important battle. There might even be an old building hidden back there somewhere, forgotten in time, vines curling around it until they made a cocoon. Hanna could definitely relate. She felt overwhelmed and choked, too. If only she could disappear into the trees as well.

Hanna took a deep breath and faced the glass door that led to her father's office, then pushed through. Her father's receptionist, Mary, took one look at Hanna and jumped to her feet. "You're not supposed to be here."

Hanna squared her shoulders. "It's important."

"Tom's in a meeting."

Hanna raised an eyebrow. "Tell him it will only take a second."

Mary set aside the pen she was using and scuttled down the hall. In moments, Mr. Marin appeared. He had on a navy-blue suit with a little American flag pin on the lapel. It struck Hanna as petty, suddenly—his daughter was going to be tried for murder, but he'd still remembered to put the flag pin on his jacket this morning.

"Hanna." Mr. Marin's tone was restrained anger.

"You're not supposed to leave the house."

"I wanted to talk to you, and you weren't calling me back," Hanna said, hating how mouselike she sounded. "I want to know why you didn't come to the police station when I was released. *Or* why you haven't spoken to me since then."

Mr. Marin crossed his arms over his chest. He gestured to the picketers through the front window. The woman carrying the huge picture of Hanna's face passed by. "Did they see you come in?"

Hanna blinked. "No. I had a hoodie on."

He rubbed his eyes. "Go out the back way when you leave."

He wheeled around and started back to his office. Hanna's mouth hung open. Then Mike stepped forward. "She's still your daughter, Mr. Marin," he shouted.

Mr. Marin stopped and gave him a vicious glare. "This is none of your business, Mike."

He looked at Hanna. "I can't align myself with you right now. I'm sorry."

Hanna actually felt physical pain shoot through her. *Align myself.* It sounded so clinical. "Are you serious?"

His gaze was on the protesters out the window again. "I've given you chance upon chance. I've tried to be there for you. But right now, it's campaign suicide. You're on your own."

"You're worried about the *campaign*?" Hanna squeaked. She took a few steps toward him. "Dad, please listen to me. I didn't kill anyone. The video the news has been showing of me beating that girl is fake. You know me—I wouldn't do that. I'm not that kind of person."

She continued to walk toward him, her arms outstretched, but Mr. Marin backed away from her, a guarded look on his face. Then the phone at the front desk rang, and Mr. Marin motioned to the receptionist to pick it up. She murmured something, then looked at him. "Tom," she said, cupping her hand over the mouthpiece. "It's that reporter from the *Sentinel*."

Mr. Marin looked pained. "I'll take it in my office." He glowered at Hanna. "You have to go now."

He turned and plodded down the hall, not even saying good-bye. Hanna stood very still for a moment, suddenly feeling like every molecule in her body was about to implode and turn her to vapor. A protester blew a whistle. Someone else cheered. Hanna squeezed her eyes shut and tried to cry, but she felt too stunned.

She felt Mike's fingers curl around hers. "Come on," he whispered, leading her back to the elevator. She said nothing as he pushed the CALL button, and they rode to the first floor. She said nothing as Mike pulled her out of the elevator and across the empty atrium to the front door. Only when she saw the protesters marching in a circle right in front of the doors did she stop and give Mike a nervous look. "He told us to go out the back way."

"Do you actually give a shit what he wants you to do?" Mike's cheeks were red. He gripped her hand harder. "I could kill him, Hanna. You don't owe him anything."

Hanna's jaw wobbled. Mike was totally, absolutely right.

Tears flowed down her cheeks as she stepped onto the curb. As the protesters surrounded her once more, she let out a single, piercing sob. Mike grabbed her immediately and hugged her tight, pulling her through the throng. And over all the shouting, one thought was clean and crisp in Hanna's mind. She *didn't* owe her dad anything. She'd thought it had sucked, all those years, when her father had chosen Kate over her.

But nothing compared to him choosing the whole state of Pennsylvania.

23

NOT ON THE LIST

That same Friday, Emily stood in the lobby of the Rosewood Memorial Hospital. Doctors swept past, looking busy and important. Emily walked over to the directory on the wall and found the cardiac unit, where her mother was recovering after her emergency heart surgery. Not that her dad or her sister had given her an update on her daily progress—they'd barely been home. Emily had had to find out through a nebulous network of doctors and nurses, who'd all seemed shocked that she couldn't just get the information from her family. Technically, she wasn't supposed to leave the house, but what could the police say if they caught her here? That she wasn't allowed to see her ailing mother?

Emily was trying to put a good face on it. It sucked that her bail cost so much money that they had to do without their cars—and a few other things, which various rough-looking dudes had removed from the house over the past two weeks, including an antique baby carriage of Emily's grandmother's and a baby Jesus statue Emily had helped her mom recover from a group of vandals last year. But Emily was still part of the family, for goodness' sake. Besides, she'd finally gotten hold of Mr. Goddard this morning, and he'd told her that after the trial, no matter the verdict, the bail money would be returned to her parents. They'd get their car back. Everyone would be able to return to college. They'd be okay.

Her heart thudded hard as she boarded the elevator and rode it to the third floor. As soon as she stepped onto the ward, she spied her dad and Carolyn slumped in chairs in the waiting room, asleep. There was an open *Sports Illustrated* magazine in her dad's lap. Carolyn's coat was half on, half off. Emily smiled faintly at them, noticing how sweet and friendly they looked in sleep. It gave her hope. Maybe, just maybe, everything would be okay.

A newscast played on the TV overhead: *Arraignment in One Week*, read a headline. Emily's school picture appeared on the screen, followed by Spencer's, Aria's, and Hanna's. Then Tabitha's father, whom Emily had come face-to-face with quite a few times in the past few months, popped on the screen. "I'm deeply saddened by the outcome of this investigation," the man said, his eyes lowered. "I want justice for these girls, but it still won't bring my daughter back."

Emily flinched. Poor Mr. Clark. She imagined him lying in bed at night, alone in his big house, thinking of that horrible video on the beach again and again. Ali wasn't just hurting the four of them by releasing that video. There were so many other victims, too. So many lives ruined. Iris flashed in Emily's mind again. Would *she* be another victim? And if she was, would Emily somehow get blamed for it? She'd been blamed for everything *else*, after all.

The news switched to a commercial about a new Ford pickup. Emily checked on her father and sister, but they hadn't stirred. Spinning around, she marched over to the nurse's station. A tired-looking woman in balloon-printed scrubs drank from a Styrofoam cup of coffee. "Can you tell me which room Pamela Fields is in?" Emily asked. "I'm her daughter."

The nurse examined Emily carefully. "Her daughter Beth?"

Emily blinked. "No. Her daughter Emily."

The nurse's eyes widened. "You're not on Mrs. Fields's list. You can't visit."

"But I'm her daughter."

The nurse picked up a phone on her desk. "I'm really sorry about this. But I was told if you came . . ." She lifted the receiver to her ear. "I need security."

Emily backed away from the desk. *Security?* For a split second, she didn't understand . . . and then she did. Her family had asked to keep her away.

She wheeled around, suddenly numb. "I'm leaving," she said, just as a figure appeared in the doorway of the waiting room. Mr. Fields was upright now, his sparse, graying hair standing in peaks atop his head, his eyes still sleepy. It looked like he'd heard the whole exchange. Emily stared at him plaintively, begging silently that he would set the nurse straight.

Mr. Fields glanced at the nurse, then back at Emily. His gaze was cold and dead but also firm and purposeful. Then he turned and walked back to the waiting room.

Well then. Swallowing a sob, Emily brushed past him for the elevator. She barely recalled the ride down, and she ran with her head lowered toward her bike.

As she unlocked her bike from the rack, her phone beeped. She pulled it out and saw Jordan's name. A news story had just broken on CNN: *Preppy Thief Apprehended in Caribbean.*

Emily suddenly couldn't breathe. She stabbed at the link. There was a picture of Jordan, tanned and beautiful but also looking stunned and upset, being led in handcuffs through a parking lot. *Katherine DeLong, on the lam since March, finally caught in a small fishing village in Bonaire. Twitter activity led to her arrest.*

Twitter activity. Emily inspected Jordan's picture again. She was staring straight at the camera, seemingly right into Emily's eyes. Her expression was rife with fury. *I know you did this to me*, her eyes seemed to be saying to Emily and only Emily. *That photo of you cheating led them right to where I was hiding.*

Emily sank into the bike's seat, feeling like everything was spinning too fast. Suddenly, her phone beeped again. A voicemail had landed in her mailbox, but she hadn't even heard the phone ring.

She dialed the voicemail access number and punched in her code. When the first and only message played back, the phone almost slipped from Emily's fingers. A piercing giggle echoed through the receiver. It stopped her heart. She'd know that laugh anywhere. It was mocking. Teasing. Tormenting. *Ali's.*

She looked around anxiously, considering heading straight to the FBI office and playing this for Fuji. But Fuji wouldn't listen. She believed what she wanted to believe. She thought Ali was dead, that the girls were liars.

It explained why Ali was laughing so hard. She knew she had them beat. And to her, it was simply hilarious. Hanna was right. They were just sitting back, letting it happen.

An idea crystallized in Emily's mind. She composed a text to Spencer, Aria, and Hanna. *I'm sick and tired of Anderson Cooper ruining everything*, she wrote, using the code name they'd come up with for Ali. *I'm back on the hunt. Are you in or out?*

She sent the text off and waited, taking steady, even breaths. All she could do now was wait. She hoped and prayed they would say yes.

24

A NEW PLAN

That same day, Aria sat in the waiting room of a lawyer's office. Well, *sort* of a lawyer's office—she'd never known a lawyer to set up his business in a strip mall between a Five Below and a Curves, but whatever. Mike sat next to her, staring at a pamphlet about an ongoing class-action drug suit. "Hey," he whispered. "Have you ever taken Celebrex? Prozac?"

"No," Aria mumbled.

"Do you have mesothelioma?" Mike asked.

"I don't even know what that *is*."

"Damn." Mike set down the pamphlet. "If you *did*, we'd be entitled to a big settlement."

Aria rolled her eyes, wondering how Mike could be upbeat. She was also beginning to second-guess this meeting—she could hear techno music from Curves thumping through the walls. This morning, Mike had knocked on her door and said, "Get up. We're talking to Desmond Sturbridge at ten AM. We'll sneak." "Who's *that*?" Aria had asked, and Mike had explained it was a lawyer who'd called the house yesterday volunteering to take Aria's case. Aria had tried to tell him that Spencer's dad was defending them, but Mike just shrugged. "It's always good to get a second opinion. Besides, we don't even have to pay this new guy unless we win."

Now, a door flung open, and a tall, skinny man with a gummy smile and hair so slicked with pomade it actually shone, beamed at them. "Miss Montgomery and friend!" he boomed. "Come in, come in!"

Aria looked nervously at Mike, but he just pulled her to her feet and led her into the office. "It'll be fine," he murmured as they followed Sturbridge down the hall. "You have a good case. He'll present the truth to the judge—how can it go wrong?"

Aria hoped he was right. She entered the lawyer's office, which was decorated with bobbleheads, signed Eagles jerseys, and a whole lot of empty Arby's wrappers. There was also a diploma from the University of Michigan on the wall, which made her feel better.

"Thanks for speaking with us," she said as she sat down.

"Of course, of course!" Sturbridge's eyes gleamed. "I think you have a very interesting case. And I have some ideas to keep you out of Jamaica."

Mike raised his eyebrows encouragingly. Aria pulled a notebook out of her bag and slid it across the desk. "We don't have too much time, since the arraignment is

Friday, so I wrote down everything that's happened so you can look it over at your leisure." Inside the notebook were also drawings she'd started for Asher Trethewey. Not that she'd need them now.

Sturbridge waved his hand. "That won't be necessary. I think I've got all I need."

Aria and Mike exchanged a look. "But you haven't got *anything*," Aria said. "Don't you want to know what really happened that night?"

"Lord, no." Sturbridge looked abashed. "Miss Montgomery, this is a tricky case. There are eyewitnesses, there's a video of you on the scene . . . it doesn't look very good. The way I see it, there's really only one way to play this case so you come out a winner."

"What's that?" Mike asked.

"We plead insanity."

He looked pleased with himself, like he'd discovered a new law of gravity. Aria blinked hard. "But I'm not insane."

One eyebrow rose. "Hallucinating that Alison DiLaurentis is alive? Sending bullying notes to yourself?"

"Those notes weren't from me!" Aria cried.

Sturbridge smiled sadly. "The police say they are."

Mike's shoulders drooped. "You're using information you read about my sister online, stuff the cops came up with. That isn't her in the video."

Sturbridge frowned. "It certainly *looks* like her."

"It's not," Aria said. "I didn't do it."

Sturbridge formed an X with his pointer fingers. "Don't want to hear it!" he singsonged. Then he passed a stapled set of papers across the desk. "If you want to stay out of a Jamaican prison, you'll sign this insanity plea. It will get you a stay and a psychiatric evaluation. It's not so bad. Chances are, you'll end up in one of those cushy mental hospitals around here, all expenses paid by the state."

"Like the Preserve at Addison-Stevens?" Aria challenged.

Sturbridge's eyes lit up. "Exactly! I hear the food is amazing there."

Aria shut her eyes and forced herself to take calming breaths.

Mike flung the papers back at Sturbridge. "Thanks for your time, but you're nuts, man." He grabbed the notebook from the lawyer and took Aria's arm. "C'mon."

"You'll regret it!" Sturbridge called out as they fled down the hall.

"Sorry," Mike said, pushing the door open. He looked miserable. "If I had known that's what he was going to go for, I would have never put you through that."

"It's okay," Aria mumbled, staring blankly at a bunch of overweight ladies congregating in front of Curves. So much for the lawyer route.

She felt her phone buzz in her pocket. She grabbed it and looked at the message. *I'm back on the hunt*, Emily had written. *Are you in or out?* In the same thread, Hanna had responded to count her in. A minute later, Spencer had said yes, too.

"What's that?" Mike asked, leaning over. Aria was about to cover the screen, but Mike had already seen the text. His face brightened. "*Yes*. You're going after Ali again?"

"You're not getting involved," Aria said quickly.

Mike slumped. "Why not? I know everything. I can help. You have nothing to lose."

Aria shut her eyes. "I'm sorry," she said. "I just can't let you help."

Mike's face fell. "In the immortal words of that freak-job lawyer, *you'll regret it.*"

Aria shoved her phone back in her pocket. No, she'd regret it if she *did* let him help. She'd lost too much already. She couldn't lose her brother, too.

It was raining when Aria biked up to the curb behind the local Wawa several hours later, after dark. She spied her old friends standing near the woods that divided the mini-mart from an apartment complex and started toward them. Her shoes immediately sank into the mud. Raindrops pelted her cheeks. She pulled her hoodie over her head and ran.

Spencer inhaled shakily when they had all assembled. "Okay. How are we going to do this? What do we have on Ali that we can look into?"

Everyone was quiet. A milk truck chugged into Wawa

and parked around the side. Then Emily cleared her throat. "I got a voicemail from Ali. She was laughing at me. At *us*."

Aria's eyes widened. "Ali *called* you?"

"Why would she do that?" Spencer whispered, her stomach swirling.

"I don't know." Emily placed her hands on her hips. "But she did."

"Maybe she thought you were the least likely to tell on her," Spencer suggested.

"Well, she was wrong." Emily pulled out her phone. They gathered around and listened to the voicemail. When Aria heard the high-pitched giggle, a shiver wriggled up her spine.

"I can't believe it," Hanna murmured, turning pale. "Do you think she meant to call you, or did so by accident?"

Emily shut her eyes. "I have no idea."

"Should we send this to Fuji?" Aria asked after a beat.

Spencer snorted. "She'll think we made it up. It probably comes from our phones for all we know."

Aria looked at Emily. "Play it again."

Emily did as she was told. Aria listened once more as that familiar laugh twirled through the air. "It sounds like she's in a crowd, don't you think?"

"And there's some sort of announcement," Hanna pointed out. "I can't tell what the guy's saying, though."

"I know, I heard that, too," Emily said. "If we were able

to isolate that part of the message, maybe we could track where Ali was when she called. Maybe it's somewhere she hangs out a lot."

"Or maybe it's another trap," Aria said sourly.

Hanna glowered at her. "Do you have a better idea?"

"I'm sorry." Aria threw up her hands. "But even if the message *did* have a clue, what can we do about it? It's not like we can stroll into Rosewood PD and say, *Hey, can we borrow your forensic equipment?*"

Spencer's eyes lit up. "Actually, I know someone who might know how to use that stuff—*and* help us."

Emily cocked her head. "Who?"

"My sister and Wilden."

Hanna burst out laughing. "Melissa? Seriously?"

"She offered her services. And think about it—of course Melissa wants Ali dead." Spencer crossed her arms over her chest. "We can take SEPTA into the city. It's so late—no one will notice us on the train. The worst thing that happens is Melissa slams the door in our faces . . . or calls the cops."

Aria stared blankly at Wawa, considering this. The wind gusted, sending the sweet smell of the convenience store's homemade donuts into her nostrils. "I'm in if you guys are in."

"Me, too," Hanna said.

"Me, three," Emily said, her eyes blazing. "Let's go."

25

SOUND BITES

"Uh, hello?" Melissa Hastings said as she opened the red door of her Victorian town house on Rittenhouse Square for Spencer and the others. It was almost midnight, and she had lavender-smelling night cream all over her face and was dressed in a frayed Rosewood Day Debate Team T-shirt and boxers printed with mini golden retrievers. Spencer had a feeling they were Wilden's.

"Can we come in?" she asked her sister. "It's important."

Melissa glanced at the other girls on the porch, then nodded solidly. "Come on."

She directed them into the house, asking them to drop their things and leave their shoes in a small coatroom off the vestibule. They walked into the living room, which was a calming yellow and had gleaming walnut floors. The furniture, knickknacks, and throw rugs matched perfectly. The room seemed familiar, and Spencer suddenly knew why. It was decorated exactly like her house in Rosewood. The TV in the living room was tuned to CNN. As usual, the reporters were talking about Tabitha's murder. *Liars' Arraignment in Seven Days*, read the banner at the bottom of the screen. Even the crawl was all about it. Melissa switched it off.

"Spencer? Hanna?" Wilden appeared at the top of the stairs, also dressed in boxers and a T-shirt. He looked nervous.

Spencer sucked in her stomach. Maybe this was a bad idea—Melissa was their ally, but was Wilden?

Melissa stepped forward. "Darren, we need to help them."

Wilden sighed and walked down to the first floor. His expression was cautious but also curious. Emily reached into her pocket and handed him her phone. "There's a voicemail I want you to check out. I'm almost positive it's Ali."

"Do you have any sort of equipment that might be able to amplify a part of the recording?" Spencer asked. "We might be able to figure out where she was calling from."

"Or even isolate her voice to prove that it *is* her," Emily added. "The cops don't believe she's still alive. We have to make them understand."

Wilden narrowed his green eyes. "I'm still not sure this is a good idea."

"Darren, *please*." Melissa sidled up next to him. "This is my sister."

Spencer swallowed a lump in her throat. It felt so good to hear Melissa say that.

Wilden glanced from one girl to the next. "All right," he said, after a moment, then took Emily's phone and sat down on the couch. "When I worked for Rosewood PD, we used a program we accessed on our intranet—all you needed was a digital file of the recording. If the pass codes to the intranet haven't changed, I should be able to get into the system."

"That would be awesome," Emily breathed.

Melissa scurried into a back room. The girls settled on the couch and waited. Melissa returned with a silver MacBook Air and a USB cord. Wilden lifted the lid and typed something on the keyboard. "I'm in." He handed Emily the phone and the USB. "Plug this in, and then play the recording back for us."

Emily did as she was told, accessing her voicemail and finding Ali's saved message. There were the sounds of a lot of voices talking at once, all of their words muffled. Then Ali's chilling laugh rang through the room. Everyone stiffened. She laughed for a good five seconds, and then the recording ended.

Melissa shut her eyes. "It's totally her." Even Wilden looked freaked out.

They played the message again. Melissa tilted her ear toward the phone. "It sounds like she's in a crowd."

"That's what we thought, too." Spencer glanced at the laptop. An audio program that broke down the voicemail into packets of information and sound waves was on the screen. Every time Ali laughed, a sound wave spiked. In the background, there was cheering and laughter. Someone made a garbled announcement over a megaphone, and a second wave peaked.

"Did you hear that?" Spencer pointed at the second wave. "We thought if we could punch up that announcement, we might be able to figure out where she's calling from."

Melissa, who had settled into the corner of the couch, hugged her knees to her chest. "I can't believe she's ballsy enough to call you from the middle of a crowd."

"Unless she's not *in* the crowd but near it," Spencer said.

Wilden listened to the voicemail one more time, highlighted the second spiky sound wave, and clicked a button at the bottom of the screen. The background noise dimmed and the announcement got louder, but it wasn't any clearer.

There was a scratching noise somewhere else in the house. Spencer shot up. "What's that?"

Everyone fell silent. Hanna's face was pale, and Emily didn't move a muscle. Something rustled. There was a teeny, tiny *creak*. Aria clapped her hand over her mouth.

Melissa half rose from the couch and peered around. "This place is a hundred years old. It makes a lot of noise, especially when it's windy."

They listened for a few moments more. Silence. Wilden

turned back to the computer. "Let me try something else," he murmured, pressing a few more buttons.

The message played again. Melissa squinted hard. "It sounds like someone is saying *Mo Mo* through a bullhorn . . . and then the message gets cut off."

Wilden hit PLAY over and over. Cheering. The loud feedback of a bullhorn. *Mo, Mo.* "Maybe they're at a sports event," Hanna suggested.

"And Ali's hiding under the bleachers?" Spencer asked, giving Hanna a doubtful look.

Wilden punched more buttons. Then a message appeared on the screen. *Unknown user*, it flashed. *Access denied.* "Shit," he said, sitting back. "I think they realized someone outside the force is using this. They kicked me out."

Spencer leaned forward. "Can you go log back in under a different name?"

Wilden closed the laptop lid and shook his head. "I don't think I should. I shouldn't be doing this at all."

Spencer looked from him to her sister. "Can't you do anything else?"

Wilden's eyes darted back and forth. "I'm sorry, girls."

Tears filled Melissa's eyes. "This just isn't fair. You girls don't deserve this. Alison shouldn't get to win."

"Have you talked to Dad? What are they saying about our chances?" Spencer asked. "Every time I ask Goddard or the other guys on the legal team, they sort of dance around the question. Do you think we'll actually get shipped to Jamaica?"

Melissa glanced at Wilden. He turned away. When she looked back at Spencer, there were tears in her eyes. "Dad's saying it's looking pretty hopeless," she whispered.

Spencer's stomach plunged. She reached out and grabbed Aria's hand. Emily laid her head on Hanna's shoulder. *Hopeless.*

"What are we going to do?" Emily moaned.

Wilden cleared his throat. "Don't do anything rash, girls. I've heard . . . rumors."

Everyone exchanged another look. It wasn't even worth asking—they all knew what the rumors were about: the suicide pact. Suddenly Spencer thought it didn't really sound like that bad of an idea. What did she have left, after all?

But then Spencer looked at Melissa again. She looked worried, almost like she could read Spencer's thoughts. Spencer placed her hand over Melissa's, and her sister pulled her into a hug. After a moment, Aria hugged them, too, and then Emily and Hanna. Spencer inhaled Melissa's clean, soapy scent. It was nice to be on Melissa's side after so many years of hating her. Even if she was no help, at least someone cared.

Because there was nothing left to do, everyone stood and headed for the door. Melissa followed them, her head lowered, looking defeated. She offered to drive Spencer and the others to the train, but Spencer waved her off. "You've done enough already."

"Call me if you need anything," she told Spencer, tears now running down her cheeks. "Even if you just want to talk. I'm always here."

"Thanks," Spencer said, giving her hand a squeeze.

And then she turned to the street. The temperature outside had dropped significantly, and the moon was now hidden in clouds. Spencer hugged her arms tight to her torso and followed the others back to the train station. No one said anything, because what was there to say? Another dead end. Another lead gone cold.

26

THE DARKEST PLACE EVER

That next Thursday, Emily woke to a headache and a perfect blue sky. She tried to get out of bed, but her legs wouldn't move. *You have to get up*, she told herself.

Only, why? Her Rosewood Day graduation was in an hour, but it wasn't like the school was allowing her to take part in it. She'd been given permission to attend, but why would she want to watch? And more than that, her mother still hadn't returned from the hospital, more expensive items were missing from her house, and the FBI still thought Ali was dead and the girls had killed Tabitha. Emily's arraignment was tomorrow, and then she'd be shipped off to Jamaica. All around her, summer was unfurling: Her neighbors were grilling and playing with their dogs and going for walks around the neighborhood. But when Emily even looked at the blooming flowers or the brilliant green grass, all she felt was dread. All of this was for other people to enjoy, not her.

She grabbed her phone, pulled up CNN, and looked again at the video. By now, eleven thousand, eight hundred, forty-two—no, forty-*three*—people had commented that Emily and her friends were evil incarnate. She winced as the shadowy girls beat Tabitha to death. It *did* look like the four of them. Besides, if the police suspected the video was a fake, wouldn't they have already blown the thing up, used all their high-tech equipment to prove it? Ali had somehow made that video foolproof.

So figure out who N could be, a voice told her.

Another impossibility. Like the staff at The Preserve was going to allow a suspected criminal to infiltrate their building. Besides, they'd already balked when she'd asked.

But she dialed The Preserve's number all the same, another matter on her mind. When a nurse answered, Emily coughed. "Has Iris Taylor returned?" she asked shakily.

"Let me check." There was typing. "No, Iris Taylor isn't here," she answered.

Emily gripped the phone hard. "You haven't found her?"

There was rustling on the other end, and a second voice got on the line. "Who is this?" a man demanded. "Are you another reporter?" And then, *click*.

The call time flashed on Emily's screen. She set her phone down on the bedside table and stared blankly out the window. Iris was out there somewhere. Who knew if she was alive or dead? And it was all Emily's fault.

Suddenly, a second voice sounded in Emily's head, this one lower in pitch and eerily hypnotic. *So give up*, it echoed. *Just stay in bed. Close your eyes. There's no point to anything.*

A door slammed outside, and Emily opened her eyes once more. Though it took a huge effort, she hefted herself out of bed and crossed the hall to the front window. Outside, her father was helping her mom out of a cab. Carolyn grabbed Mrs. Fields's bags, and Emily's sister Beth and brother, Jake, fluttered around, trying to be useful.

She watched her mom hobble to the front door. Mrs. Fields looked gray and old, clearly sick. The door creaked as it opened, and Emily heard voices downstairs. "Sit right here," Mr. Fields encouraged softly. "See? Isn't that nice?"

"Can I get you something, Mom?" That was Beth's voice.

"How about some ginger ale?" said Jake.

"That would be lovely," Mrs. Fields said. Her voice was scratchy, like a grandmother's.

There were quick footsteps, the kissing sound of the fridge opening and closing. Emily hesitated at the top of the stairs, more nervous than she'd felt on the blocks before the state-championship swim meet last year. After a few heaving breaths, she squared her shoulders and walked down the stairs.

Beth and Carolyn were sitting on the couch, their

hands in their laps, their smiles twitchy. Jake returned from the kitchen with a tall glass of ginger ale. Mr. Fields was squatting by the TV, doing something with the cable box, and Emily's mom was sitting on the recliner, her face pale and lined.

When Emily reached the bottom of the stairs, everyone froze. Carolyn's lips puckered. Jake shot to his feet. Beth looked away, which made Emily feel especially awful.

Emily stepped toward her mom. "It's so nice to see you home," she said shakily. "How are you feeling?"

Mrs. Fields stared at her hands. All at once, her breathing began to quicken.

"Tired?" Emily tried. "Did they feed you okay in the hospital?"

Mrs. Fields was actually wheezing now. Carolyn let out a whimper. "Dad, *do* something."

"She shouldn't be here," Beth said quickly, sharply.

Mr. Fields rose from the TV stand. He had disconnected the cable box from the television. Were they so broke that they couldn't even afford cable anymore? "You need to go back upstairs," he said firmly to Emily, his eyes cold.

"I'm sorry, everyone," she eked out. "I'm really, really sorry."

Then she fled back upstairs, holding in her sobs only until she was safely behind her closed door. Her phone was flashing on the bed. GOOGLE ALERT FOR THE PREPPY THIEF, said the screen. Emily scanned the headlines.

Jordan's sentencing trial was scheduled for next week. *Experts say her sentence will be somewhere between twenty and fifty years.*

Emily threw the phone against the wall. Jordan would have been fine if it weren't for Emily. She'd ruined her life, too.

All at once, she thought of Derrick, her pal from last summer. How many times had he held her hand in the break room when she'd poured her heart out about how scared she was about having the baby? How many times had she called him in the middle of the night because she couldn't sleep? She'd seen him not too long ago, when A was tormenting her about Gayle, so she knew he was still around. Maybe he'd listen. Maybe he'd understand.

She scooped up her phone from the carpet and dialed his number, but the call went to voicemail. Emily hung up without leaving a message. What if Derrick saw her number and hit IGNORE? Maybe he thought she was a killer, just like everyone else did. Maybe he was still upset that she'd cost him his job with Gayle, because she hadn't given Gayle her baby—the last time she'd seen him, he'd mentioned it. She'd negatively impacted Derrick's life, too.

She was the opposite of King Midas—everything and everyone she touched turned rotten, and there was so little now she could fix. Suddenly, something occurred to her. A lot of this was out of her control, but there was a way she could make her family happy again, get their money back, and heal their mother. She could disappear completely.

But did she dare even think it?

Emily squeezed her pillow hard. If she weren't here right now, if she weren't a constant stressor, her mom would recover. But when she thought about vanishing, she didn't mean simply leaving town. It was a bigger, scarier, more definite decision than that.

She'd save her family. And who would miss her?

A laugh exploded from downstairs. Someone opened a door and shut it again. Emily rose from her bed and stood in the middle of the room, fingertips twitching. All at once, she couldn't get the thought out of her mind. It made so much sense. She couldn't live like this. She couldn't let her family suffer. She couldn't go to Jamaica, either. Maybe the rumors weren't swirling because Ali and her helper planted them. Maybe everyone thought it was the next logical step.

Emily shut her eyes and thought for a moment. The Rosewood covered bridge came to mind. Most of the bridge had a roof over it, the inside walls coated with graffiti, but there was a tiny walkway on the outside that was open to the water below. The stream was deep this time of year from all the melted snow. It would still be cold, too. Numbing.

Heart pounding, she pulled on jeans and a T-shirt. Then, gathering up her courage, she hefted open her window, crept onto the roof, climbed onto the oak tree, and slid down the trunk, the way she always did when she snuck out. The bridge was about a twenty-minute walk. By the time her father checked on her—if he even *did* check on her—she'd be long gone.

27

FRIENDS DON'T LET FRIENDS JUMP

That same morning, Spencer and Melissa stood on the Rosewood Day Commons. All one hundred and six of Spencer's senior classmates, dressed in white and black graduation gowns and blue-tasseled caps, sat on folding chairs in front of a makeshift stage. Spencer, however, was in a plain cotton dress and wore no cap at all.

Faces of kids she'd spent the last twelve years with lined the rows. Phi Templeton sat next to Devon Arliss. Spencer's field-hockey friend, Kirsten Cullen, giggled with Maya St. Germain. Noel Kahn, still looking a little weak, sat with his lacrosse buddies. Naomi Zeigler, Riley Wolfe, and Klaudia Huusko whispered to one another. Cast members from countless school plays Spencer had starred in fiddled with their tassels. Her cohorts on newspaper and yearbook fanned themselves with their programs. None of them glanced back at her. There weren't even four empty seats, indicating where Spencer, Aria, Emily, and Hanna should be sitting. It was like Rosewood Day had wiped them clean from its memory.

Spencer looked around, wondering if any of the others had come. She finally spied Aria and her mother on the other side of the field. Hanna was under the bleachers. Emily wasn't anywhere. Maybe she had the right idea.

Principal Appleton cleared his throat on the stage. "And now, I present to you, our valedictorian, Mason Byers."

There was thundering applause as Mason rose from a seat in the front row and took the stage. Spencer shook her head ever so slightly. Mason Byers? Sure, he was smart, but she had no idea he was next in line for valedictorian. *She* was supposed to be up there right now. She'd had a speech prepared since sophomore year. Knowing Mason, who never stressed about anything, he'd probably written the speech last night.

Melissa reached over and squeezed Spencer's hand. "It's going to be okay."

Spencer swallowed a lump in her throat, grateful to have someone next to her who understood how painful this was. But it was too much. "Let's get out of here," she grumbled, walking toward the parking lot.

Melissa followed her. As they passed the big fountain in the front of the gym, she coughed. "Listen, we're working on finding you a top-notch lawyer from Jamaica. Darren has some contacts down there, and so does Dad."

Spencer pinched the bridge of her nose, hating that

the lawyers weren't even considering the possibility of trying the case in the United States anymore. "Do you know how long it takes for a case to go to trial in Jamaica?"

"I've gotten conflicting answers." Melissa's heels clicked on the sidewalk. "Some people said only a few months. Others said years."

Spencer made a small whimper.

A cheer rang out from the Commons. Melissa stopped in the middle of the jammed parking lot. "I'm sorry," she said with a pained look on her face. She glanced around the lot, then leaned closer. "If you do get sent to Jamaica, I'll look for her after you're gone. I don't want to stop until she's dead."

Spencer shook her head. "Don't. It's awesome that you'd offer, but she's dangerous. She'll kill you, Melissa. I couldn't live with that."

"But . . ." Melissa trailed off and sighed. "It's just not *fair*."

Spencer didn't think it was fair, either. And this was so ironic: Just when she and Melissa were really, truly bonding, becoming the sisters Spencer had always hoped they'd be, her life was ending.

Her phone beeped loudly. Spencer looked at the ID. EMILY. As Melissa unlocked the car, Spencer answered it. There was no reply, only the sound of wind. "Hello?" Spencer said. "Em?"

And then she heard crying. The sobs were soft at first, but then they intensified.

"Emily!" Spencer shouted into the phone. "Em, are you there? Why aren't you at graduation?"

The sobbing stopped. There was some rustling, and then Emily sniffled loudly into the receiver. "S-Spencer?" she bleated.

Spencer sat up straighter. "Why aren't you at graduation?"

"I just wanted to call to say good-bye."

More wind blew against the speaker. On Spencer's end, the band had just struck up the beginning notes of "Pomp and Circumstance."

"What's going on?" All at once, it sounded like Emily was crying again. Spencer clutched the phone tighter. "Em. What's wrong?"

"I just can't do this anymore," Emily said. Her voice had no intonation to it. "I'm really sorry. I'm just . . . done."

Spencer's skin prickled. She'd heard Emily despair before, especially after she'd had her baby. But this seemed different, like Emily was in a dark, dark place and had no idea how to save herself.

"Where are you?" she demanded, gripping the phone hard. Melissa paused from getting into the car, giving Spencer a curious look.

"It doesn't matter." There was a swish, maybe a car passing. "You'll never get here in time."

Spencer's heart pounded. "What do you mean?" she demanded, even though, horrifyingly, she thought she knew. She spun in a circle, feeling helpless. "Em, whatever you're thinking of doing, don't. I know things are tough right now, but you have to hang on. Just tell me where you are, okay?"

Emily laughed bitterly. "I probably won't even drown, you know. That's the thing I was thinking just before I accidentally called you. I picked a bridge—and I'm a freaking *swimmer*."

"A bridge?" Spencer's eyes darted back and forth. Melissa was now standing next to her, her eyes wide and full of question. "Which one? The covered bridge?"

"No," Emily said quickly, but Spencer could tell she was lying. "Don't come, Spencer. I'm hanging up now."

"Em, don't!" Spencer screamed. The call ended. Spencer tried to dial Emily back, but it rang and rang, not even going to voicemail.

"*Shit*," Spencer said out loud.

"What's going on?" Melissa asked.

Spencer's throat felt dry. "It's Emily. She's on a bridge. I think she's going to . . ." She trailed off, but by the look on Melissa's face, it was obvious she knew what Spencer meant.

"Which bridge?" Melissa demanded.

"The covered one on the other side of town," Spencer said. She stared at Melissa. "Can I take your car?"

Melissa pursed her lips. "I'll go with you."

Spencer swung around. "I don't want to involve you in this." What if Ali had led Emily there? What if it was dangerous?

Melissa's eyes were firm. "Stop it. Come on."

On the lawn, kids were marching up the stage and collecting their diplomas to thunderous applause. Spencer got into the car and slammed the door. Melissa started the engine and gunned out of the lot onto the mercifully empty street. "It won't take us long to get there," she said, staring steadily at the road.

As Principal Appleton called out Chassey Bledsoe's name, Spencer dialed 911. "A friend of mine is going to jump off the covered bridge in Rosewood," she shouted to the dispatcher, when she answered. "Send an ambulance, now!"

Melissa turned out of the school's main drive. Spencer then dialed Aria and Hanna; she hadn't wanted to waste precious time finding them back at the ceremony. Hanna answered on the second ring. Spencer could hear applause in the background. "We need to get to the covered bridge," she shouted. "Emily's in trouble."

"What do you mean?" Hanna asked.

"I don't know." Spencer bit her lip. "But I think we need to go to her. Find Aria and meet me there, okay?"

"Definitely," Hanna said urgently, and hung up.

Melissa gunned around another turn. She gave Spencer a sidelong glance. "What if we get there and it's too late?"

Spencer chewed hard on her thumbnail. "I don't know."

The car sped down the country road that led to the bridge, whipping by a cheese farm, an enormous estate surrounded by acres of lawn, and a fancy restaurant tucked into an old barn. When Melissa was just one hill away from reaching the bridge, Spencer looked ahead on the road, then behind them. "Why don't I hear an ambulance?" she said aloud.

"I was just thinking the same thing," Melissa murmured. But then she pressed on the gas. "It'll be okay," she said almost angrily. "We'll get there."

They made the final turn. *Please don't jump*, Spencer repeated over and over again, a sick feeling welling in her stomach. *Please, please, please, Em, don't jump.*

The rustic, graffiti-covered bridge loomed in front of her. There were no police or paramedics anywhere. As soon as Melissa pulled onto the shoulder, Spencer sprang out of the car and ran to the small ledge that surrounded the bridge. She peered onto the left side, then the right. There was no one there.

"Emily?" Heart in her throat, Spencer gazed down at the rushing water beneath, expecting to see a flash of Emily's gold-red hair in the rapids.

Aria's car roared up next, and she and Hanna jumped out and sprinted toward the bridge. "There she is!" Aria cried out. A board jutted out from the bridge; Emily was scrunched behind it. The wind blew her hair around her face. Tears stained her cheeks. She leaned over the water, her chest heaving.

"Emily!" Spencer screamed. "Don't!"

Emily looked over at them, and her face crumpled. "Leave me alone. I have to do this."

"No, you don't!" Hanna screamed, crying, too.

Emily stared despondently into the rapids. "No one wants me. My family wishes I was dead."

"They're just upset," Spencer urged. "They don't feel that way for real."

Emily pressed her hands over her eyes. "Like you guys haven't been thinking about it? We're as good as dead. Of course we want to end it all."

Spencer exchanged a horrified glance with the others.

"Don't you see what's happening?" Hanna wailed. "Ali arranged for all of this. She was the one who sent those suicide notes from our phones to our friends and families, making it look like we wanted to kill ourselves. It's so *obvious*, Em."

Emily shrugged. "So? It still doesn't change anything."

"Yes, it does!" Hanna banged her fist against the bridge wall. "For months—*years*—we've let Ali manipulate us. We've let her make us think people we love are A. Aria lost Noel because of it. And Spencer suspected her *mom*, remember? Now Ali's using the power of suggestion to make us think we should commit suicide—and we're letting her. Are you really going to let her get to you like that?"

Emily peeked at Hanna. "But why would she want us to commit suicide? She already won by getting us sent to Jamaica."

"Maybe she worries we'll be acquitted," Spencer shouted onto the bridge. "Or maybe she worries we'll continue to investigate while in prison and find her for real. This is her safest option. We die by our own hands. She doesn't have to lift a finger."

Emily's chin wobbled. "I don't know if that makes sense. How could we investigate her in Jamaica?"

"I'll help!" Melissa called out from a few feet away. "I'll do whatever I can!"

Spencer gave her a grateful look, then turned back to Emily. "We need you, Em. We need to stick together if we want to beat A."

Emily shut her eyes tight, overcome with emotion. "Guys . . ."

"Please," Spencer begged.

Suddenly, *finally*, sirens screamed behind them. An ambulance pulled onto the embankment, and several men in EMT jackets jumped out. "Where is she?" shouted the first one, a young man with stubble on his face.

"There!" Melissa pointed to the ledge.

The EMT nodded, then conferred with the two other men who'd jumped out of the vehicle. One of them requested backup on a walkie-talkie. The second one started to pull medical equipment out of the car.

The first man squared his shoulders, wrapped a rock-climbing tether around his waist, and hooked one end of the line to a post on the bridge for stability. Then he inched onto the narrow ledge. "Come here, honey," he said gently, almost lovingly. "You're safe."

Emily looked at him, her eyes wild.

"Take my hand," the EMT begged. "Please don't jump."

"We need you, Em," Hanna called out.

"We love you!" Spencer called.

The two other EMTs were stationed near the water, ready to take the plunge in case Emily jumped. The man on the bridge inched closer to her, the rope around his waist stretching taut. Emily didn't move. Finally, he was close enough to wrap his arms around her. Emily crumpled into him, her face twisted with anguish. He lifted Emily up and slowly inched backward to the front of the bridge. When they were on solid ground, he gently set Emily on the grass. She was sobbing.

Spencer ran over to her and engulfed her in a hug. Aria and Hanna did the same. They all started to cry. "Oh my God," Spencer said over and over.

"How could you have done that?" Hanna wailed.

"We could have lost you," Aria added.

Emily was crying so hard, she couldn't speak. "I just . . . couldn't . . ."

Spencer squeezed her tight. Hanna wrapped her sweatshirt over her shoulders. One of the EMTs brought out another blanket and laid that over Emily, too. The man who'd saved Emily radioed that they no longer needed backup—the girl was safe. Then he sat down next to the girls and checked Emily's pupils to make sure she wasn't going into shock. He made no reference to who the girls were or what they were facing—maybe he didn't even know.

Emily's sobs dissolved into sniffles. All the girls clung to her tightly, as if they were afraid they might lose her again. Even Melissa joined in the hug, stroking Emily's hair and telling her that she was going to be all right. Spencer took a moment to imagine what things would have been like if they hadn't caught Emily in time. The breath left her lungs. It terrified her to even consider it. If one of them died, a part of Spencer would die, too. It was one small silver lining about going to Jamaica—at least they'd be going together. They wouldn't be facing this alone.

Her thoughts turned to Ali again. Of course she'd planted suicide into all their minds. And look what it had almost done. Look at who it had almost taken. This bitch deserved to go *down* for all of this. Now more than ever.

Melissa headed back to the car, giving the girls a few minutes alone. A minivan rounded the bend, slowing at the sight of the ambulance. Spencer didn't recognize the woman behind the wheel, but there was a faded ROSEWOOD DAY LACROSSE bumper sticker on the back. Spencer gasped.

"What?" Aria asked, looking at her quizzically.

"I thought of another way we could hunt for Ali," Spencer said. "But you're not going to like it."

Aria frowned. "What do you mean?"

A chilly breeze swept down Spencer's back. "I mean Noel."

Aria's face hardened. "What *about* Noel?"

"Maybe he knows something else about Ali. Maybe he didn't tell you everything."

Aria looked shocked. "You want me to talk to him?" Spencer nodded. Aria shook her head. "No way."

"I think Spencer's right," Hanna said. "Maybe Noel doesn't even realize what he knows. What if this leads us to her?"

"I'll do it, if you don't want to," Spencer volunteered. "I wouldn't mind giving that jerk a piece of my mind."

Aria lowered her eyes. "He's not a jerk," she said quietly, almost automatically. She sighed. "I can handle it. But only if Emily—and the rest of you—never stand on the edge of a bridge again. Losing you guys is way worse than going to prison."

"I won't," Emily said softly.

"I won't, either," Hanna said, and Spencer nodded. Aria was right. They couldn't abandon one another now, not when things were so critical and dangerous.

Not when they had so much to lose.

28

THE SECRET CODE

"Oh my God," Mrs. Kahn bleated, when she opened the door to the Kahn estate later that afternoon. Her blond hair was expertly blown out, her makeup was perfect, and she wore a new-looking ivory cashmere sweater, curve-hugging skinny jeans, and scuff-free Tod's driving loafers. But her face was pale, and cords stood out in her neck. She stared at Aria in fear, and Aria knew instantly that Mrs. Kahn believed everything the news was saying. This was a woman who had once, at a family wedding Aria and Noel had attended, pulled Aria into a hug and said, *You know, I think of you as my daughter*. It was amazing how a couple of news stories could sway an opinion.

For the millionth time in the past hour, Aria wished she hadn't agreed to this. But she was here now. The damage was done. She took a deep breath. "Can I speak to Noel for a few minutes?"

Mrs. Kahn backed away. "I don't think so."

Unbelievable. Aria grabbed the door before Noel's mom could shut it. "My mom is right there. It's fine." She gestured toward the curb, where Ella was waiting in the Subaru. Aria was surprised Ella had said yes about bringing her to Noel's, given that Aria had disappeared from graduation. But maybe Ella figured that there wasn't really anything *worse* the cops could do to Aria that they weren't already doing. Her mother had spent a good deal of time crying over the last month, but now she just seemed kind of spent and exhausted.

"We'll talk out here, and she'll watch us the whole time," Aria added to Noel's mom.

Mrs. Kahn squinted at the Subaru but didn't wave—she probably thought Ella was a criminal by association. "Five minutes," she said tightly. "Then we have to get to a graduation party."

She shut the door halfway. When it opened again, Noel stepped out. "Aria," he said. His voice cracked. He was holding his graduation cap in his hands.

"Hey," Aria said softly, her heart pounding fast.

It felt like ages since she'd talked to him. Suddenly, here they were, standing within inches of each other on his porch. Part of her wanted to give him a huge hug. Another part worried he'd push her away—she hadn't heard from him since the arrest. Another part, an angry part, yearned to run.

When he met her gaze, his eyes were soulful, concerned, and uncertain. The bruises on his cheeks had faded to yellow, and the stitches on his jaw were no longer puffy and Frankenstein-monster-like. He had a cast on his arm, too, but he was mostly the Noel she remembered. Aria glanced at the Nike lacrosse T-shirt, feeling an ache. He'd worn it the day she'd returned from Iceland, the first day they'd sort of talked. Did he remember that? Was he wearing it today on purpose?

"Are you . . ." Noel started.

"Have you . . ." Aria said at the same time. She stopped. "You first."

"No." Noel swallowed. "You."

She stared at the basket-weave brick pattern on the porch floor. All at once, she had no idea what to say. "Congratulations," she finally mustered, pointing to the cap.

"Thanks." Noel set it down and shoved his hands into the pockets of his jeans. A hawk screamed loudly in the sky overhead. "I don't believe it, you know," he said quietly. "I don't know what happened, and you don't have to tell me, but I think I know who's behind this. Am I right?"

Aria nodded, her insides twisting. "That's why I need your help."

Noel's brow furrowed. *"Me?"*

"You were her friend. Are you sure you don't know where she could be?"

Noel shook his head vehemently. "I have no idea."

Aria sighed. Above them, bronze wind chimes knocked together. The sun came out from behind a cloud, making slanted stripes across the vast front lawn. "Okay, then," she said, turning. "I guess I'll go."

"Wait." Noel's voice was like an oar cutting through water. Aria turned, and there was a strange, tortured look on his face. "There was no e-mail or phone at The Preserve, so we used to have a secret code for when she needed to talk."

Aria sucked in her stomach. "Have you used this code recently?"

"Of course not. Even if I did know she survived the fire, I would have done everything in my power to *hurt* her, not help her."

Aria walked back to the porch. "Could you use it now?"

Noel glanced around the front yard, as though he thought Ali might be watching. "I don't know. She might not fall for it."

Aria wrapped her hands around the railing that surrounded the porch. "We've been getting A notes—from *her*. But no one believes us. We're grasping at straws. Believe me, I didn't want to ask you, but you're our last hope. We don't want to go to Jamaica."

Noel slumped against one of the Adirondack chairs. "*I* don't want you to go to Jamaica."

"Then *help* us."

The door opened behind him, and Mrs. Kahn stuck out her head. "Noel? We need to get going."

Noel glanced at his mother, annoyed. "One sec, okay?"

Mrs. Kahn reluctantly shut the door again, though

Aria could tell by the light through the window that she was hovering close by. Noel pulled out his cell phone, then called up an electronics website on his browser. Aria watched as he ordered a single package of AA batteries. On the order page, he listed his name as Maxine Preptwill and that his address was the Rosewood Public Library. In the special instructions section, all he wrote was: 9 PM *tonight*.

"Who's Maxine Preptwill?" Aria whispered.

Noel shrugged. "I don't know. Ali suggested it." He gestured to his phone. "It's a dummy site. Somehow it always gets to her." He slipped his phone back into his pocket. "It's done. We're meeting up tonight at nine at the Rosewood Public Library."

Aria's heart thudded fast. She was at Byron's tonight. It would be easier to sneak out. "Will you be able to get away from your graduation party?"

"I'll figure something out."

Aria nodded. "Okay. We'll be hiding nearby, waiting."

Noel looked alarmed. "Just you guys? Shouldn't you call the police, too?"

Aria shook her head. "She'll never come if a bunch of cop cars are there. We'll all ambush her. Jump on her. Throw her in my car. And *then* we'll take her to the police station."

An uncertain look clouded Noel's face. "That sounds so dangerous. *And* violent."

Aria swallowed hard, hating that she'd become

someone who even considered throwing another person into the back of her car. "I know," she admitted. "But I don't know what else to do. This might save us."

"Okay. I'm in." Noel nodded, then turned for the door. His mom shifted inside. "See you tonight."

Aria nodded, too, pivoting toward the waiting Subaru. She was about to step off the porch when Noel called, "Why didn't you tell the cops what I knew about Ali?"

Aria whirled around and looked at him. His eyes were wide. His face was open and vulnerable. His beautiful, kissable, pink lips were parted just slightly.

"I-I couldn't," she admitted. "I wouldn't do that to you."

Noel stepped toward her. When he was close enough to give her a hug, he reached out and touched the edge of her chin, tilting it up. "I miss you so much," he whispered. "If I could take all of this back, I would. I wish they'd find Ali. I wish they'd kill her. And I wish, when it is over, that we could be together again."

His green eyes met Aria's, and the look brought back hundreds of memories. How hard they'd laughed in cooking class. How Aria had had to hold Noel's hand on the Batman roller coaster at Great Adventure because he was secretly terrified. The look on his face when he'd picked her up for homecoming. The first time he said he loved her.

She reached out for Noel, but she hesitated before taking his hand. Her fingers remained open in space for a few long beats, just inches from his. All sound fell away. All

Aria could see were Noel's thick eyebrows, his square jaw, his strong shoulders.

"I wish we could, too," she blurted. And then she ran to her mother's car as fast as she could. If she'd have stayed on that porch for a second longer, she would have never been able to leave.

29

STAKEOUT

Later that same night, as the digital clock in the bank across the street clicked to 8:56 PM, Emily, Aria, Spencer, and Hanna stood behind a line of bushes at the Rosewood Public Library, a stone building in the same complex as the King James Mall. A spotlight illuminated the library's front walk. Another light shone on the book return slot, which had been decorated with a blue-and-white banner that said, CONGRATULATIONS, ROSEWOOD GRADS! Inside, the place was locked up for the night. The aisles were empty, the desks unoccupied, all the seats pushed in. Not a single car was in the lot; Noel had picked the girls up in his Escalade then parked it by the mall. Now, a few paces in front of them, Noel sat on a bench in the shadows, knocking his cast-bound arm against the wooden seat again and again.

Emily's stomach jumped just looking at him. She couldn't believe they were doing this. Then again, *every-*

thing was a bit unbelievable these days, including what she'd almost done on the bridge. She was so thankful that her friends had come to her rescue, and she felt much calmer. But the teetering danger of the situation resonated with her. What if Ali fell for it? Could they really capture her? What if they actually *got* her?

What if they didn't?

"He seems nervous," Hanna whispered, brushing against one of the bushes. The shrubs were a bit thorny, but they wanted to be close to Noel if he needed them–*if* Ali actually showed up.

"I would be, too, if I was going to come face-to-face with the person who left me for dead," Spencer mumbled. Aria shuddered. Emily squeezed her hand. "Are you okay?"

Aria shrugged. She'd been quiet this whole time, and Emily had noticed that she and Noel had shot each other a few shy glances. But then, after each look, Aria seemed to pull away sharply, as if ashamed.

Aria peered at the others. "So let's run through the plan one more time. In a few seconds, we all spread out. When Ali shows up, Noel will give the signal that it's her. Then we ambush."

"Aria and I pile on her, then drag her to the car," Emily added.

"Hanna and I are on the lookout for Helper A," Spencer said. "And Noel's in charge of calling 911."

"If Helper A *does* show up, we bolt," Aria said.

"But not before we get a picture of Ali with our phones," Emily recited. "Proof that she's alive has got to help us."

"And if they catch one of us, we immediately call the police," Spencer said.

Emily looked at Noel again, her heart thumping. She hated the idea of Ali or her helper hurting one of them. Still, it was a possibility. They had to consider every angle.

The bank clock ticked to 9:00 PM on the dot, and the girls took their places. Emily's nostrils twitched with the smell of fresh mulch and some sort of fertilizer. She scanned the area, but no one appeared at the library entrance. Mall traffic whizzed past them. An eastbound SEPTA train clacked on the tracks. Noel shifted on the bench and checked his phone. The minutes crawled by. The bank clock clicked to 9:05, then 9:06. Dread blossomed in Aria's stomach.

Suddenly, a blond figure in a hooded sweatshirt appeared and walked toward Noel. All four girls leaned forward. It was a girl.

Emily felt a million emotions rush over her at once. Disbelief. Fear. Hatred. She looked at the others. Hanna clapped her hand over her mouth. Spencer widened her eyes. Emily looked at Aria. *Should we do it?* she mouthed.

The figure stopped in front of Noel; no one could see his expression. Nor did he give the signal: three fingers held up behind his back.

Still. It *had* to be Ali. Right? *Go*, Aria mouthed to the group, pointing toward Noel.

They burst out of the shrubs. Emily's heart pounded faster and faster as they approached the figure, who was still talking to Noel. *In just seconds, I'm going to look directly into Ali's face*, she thought.

Suddenly, the figure moved away from Noel and started running. Emily still couldn't see who it was, only the dark hoodie over her head. "Hey!" she screamed, chasing after her. The others followed. The figure raced across the two-lane road that connected the library to the mall and dove into a line of bushes. *We've nearly got her*, Emily thought excitedly. Getting out of those bushes would slow her down.

They crossed the street, and there was a horrible screech. Headlights shone in their faces. Emily screamed as a car barreled toward them. "Oh my God!" she cried, the light illuminating Hanna's outline in front of her. She reached out and shoved Hanna out of the way. The car zigzagged past, missing Emily by mere inches. She tumbled to the grass, scraping her knee on the curb. Spencer fell face-first next to her, and Aria crashed into a road sign. Hanna sat in the middle of the road, looking stunned.

"Are you okay?" Emily asked, scrambling up and running to her.

Hanna nodded shakily, staring at the car's taillights in the distance. "It came right for us. It could have *killed* us."

Emily helped her up, then ran toward the bushes into

which the figure had disappeared. She wasn't there anymore. No one was darting through the parking lot, either.

Then Emily turned back to Noel on the library bench. He was standing now, staring at them in alarm. She followed Aria and the others over. "Was that her?" Aria asked him. "What did she say?"

Noel shook his head dazedly. "It wasn't her. Just a random blond girl asking if I had a light. And then she saw you and took off. Are *you* guys okay?"

Emily and Hanna exchanged a look. "I don't know if any of this was random," Hanna said shakily.

Noel nodded, fear in his eyes. "Do you think this was a setup?"

Everyone stared at one another, then down the lane where the car had disappeared. No one had thought to get a license-plate number.

"Yes," Aria whispered. "It was Ali." Maybe she'd paid a blond girl to walk up to Noel to distract them. She'd probably sensed their plan all along.

Emily looked at Noel, suddenly desperate. "Can't you try to contact her again? Maybe we can set up another meeting, before the arraignment."

Noel stared at her. "She already knows it's a trap. She might try to hurt you again."

"Yeah, it's not a good idea," Spencer added.

Aria looked at Noel challengingly. "No, Emily's right. We've already come too far. We have to do *something*. Please contact her again."

Noel's shoulders lowered. In a defeated voice, he tapped something into his phone. After a moment, his expression wilted. "Site not found."

He tilted the screen toward the girls. Aria shook her head. "It's got to be a mistake."

"That's the site. I'm positive."

Emily watched as Aria took the phone from him and pressed the search button once more, but the same results popped up. Her lip trembled. Emily's heart sank.

"The site's gone, because Ali took it down," Noel said woodenly. "There's not going to be another meeting. She's gone."

Everyone blinked hard, absorbing the shock. The writing was on the wall: This had been their last chance, and they'd blown it. They were out of options. Their arraignment was tomorrow, and they were going to Jamaica—to *prison*—no matter what.

30

THEIR LIVES END HERE

Friday morning. Arraignment day. Hanna stood in the middle of her silent bedroom, looking at all the items on her shelves. She might never see any of this again. She began to say good-bye to all of it, just like how she used to say good night to all her stuffed animals when she was a baby. *Good-bye, Dior perfume. Good-bye, Louboutin heels. Good-bye, fluffy bedspread and earring tree. Good-bye, picture of Ali.*

She frowned and plucked it from the corner of her mirror, having forgotten it was there. She stared at Ali's teasing smile and mocking eyes. Sure, this was Courtney, *her* friend, but if it weren't for her—if it weren't for that stupid Time Capsule flag and that switch and Hanna caring so, *so* much about being popular, none of this would have happened.

"Hanna?" her mother called from downstairs. "It's time."

There was a lump in Hanna's throat as she walked to the first floor. She gazed at her expression in the big mirror in the foyer. Would this be the last time she'd wear a Diane von Furstenberg dress, gold earrings, and leather boots? Tears filled her eyes as she leaned down and gave her miniature Doberman, Dot, a huge hug. "I'll miss you, big guy," she whispered, barely able to get the words out.

And then she walked to the car, where her mother was waiting. "You ready?" she asked, tears in her eyes.

Hanna shook her head. Of course she wasn't.

Ms. Marin drove them without a word, mercifully keeping the radio off for the trip to the courthouse, which was only a few miles away at the very top of Mount Kale, just past a cemetery and the Botanical Gardens. Hanna gazed over the cliff that overlooked Rosewood and Hollis, feeling nostalgic and lonely. There was Rosewood Day and its sports fields—she'd never sit at a lacrosse game again. There was the Hollis Spire and surrounding buildings— she'd never go to another bar. Even Ali's old house was visible through the trees. Okay, she wouldn't miss that place very much. All it held were bitter memories.

A shiver ran up her spine as she remembered the last time she'd been at the courthouse. It had been for Ian's arraignment almost a year and a half ago. When they'd come back outside, Emily had grabbed them, swearing she saw Ali's face in the back of a limo. Of course no one had believed her. But they should have.

The car pulled into the courthouse entrance. As usual,

protesters marched in a circle on the sidewalk. The same line of news vans was parked by the entrance. Immediately, a gaggle of reporters swarmed them, staring at Hanna through the window. "Miss Marin!" they screamed, slapping at the windows. "Miss Marin! Miss Marin, will you answer a few questions?"

"Ignore them," Hanna's mother said.

It was no surprise that the reporters surrounded Hanna as soon as she got out of the car. They thrust their microphones at her and pulled at her sleeves. Their questions were still the same—stuff about Hanna being a killer and Mr. Marin's campaign and predictions about going to Jamaica. Hanna's mom draped an arm around her shoulders and led her toward the doors. Hanna's ankle twisted as she climbed up the first step, but she barely felt it and kept going. She barely felt anything.

Up ahead, Aria, Spencer, and Emily were scrambling inside. After the double doors shut, the shouts and screams and crowd noise disappeared almost completely. Hanna blinked in the marble lobby. Stone statues of Rosewood founders surrounded them. A Pennsylvania and an American flag hung from the balcony. Aria's parents and Spencer's mom stood in the metal-detector line, digging stuff out of their pockets. Beyond them stood their legal team, including Spencer's father and Mr. Goddard. Hanna was surprised to see Kate on the other side of the conveyor belt, dressed in a blue blazer and pinstriped pants. Hanna's father was noticeably absent. Hanna reached for that familiar stab of sadness, but it didn't come. Maybe because she wasn't really surprised.

As Hanna joined the metal-detector line, a hand slipped into hers. Mike's ice-blue eyes were full of tears. "I know you were trying to find her," he whispered. "You should have let me help."

Hanna shook her head. "I couldn't."

"Did you have any luck?"

Hanna almost wanted to laugh. "What do you think?"

Mike answered by squeezing her hand harder than ever before.

After the scanners, the legal team joined the girls, and they walked to the courtroom as a group. As soon as Mr. Goddard opened the double doors, a hundred heads turned around. Hanna recognized every face: There was Naomi Zeigler and Riley Wolfe. Boys from Mike's lacrosse team and girls from Hanna's old cheerleading squad. A girl named Dinah she'd met while doing a boot-camp program last Christmas. Sean Ackard, Sean's father, Kelly from the burn clinic. Phi Templeton, Chassey Bledsoe, and then—horrifyingly—Mona Vanderwaal's parents, both of them looking older and much more haggard since Mona's death a year and a half before.

Everyone stared at Hanna as though she'd already been convicted. Hanna hadn't felt this vulnerable since Mona-as-A had broadcast that video of Hanna's court dress ripping at the seams at Mona's Sweet Seventeen. Hanna leaned into Mike. "You don't have to stand by me,

266 + SARA SHEPARD

you know. Save yourself. Go sit with your friends."

Mike pinched her palm. "Shut *up*, Hanna."

Mike held fast to her hand as they walked down the aisle to the front bench. Hanna sat next to her lawyer, the wood cold through her thin dress. Mike retreated to the bench behind her. Emily, Spencer, and Aria slid into the front bench as well. They all exchanged a glance, but no one bothered to say anything. The defeat was clear on their faces. They'd tried every avenue to find Ali, and they'd failed again and again.

The heavy doors slammed shut, and a bailiff ordered everyone to rise. A rotund, balding judge in flowing black robes entered and settled down on the bench, gazing wearily at the girls. After a few beginning remarks, the district attorney rose. "There is reasonable evidence to prove that Miss Hastings, Miss Marin, Miss Montgomery, and Miss Fields murdered Miss Tabitha Clark at a resort in Jamaica last April."

The judge nodded. "Their trial will take place there, as will their sentence. Extradition to Jamaica will happen immediately."

The lawyers and the judge said more than that, but that was all Hanna heard before the sound of her heartbeat drowned out their voices. She shut her eyes, seeing only darkness. When she opened them again, Mr. Goddard was standing. "I motion to allow my clients one more night in Rosewood with their families."

"Motion granted," the judge decided. "All of the girls

must leave the country tomorrow. Flights will be arranged, paid for by their families. US marshals will accompany each prisoner."

And then the gavel banged, and everyone was standing again, and then Mr. Goddard was rushing them out of the courtroom and into a conference room where they could talk. The same reporters had made their way into the halls; they clawed at Hanna fiercely as she passed. Hanna glanced over her shoulder for Mike, wanting to spend every remaining second with him before she had to leave the country, but all she saw were angry faces.

Emily appeared by her side. Spencer caught up next, then Aria. Mr. Goddard made a circle around them with his arms, barricading the reporters, and as the girls looked at one another, they all burst into tears. Spencer grabbed Hanna tightly and hugged her. Aria and Emily wrapped their arms around them, too. They sobbed as one, their breaths sharp and uneven. Flashbulbs popped. The reporters didn't pause for a second from questioning. But for a few moments, Hanna didn't care what the photos would be. Who *wouldn't* show emotion when she was extradited to a foreign prison for a crime she didn't commit?

"I can't believe it's come to this," she murmured into her friends' ears.

"We have to be strong," Spencer said, her voice cracking.

Hanna gazed back at the courtroom doors, surprised at how many people were streaming out. Mona's parents hurried down the steps, probably worried they'd be stalked by the reporters themselves. Naomi and Riley flirted with a few lacrosse players, treating this as a social event. Kate looked a little lost as she walked to the window. Hanna wanted to call her over and give her a big hug.

Mr. Goddard directed them into the conference room and shut the doors. "I'll be right back," he said. "We're filing an appeal immediately. And we're working on getting you the best lawyers in Jamaica." Then he shut the door behind them, leaving the girls alone.

For a few moments, Hanna sat numbly at the table, scratching her nails against the wood.

Suddenly, something out the window caught her attention. The view was of the empty parking lot, but voices rang out from somewhere below. "*No more*," someone said through a bullhorn.

"No more," more voices echoed.

"No more murders in Rosewood!" the first voice said.

She cocked her ear. If you weren't paying attention, if you didn't know what you were listening for, that first part kind of sounded like *Mo, Mo*.

"No more!" the first voice said through the bullhorn.

"No more murders in Rosewood!" echoed the protesters again, waving their picket signs.

Hanna clapped a hand over her mouth. "Guys." She wheeled around and motioned for Spencer, Emily, and Aria to come to the window. They moved toward her, their brows furrowed.

"*The protesters*," Hanna said. She peered all the way to the left, and there they were, making a big circle on the front lawn. *No more murders in Rosewood*, they chanted. "That's the announcement from Ali's voicemail," Hanna said.

Emily blinked hard. "Really?"

Hanna nodded, suddenly never more sure of anything in her life. "It's the same voice. The same protest message. We only had a piece of it before Ali hung up. But this is it."

Spencer made a face. "Ali was in the middle of a protest march . . . about the murders *she* committed?"

"Maybe she was *near* a march," Hanna said.

Spencer paced around the room. "There have been marches all over Rosewood for the past week. When did you receive that message, Emily?"

"Last Friday."

Aria looked at Spencer. "Is there any way we could figure out where the protesters were that day?"

Hanna suddenly realized something. "I know where they were." The last time she'd gone to his office, he'd been more concerned with whether the protesters had seen her come in than with the fact that she needed his help.

When she explained this to her friends, Spencer gasped. "You're sure?"

"Positive." Hanna's heart beat faster and faster. "She was calling from near my dad's campaign office."

Hanna gazed at her friends, a tiny candle of hope

burning inside her. They had one more day until they were going to Jamaica. One more night to stake this out. It would be next to impossible to get out of the house, but they had to, somehow. When she saw the determined expressions on her friends' faces, she knew they were thinking the exact same thing.

Spencer's gaze flicked toward the trees. "One AM?"

Hanna nodded. It was on.

31

FINDING HER

At 12:20 AM, Spencer's phone alarm buzzed on her nightstand. Her eyes popped open, and her body was suddenly alert. Though her bedroom was dark and she was tucked under the covers, she was fully dressed in a black hoodie, black tights, and even black New Balance running sneakers she'd found in the closet in Melissa's old bedroom. She was ready.

She slid the covers back and tiptoed to the door. The house was silent. Her mom and Mr. Pennythistle were presumably sleeping, probably zonked out on Xanax. Spencer padded over to the window that faced the front of the house. There was no police car at the curb.

Spencer made a lump of pillows in her bed to look like she was still sleeping. Then she snuck downstairs, opened the alarm unit on the main floor, and disarmed one of the exits, silencing it before any sort of announcement could be made to the rest of the house. Finally, she crept to the only unfinished room in the basement, which held cases of wine and an extra fridge the Hastings used for big parties. Normally, Spencer didn't like going into the room—it smelled musty, was full of spiders, and was where Melissa used to "banish" her when they played Evil Queen and Prisoner when they were little. But tucked into the corner was a small set of stairs that led to a flat door flush with the backyard. No one would be watching it. The cops probably had no idea it was there.

Her heart pounded as she climbed the dark cellar stairs toward the door. She didn't dare breathe as she pushed it up and open. A sprinkler hissed pleasantly. The hot tub bubbled to the left. Spencer squeezed out, keeping low to the ground and out of the floodlights as she dashed to the woods. From there, she was free.

It was at least three miles to Hanna's dad's campaign office, which was in a building on Lancaster Avenue near the train station. Spencer had considered taking her bike, but she hadn't had time to plant it in the woods behind her house, so she had to go on foot. She shot into the next development, ran on the streets for a while, but ducked into a yard whenever a car turned onto the road. Every footfall was like a chant: *Must Get Ali. Must Get Ali.*

Running along Lancaster was much more difficult—even though it was late, there was still some traffic, and Spencer had to keep on the inside of the guardrail at all times. Whenever she saw headlights, she ducked behind a tree or a strip-mall sign. Once, when she saw a cop car at the intersection, she hid in a ditch. Still, she arrived at the office shortly before 1:00 AM. A thin sheen of sweat covered her body. Dirt caked her tights and shoes. She was pretty sure she'd twisted an ankle diving into a ditch. But it didn't matter. She was here.

She stared at her reflection in the building's flat panes of glass. Exit lights above the doors glowed, but otherwise the atrium was dark. She peered at the underground parking lot, then at the woods in the back, and then at the neon sign of Jessica's Consignment Shop next door, where the Rosewood Day Drama Department sometimes got costumes for school plays. Was it really possible Ali was around here? How could she have hidden somewhere so public for so long?

"I bet you're thinking what I'm thinking."

Hanna stood behind her, similarly dressed in black and breathing heavily as if she'd run here, too. "Ali isn't here, right? She wouldn't hide near an office building right in the middle of Rosewood."

Spencer shrugged one shoulder. "It doesn't seem very likely."

Hanna sat down on the planter next to the front door. "This is where the protests were on Friday. This is where she called Emily from."

Within minutes, Aria and Emily arrived on bikes. Spencer filled them in on what they were talking about. "I've thought about this being a mistake, too," Aria admitted, carefully stashing her bike in a shrub. "I mean, if we're wrong, what are the cops going to do when they find us?"

"It's not like they can punish us any more," Spencer said emptily.

Emily looked at Hanna. "What if Ali was only here for a little while? Maybe she knew you'd figure it out, Hanna, and she called from here just to send us on a wild-goose chase?"

"But what if she didn't?" Hanna said. "It's worth the risk."

Spencer pulled at the bar on the front door, but it was locked tight. "So where do we go from here? It's not like we can get inside and check if Ali's in any of the offices."

"She wouldn't be," Hanna said thoughtfully. "I've been here so often that I know everyone in all of the offices throughout this building—no one is hiding Ali in a back room, I'm sure of it."

"What about the basement?" Emily suggested.

Hanna shook her head. "There are maintenance guys patrolling this place during the day—I doubt she's set up camp there."

Spencer put her hands on her hips and did a full circle, once again taking in the building, the parking lot, and the road.

Hanna's gaze fixed on the lot next door. "What about that building?"

Everyone turned and looked. "Jessica's Consignment Shop?" Emily asked.

"No, the thing *before* Jessica's." Hanna pointed at a

cluster of trees that made a barrier between the office building and the consignment store's parking lot. And suddenly, Spencer saw it: Set back from the road, peeking out above the brambles, was what looked like a rooftop.

"Oh my God," Aria breathed.

"I noticed it when I was here the other day, talking to my dad," Hanna whispered. "I don't know what it *is*, though."

They walked closer, down a path hidden in the tall grass. A hundred yards back, mostly concealed by overgrown trees, loomed a building—a fallen-down barn, perhaps, or an old stone house left to disintegrate. Spencer opened the flashlight app on her iPhone and shone it against the weathered clapboard frame, a broken window, a drooping gutter. The ground was overrun with weeds, as if no one had touched it in years.

Hanna squinted. "Gross."

A hush fell over the group. They peered at the looming house. A shiver slunk up Spencer's spine. Suddenly, this felt like it. "Come on," she whispered. "Let's go."

32

THE BOY

One by one, Hanna and the others climbed through the hedges. Up close, it was even more disgusting than it had looked from the parking lot. The windows were boarded up with rotted pieces of wood, and a front porch was covered in spiderwebs and trash. A rusted, rooster-shaped weathervane on the roof spun slowly and creakily with the wind. Vines and weeds grew up and into the walls as if they were trying to swallow the house completely. The foul stench of a rotting animal carcass wafted out from somewhere inside.

Hanna covered her nose with her sleeve. "How could she live in a place like this?"

"The same way she could kill five people," Aria reminded her. "She's crazy."

Spencer climbed up a crumbling ridge to the front door. The hinges were so old that it gave way easily, letting out a loud screech as it opened. Hanna bristled and covered her head as though a bomb were about to go off. After a few seconds, she dared to open her eyes. The door was ajar. No one was there. Spencer was stock-still in the doorway, her face a mask of fear.

Emily scurried up the ridge next to Spencer. Hanna followed, and they all peered inside. It was very dark. The dead-animal smell was stronger, though, almost dizzying.

"*Ugh*," Hanna said, turning away.

"It's really bad." Spencer gagged. Emily pulled the collar of her shirt over her nose.

Aria pulled out her phone and shone the light around the room. The floors were covered in dust, plaster, pieces of wood, and dirt. When she shone the light into a corner, something skittered out of the way, squeaking as it went. The girls screamed and jumped back again.

"It's just a mouse," Spencer hissed.

Trying not to breathe, Hanna took a tentative step into the room. The floor seemed to hold her weight, so she ventured a few more steps through an archway. The next room contained an old metal sink and a black, three-legged stove like something out of "Hansel and Gretel." An old newspaper lay near a huge hole in the wall that might have once been a back door. She picked it up and squinted at the headlines, but the page was so faded, she couldn't tell what it said.

She poked her head into a bathroom. A rusted bathtub sat in the corner, a toilet without a seat against the wall. There were holes where a sink might have been, and much of the tile was chipped away. A window was propped open, the stiff breeze blowing in. Hanna stepped back. The air smelled dirty and contaminated.

The other girls wandered the rooms, peeking into closets. They would have climbed the stairs to the second floor, but half the risers were missing. "There's no one here," Spencer whispered. "It's totally empty."

"Is there a basement?" Emily suggested.

Spencer shrugged. "I haven't seen any stairs leading down."

Aria whirled, her eyes wide. "Did you hear that?"

"What?" Hanna asked shakily, standing very still.

No one said a word. Hanna listened very hard. She didn't hear a thing. She stared around at the dark, empty, creepy space. "Maybe this isn't it," she said. "I don't see any evidence of anything. I don't think Ali's here."

Spencer breathed out, too. "Maybe we were wrong."

There was a creaking sound above them. It sounded like branches scraping across the roof. "Maybe we should go," Emily said, tiptoeing toward the door. "This place is freaking me out."

Everyone nodded and moved toward the exit. But then footsteps sounded behind them, this time for real. Hanna spun back around, her muscles stiffening. Suddenly, someone was standing in the shadows near the back of the room.

The others turned, too. Spencer gasped. Aria made a small *eep*. Emily cowered against the wall. "H-hello?"

Hanna called out shakily, trying to make out who the figure might be.

A flashlight snapped on. Diffused, yellow light scattered throughout the room. The mouse squeaked and scampered. The house creaked and groaned with the wind. Finally, the figure holding the flashlight flipped it upward, shining it on himself. "Hello, girls," a guy's voice said.

Hanna blinked at his face in the light. He had brown eyes, a sloped nose, and a pointy, clean-shaven jaw. There was a gun in his right hand, aimed at them.

As he drew up to his full height, Hanna realized with a jolt that she knew him. Madison had just shown her his picture.

"*Jackson?*" she exclaimed. The bartender. The one who'd overserved Madison and laughed when Hanna suggested they call her a cab.

Only . . . what was *he* doing here?

"Derrick?" Emily said slowly, next to her.

Hanna frowned and studied the look of shock on Emily's face. Who was Derrick?

Spencer was twitching, too. "Phineas," she said dazedly, staring at the boy. "Easy A Phineas from Penn."

"*Olaf,*" Aria said at the same time.

Hanna recoiled, too many neurons firing at once in her brain. "Wait. Olaf from *Iceland*?"

"Yeah," Aria said slowly, her hand half covering her mouth. "That's him."

Hanna shook her head vehemently. "*That's* not Olaf.

I *met* Olaf." Her night at that dive bar in Philly had happened before Iceland—she would have known if the same guy who'd waited on her the night of Madison's accident was also hitting on Aria halfway around the world.

Or . . . *would* she? She stared at Jackson's dark eyebrows and thin lips. Come to think of it, he *did* sort of look like Olaf. But she never would have thought to connect the strange Icelandic guy with a preppy bartender in the States.

"I-I don't understand," Spencer croaked.

"What the hell is going on?" Hanna said at the same time.

The boy stepped forward. "My name is Jackson," he said. "*And* Derrick. *And* Phineas, and yes, even Olaf. But my real name is Nick. Or Tripp to my friends. Tripp Maxwell."

Emily blinked hard. "Tripp," she whispered. "Oh my God."

Spencer looked at her. "Who's Tripp?"

Emily's jaw trembled. "Iris liked a boy named Tripp Maxwell. He was a patient at The Preserve."

"Oh, Iris." Nick rolled his eyes. "She always had such a thing for me."

Hanna's head spun. He was a Preserve patient. His name started with an *N*. This was Ali's boyfriend. He was the person who Graham was talking about. He'd hurt Noel, too. Killed Gayle. Murdered Kyla.

He was Helper A.

Panic rose in her chest. She peeked over her shoulder. They were only a few steps away from the door—maybe they could make it out without Nick getting any of them. She grabbed Spencer's arm and yanked her around. Emily and Aria made a break for it, too. Hanna took one step for the door, then another, reaching out her arms for the wobbly knob.

But then, seemingly out of nowhere, a body shot forward and stood in front of the door, barring their exit. "Not so fast," said an icy voice.

This voice Hanna *knew* instantly. All at once, the scent of perfume wafted through the air. Hanna's blood ran cold. *Vanilla* perfume.

Slowly, dramatically, Nick trained the flashlight on her. Scars covered her neck and arms. She still had huge blue eyes and a heart-shaped face, but there was something hard and mean about her. She was thinner, reedy, stripped down, and very sick-looking. Her eyes were cold and mocking, without the slightest bit of joy. Hanna drew in a breath.

"Greetings, bitches," Ali whispered, pulling out a gun as well. "You're coming with us."

33

THE SWEET SMELL OF DEATH

Emily trembled as she felt Ali's steely, murderous gaze upon her. Here she was, finally. Real. Alive. Sickly and way too thin, her jeans hanging off her hips, her arms like toothpicks, cords and veins standing out in her neck. There was dirt all over her face, her hair was matted, and one of her front teeth had rotted, spoiling her smile. It was like scribbling over the *Mona Lisa*. A beautiful girl, the *most* beautiful girl, envied by everyone, adored by Emily herself. Now she was just a tarnished ruin. A twisted freak.

Then she spun around again and looked at Nick. *Derrick.* It made no sense. Emily couldn't believe this was her sweet confidant, the boy who'd helped her through a bleak summer. He'd offered to rescue her from Carolyn's dorm. But he was looking at her coldly now, an eerie, unfamiliar smile on his face. And something else occurred to her, too: Derrick *knew* Gayle. He had worked as her landscaper that same summer. It was why Gayle spoke to

Derrick with some familiarity the night he'd killed her. She'd probably wondered what Derrick, of all people, was doing in her driveway.

Ali waved the gun, her body still planted firmly against the front door, their only exit. "There's a trapdoor in the corner. Go there. *Now.*"

They marched the girls to a hidden door in the floor. Nick pulled at a rusty hinge and yanked it open. A set of stairs descended to a basement. A strip of dim light shone on a carpet. A strange, sweet smell wafted out, causing Emily to cough. "What *is* that smell?" she sputtered.

"No questions. Climb down," Ali demanded, pressing the butt of the gun into Aria's back.

Trembling, Emily staggered down the stairs, nearly falling twice. Spencer, Aria, and Hanna followed. Emily's feet touched the bottom, and she looked around. They were in a narrow corridor. There was nothing down here except for four walls. The sweet smell was stronger, cloying and almost suffocating, and there was an unsettling *hiss* in the air, perhaps of more of the sweet poison filling the space. Emily coughed a few more times, but it didn't seem to help. Spencer took heaving breaths. Aria looked pale.

Ali's and Nick's shapes danced before them as they climbed down the ladder last and shut the trapdoor. "So, girls," Nick said, grinning like a crocodile. "Are you still confused?"

No one dared to speak, though Emily was sure they were all as confused as she was.

"You followed me to Iceland," Aria stated.

Nick shrugged. "I guess I did."

"Were you there, too?" Aria asked Ali, peeking at her in the dim light.

Ali just smirked, not answering. Probably figuring she didn't *have* to answer.

"Did you put Noel in that shed?" Aria whispered, tears coming to her eyes.

Nick crossed his arms over his chest. Again with that sly smile.

Then Emily cleared her throat. "You stole that money from Gayle. And you killed her. And you came on the cruise with us. You told the Feds about Jordan."

"*And* you bombed the ship," Aria added. "You almost killed me."

"You *did* kill Graham," Hanna said.

Nick and Ali glanced at each other, looking proud. They seemed almost giddy.

Emily reached for Aria's hand. The extent of everything he'd done knifed through her, hot and sharp. It was bad enough what Nick and Ali had done to Noel. But the two of them had killed Ian, too. And Jenna. He'd helped set fire to Spencer's yard. He'd more than likely been in the Poconos when Ali tried to kill them, too. He'd helped Ali escape.

Even though it made no sense, even though it was *crazy*, somehow this guy had been four people at once, different people to all of them.

"I trusted you," Emily whispered, staring at Nick. "And because of you, I almost gave my baby away to a crazy person."

Nick's eyes hardened. "I didn't *force* you to make that deal, Emily. You did it yourself. That's the beauty of this, girls—I got you all into trouble, but you were the ones, ultimately, who sealed your fates."

Everyone exchanged a doomed glance. He was right. They were culpable . . . and ultimately responsible. Somehow Nick had figured out their weaknesses and exploited them.

"You killed Tabitha, too, didn't you?" Emily sputtered.

Nick glanced at Ali, and she snickered. "We just did what we had to do," Nick said.

"And what about Iris?" Emily whispered.

Nick shrugged. "No more questions. We're done."

He brushed past them and located a small bump in the wall. He twisted it once, grunted, and the whole wall shifted, revealing a hidden room. Light spilled out from a bare bulb in the corner. "Go," he demanded, pushing Emily and the others inside.

Emily walked shakily into the space. It was a small, damp, basement room that smelled of mildew and that horrible sweetness she couldn't identify. There was an old tweed couch pushed against the cinder-block wall, a table at its side. And on the walls, covering every inch, were pictures of Ali.

Old school pictures from seventh grade. Snapshots

from yearbook in fourth and fifth grades, candids of her when she'd returned to Rosewood after Ian was arraigned, family portraits Emily remembered from the DiLaurentis front hall, only one DiLaurentis twin smiling a gap-toothed smile. The pictures covered every inch of the space. Newspaper articles about Alison returning to Rosewood, Alison going missing after the Poconos fire, and Alison sightings all over the country were plastered on the walls as well, certain lines of text highlighted, other things circled with red pen. WE LOVE YOU, ALI, read sparkly letters along the top border of one wall. WE MISS YOU, ALI, read letters on the opposite wall.

Emily stepped back. "What *is* this?"

"Like it?" Ali asked behind them, her gun still pointed at their backs. "You should. *You* made it."

Emily blinked, her head lolling on her neck. She couldn't feel her legs, exactly. "What do you mean by that?"

"When they find you," Ali explained in a pleasant voice, "they'll figure it's your shrine to me."

Spencer's eyes blazed. "We would *never* make a shrine to you."

"Oh, please." Ali rolled her eyes. "You love me. You've *always* loved me. I'm all you've been thinking about these past few years. That's what the cops will think when they find all of you dead here. Your own little death plan, a final tribute to *moi*."

It took Emily a great effort to swing around and give

her best friends a horrified look. Her brain was moving slowly, but the pieces fit. *The cops. An Ali shrine. A death plan.* When the cops found them—*if* the cops found them—it would look like they'd killed themselves because of—or in honor of—Ali. Because they were haunted and enchanted by her.

Emily clutched her head, which was now pounding. "What did you do?" she asked Nick. "You pumped something into the air, didn't you? Something poisonous that will kill us."

"Maybe, maybe not," Nick teased.

"I can't breathe," Spencer sputtered. "Make it stop."

Nick shook his head, then reached behind him and placed an object over his face. It looked like a gas mask. He handed a second one to Ali, and she put it on, too. Their bodies relaxed as they took deep breaths of clean air. Mist appeared against the plastic. He breathed again and again, mocking them.

All the while, every breath Emily took hurt. She could feel her cells fizzling, sputtering, giving up. Her friends writhed, too, equally suffering. Tears filled Emily's eyes. This was it. She could feel it. *But I need more time*, her brain screamed. She couldn't die now. She couldn't let Ali win.

But this was the end. Spencer let out a helpless whimper. Aria dropped to the floor, half-conscious, her eyes rolling to the back of her head. Nick and Ali clasped hands and bounced on the balls of their feet like children. They were *loving* this.

Emily stared at them. They were savages. Inhuman. Suddenly, energy from somewhere deep inside filled her, and she sprung for Nick, her arms outstretched. He screamed as he landed on his back. She ripped off his mask and tossed it across the room, then grabbed the gun and flung it away, too. When she looked at him again, his neck was twisted, his eyes closed, his lips parted. He took even, steady breaths. She'd knocked him out.

The gun glinted across the room. Emily didn't know where she found the energy, but she lunged for it and grabbed it with both hands. It was heavier than she expected, the metal cold to the touch.

"Well, well, well. Look who's tough."

Emily looked up. Ali peered down at her, the mask still over her face.

"Get away." Emily pointed Nick's gun at her.

Ali shrugged and aimed her gun at Emily. "Now, now, Em," she said kindly, her voice muffled. Then she took off her mask and smiled, showing that horrible gap in her teeth. She dropped to her knees next to Emily. "It doesn't have to end like this. We can be friends again, can't we?"

Her breath was hot and sour-smelling on Emily's cheek. Emily cringed, not wanting Ali to touch her. She glanced at Nick on the floor. He was out cold. Then she peeked at her friends across the room. They were staring at her fearfully but also dazedly, too weak to move.

"I'll hurt you," Emily warned Ali.

Ali placed the mask back on her face, then rolled her

eyes. "No, you won't, Em. I know how you feel about me. I know I'm not as pretty as I used to be, but I'm still the same Ali. I know you've still been thinking about me. I've been thinking about you, too. Especially the last time we saw each other. When you let me out of that house just before it exploded. I've never properly thanked you for it."

There was a knot in Emily's throat.

Emily gripped Nick's gun hard and brushed Ali off of her. "Stay away from me."

Ali sat back on her butt, looking amused. "Does poor widdle Emily not love me anymore?" she said in a pouty, babyish voice, partly muffled by the mask over her mouth.

Emily looked her in the eye. "I *never* loved you," she hissed.

Ali drew back her hand and slammed Emily across the cheek. Red streaked across Emily's vision, her face screamed with heat, and she wheeled backward. The gun flew from her hands and skidded across the floor once more. Emily reached for it, but Ali caught her and pulled her back with surprising strength.

"Say you never stopped thinking about me," Ali growled, her gun at Emily's temple now. Her mask came loose and dangled around her neck. She held it against her mouth, her nostrils flaring. "Say you would have betrayed even your best friends if it meant getting me back."

Emily's cheek stung. She couldn't eke out a response. She glanced again at Spencer, Aria, and Hanna. They were barely conscious, their skin gray, their breath ragged. Each had a look of desperation on her face—it was clear they wanted to help Emily, but they simply couldn't. The gun rested in the corner, out of their reach.

"*Say* it," Ali demanded. "Tell your friends just how much you wanted me to live. Tell them you betrayed them. We'll see how much they love you then."

"She already told us, Alison," Aria said weakly. "We don't care. Emily's still our friend."

Ali pressed the gun into Emily's flesh. "Say it, anyway."

"Leave me alone." Emily's lips trembled. Even though she knew this was the end, even though she'd probably be dead in a few minutes and Ali would escape *again*, she didn't want this to be the last thing she ever said. She didn't love Ali. No frickin' way.

There was a click as Ali lifted the safety latch. "*Say* it," she growled. "Say how excited you were when you guys were looking for me. Say how much you wanted to find me so you could kiss me again."

"Stop it!" Emily screamed, curling into a ball.

Ali moved the gun to Emily's temple. "Well, then, say good-bye."

Emily started to sob. Every muscle in her body trembled. She looked around the room, first at her friends, then at Nick's limp body, and then at all of those awful Ali photos on the walls, and then, finally, at Ali herself. "I hate you," she whispered.

"What was that?" Ali growled, looking alien in her gas mask.

Emily was about to say it again, but suddenly, there was a faint sound from upstairs. Ali cocked her head toward the ceiling. Emily did, too. The sound grew louder. It sounded like . . . *a police siren.*

Ali gasped. She glared at Emily. "Did you call the cops?"

Emily looked at the others. Were the cops coming for them? Did they know? Would they be here in time?

But the sirens were still so far away. Even if the police *did* reach the house, they'd never find the basement. Tears ran down Emily's cheeks. Help was so close . . . yet so far away. Ali was going to win this time . . . for real.

"Too little, too late," Ali said in a soothing voice, pushing the gun against Emily's head. "Say good-bye, Emily, dear."

Emily shut her eyes and tried to think of something good and pure. And then, *bang.* The sound reverberated off the walls. Emily flattened to the ground, terrified of the power.

And then all she saw was darkness.

34

SOMEWHERE OUT THERE

Aria was swimming in a beautiful blue ocean. Colorful fish flanked her sides. Coral waved in the ocean current. A figure treaded water in the distance, and she kicked toward him. When she surfaced, she saw Noel. The sun danced across his cheekbones. His eyes sparkled. But his smile was sad and lonely. There were tears in his eyes.

"Aria," he said, his voice full of pain.

"Noel!" Aria paddled toward him. "I've missed you. I thought I'd never see you again."

Noel blinked and pressed his lips together. "That's the thing, Aria. You won't. This is the last time."

"W-what do you mean?" Aria asked. Why did he look so miserable?

And then she remembered. That basement room full of Ali. That poisonous gas. Ali and Nick and those guns. That *bang*.

It all flooded into her memory, twisting her into knots.

She looked at Noel in horror, waves lapping around them. "Am I . . . *dead*?"

Noel's chin trembled. Tears spilled down his cheeks.

"No!" Aria exclaimed, waving her arms, suddenly hyperventilating. "I-I *can't* be dead. I feel so alive. And I'm not ready." She stared at her ex-boyfriend, full of purpose. She *wasn't* ready. She wanted to live; she wanted him back. She didn't care about that Ali shit anymore. Everyone lied. Everyone made mistakes. They'd get over it, the way they'd gotten over everything.

She reached for him, but Noel ducked under the water. "Noel!" Aria cried out. He didn't surface. "Noel!" She ducked under, too, but all she saw was darkness. No more fish. No more *nothing*.

"Aria? Honey?"

Aria blinked hard. When she opened her eyes again, she was lying on a bed in a bright room. A sheet covered her body, and a monitor beeped at her side. A blurry face loomed over her. When her eyes adjusted, she saw it was Agent Fuji.

Aria licked her dry lips. Was this another hallucination? Was she in some sort of post-death limbo? "W-what's going on?" she heard herself say.

Agent Fuji glanced over her shoulder. Two more blurry figures shot forward. One of them was Byron, the other Ella. "Oh my God," they both cried, clasping Aria's hands. "Oh, honey, we were so worried."

Mike appeared, too. "Hey," he said sheepishly. "Good to have you back."

Aria swallowed hard. When she shifted, her head pounded. Did dead people get headaches?

"I'm . . . alive?" she asked tentatively.

"Of course you're alive," came a voice next to her. Aria looked over. Emily was propped against a pillow, her eyes open and a wan smile on her face. Her sister Carolyn was next to her, tears in her eyes. Hanna was lying on her side, her mom holding one hand, Kate holding the other. Spencer had a bandage on her forehead and looked pretty out of it, but when she saw Aria's gaze land on her, she weakly waved.

They were *all* alive. They'd all made it out, somehow. "How long was I out?" Aria said shakily.

"Two days," Mike said. "But it felt like two *years*."

Fuji materialized at the foot of Aria's bed. "We pulled you girls out of that room just in time. The amount of cyanide in the air was staggering. If we would have arrived a few minutes later, you wouldn't have lived. It's a good thing we were keeping tabs on you that night. Someone followed you to that house. When you didn't come out, our agent called for backup." She patted Aria's leg. "But we got him, honey. He's in custody. It's all over."

"Him," Aria said thickly. *Nick.* She thought of his eerie, wolflike smile. The gun trained in his hands. His body falling to the ground, a dim recollection of Emily knocking him out.

"He nearly killed you girls," Fuji said. "I guess he figured out you were getting too close. Some members of my team figured out the Nick link just about the same time he captured you girls. They brought it to our attention just as he trapped you in that house."

"How did you figure out it was Nick?" Aria asked.

Fuji rubbed the fine lines around her eyes. "One group of forensic experts was doing the computer piece, and they were able to trace everything back to Nick's phone—all those A notes, and also the rerouting of the A notes to *your* phones." She glanced at Spencer. "We *did* listen to you—we cross-referenced Preserve patients to see if someone from inside the hospital might be a suspect. Nick was on our list. We had other experts looking at DNA, and Nick came up a match there, too—his DNA was on record from a prior offense before he was at The Preserve. We finally ID'd the third face in the cruise basement where that bomb went off. And last night, we found Iris Taylor tied up in the woods, half-dead. She confessed that he hurt her. It was Nick. It was *all* Nick."

"Iris?" Emily cried out. "So she's . . . okay?"

"She will be," Fuji said. "But it was a close call."

"Wait." There was a gap in Aria's brain. "What about . . . Ali? Did you find her?"

Byron and Ella glanced at each other. Fuji set her mouth in a line. "Ali wasn't there, Aria."

Aria struggled to prop herself up on the pillows. Her head throbbed. "Yes, she was. We all saw her. You said there were people watching us at the house. They must have heard her voice."

"Honey," Ella said gently. "You're just confused."

"No, it's true," Spencer croaked. "She tried to kill us alongside Nick. They did this together."

"She shot me," Emily said. Aria watched as she touched her head. There was no wound. "At least I *thought* she did," Emily said, after a moment.

Fuji sighed. "Girls, Nick drugged you with a dangerous mixture of toxins. You saw Alison because that was who you feared you'd see—*and* because her picture was all over those walls. Nick built a shrine to her. He was obsessed over her death, and he was trying to get revenge."

"Nick and Alison were boyfriend and girlfriend," Melissa Hastings, who was sitting by Spencer's side, piped up. "He came after you because his girlfriend was killed. He knew Tabitha Clark—they were friends from the hospital as well—and clearly got her to impersonate Alison to scare you girls. And that's where it all started."

"But Iris said she hadn't seen Tripp—Nick—in years," Emily protested. "She just led me on a wild-goose chase to find his house."

"People lie," Fuji said. "And Iris isn't exactly a healthy girl."

Aria stared at her, blinking hard. "So what about that video from Jamaica? The one of Tabitha?"

Fuji shifted her weight. "A second video came in the same night you girls snuck out, proving your innocence. It's more footage from the night Tabitha was murdered, and it shows one person acting alone, beating the girl to death—Nick. Our forensic and digital experts are certain it's the real one. The other *is* a fake."

A shock wave went through Aria. "Who sent that video?"

Fuji shook her head. "I don't know."

Aria looked at the others, and they seemed just as stunned. "What if *Ali* sent it?" Emily cried. "Don't you see? She had it in her back pocket all along. She sent it to frame Nick when she knew they were caught!"

"And what about your theory of two people tying Noel up?" Aria asked. "If it wasn't Ali helping Nick, who was it?"

"It could have been anyone," Fuji said. "Nick had other friends. It's possible he lied and said Noel pissed him off, or that he was doing this as a prank."

Aria shut her eyes and thought of the night she, Noel, and the others had tried to trap Ali at the library. A blond girl had served as a decoy, clearly Nick's helper. What if whoever was aiding in his crazy rampage wasn't Ali at all?

But no. They'd *seen* her. *Talked* to her. Aria was sure of it.

Fuji stuck her hands in her pockets. "Let it go, girls. I know you wanted closure, but you really didn't see Alison in there. Our experts are combing the basement, making sure, but I'm positive we'll find no trace of her. She's dead—and has been for a long, long time. Honestly. It's better to just accept it and move on." She looked around at all of them. "Just get some rest, okay? You're going to have to answer a lot of questions from reporters soon enough."

And then she walked out of the room and shut the door. Aria glanced at her best friends. Everyone stared at her blankly. But it wasn't like they could talk about any of this now—not with all their family around. Of course everyone would think they'd hallucinated Ali, too. Maybe they *should* let it go, Aria wondered. Maybe this really *was* the end.

The door swung open again, and Aria turned her head, worried it might be a nosy reporter wanting to ask questions. But Noel stepped through instead. As soon as he saw Aria, his face crumpled. He ran to her bedside. Byron and Ella moved apart to let him get close.

"H-hey," he said, trembling.

"Hey," Aria said. All at once, the dream rushed back to her. Sinking underwater and finding Noel nowhere. Never getting to touch him again. She reached out and squeezed his hand, and he squeezed back. And then he leaned forward so that his face was close to hers. At first, Aria thought he was going to kiss her—and she wanted him to.

He moved toward her ear instead. "You saw *her*, didn't you?" he whispered.

Aria's eyes widened. She nodded, then glanced toward the door, where Fuji had disappeared. "But no one believes us."

"I believe you. I'll *always* believe you."

He drew back, and Aria stared at him, half in shock,

half grateful.

Thank you, she mouthed, her eyes full of tears.

But she wanted to tell Noel to forget about Ali. She wanted *everyone* to forget about her. Her mind went to a dark, terrible place. *We won't find a trace of her*, Fuji had said. All at once, Aria knew they wouldn't. No fingerprints on the gun she was holding. No blood on the floor. No long, blond hairs on the carpet. Not because Ali hadn't been there.

Because Ali was smarter than all of them.

A nurse poked her head into the room and frowned at all of the guests. "Okay, visitors, everyone out," she demanded in a no-nonsense voice. "These girls need their rest."

Noel patted Aria's hand. "I'll be right outside," he said. Aria nodded, then watched as everyone else trailed out, too. The nurse dimmed their lights, and for a moment, the room was silent. Then Hanna reached for her remote and turned on the TV that hung from the ceiling. *Serial Killer Taken into Custody*, blared a headline on CNN. Of course it was all over the news.

The camera showed the outside of the old farmhouse. A cop shoved Nick into the backseat, his hands pinned behind his back. Ambulances whirled in the background. Aria wondered if she'd been inside one of them, unconscious.

"I hate him," Spencer said quietly, when a mug shot of Nick popped up.

Aria nodded, saying nothing. He totally deserved this.

But he was only half the problem. If only the cops had caught Ali, too.

The police car rolled away on the screen, but the cameras remained on the police activity on the farmhouse for a moment. It was crawling with police officers, forensic teams, and dogs. Aria listened hard over the sounds of sirens for that telltale high-pitched giggle, anything that would prove Ali was still here. But there was nothing. Of course there wasn't.

"What now?" she asked, when the news cut to commercial.

Spencer sighed. "It's hard to know. We lost everything. But now maybe we can do anything."

Anything. They stared at one another, absorbing the possibilities.

Hanna looked down at her phone, which was still tucked in her pocket. "I keep expecting this to go off any second."

"With a text," Spencer whispered.

Aria stared at her phone, too, but no texts came. They wouldn't, of course. Ali wasn't dumb enough to send one right then.

Aria looked at her friends nervously. "Do you think we'll ever hear from her again?"

Hanna shook her head, a look of determination on her face. "No. It's done."

"Definitely," Spencer agreed.

But Aria knew they didn't quite believe it. They might

not hear anything from Ali for a while—maybe a long while. But she wasn't gone from their lives forever. She was still out there . . . and they were still alive . . . and that meant her job wasn't done. Knowing her, she'd only stop when she got what she wanted. She'd only stop when they were dead.

It was just a question of *when*.

ALI, INTERRUPTED

Alison ran and ran until her muscles ached and her lungs burned. The more she ran, the less she thought, and the less she thought, the less she cared. And by the time she was where she needed to go, she was resolved in her decision. This was the only solution. She'd saved herself.

She walked up to the place she'd set up weeks before without Nick knowing, the place that was all her own. She pulled the keys out of a secret pocket sewn into her jeans and unlocked the door, striding down the dark hall and sinking into the freshly made bed without even glancing at the pile of mail she'd left there the last time she'd come in, all addressed to Maxine Preptwill, her new alias. It was always a name she'd found funny, sort of an anagram of Nick Maxwell and also the name she'd used with Noel for their secret communiqués. For a long time she'd thought about what sort of person Maxine would be. A quiet girl who kept to herself. A friendly face around the neighborhood, a standout at the community college she would eventually enroll in with the remaining cash from Nick's trust—she'd tucked away small amounts every time she came here, building up a nest egg. She'd use it to get her teeth fixed, too. Her hair properly cut. Plastic surgery for the burns. She'd become beautiful and irresistible again. She needed to put someone new under her spell.

She lay there for a long time, staring at the ceiling, her mind working over the day's events. She poked at the Nick wound, but she felt nothing. Well, good. It was better to feel nothing. No regrets. No entanglements. She was free.

She thought about turning on the television—she'd jerry-rigged the antenna with aluminum foil so she could at least get the news. But she wasn't sure if she was ready to see the carnage yet. *Man Arrested for Clark Murder. Pretty Little Liars Finally Tell the Truth.* And there would be Nick's mug shot, his hollowed eyes, his dazed expression. He was the smartest guy Ali knew, but he still wouldn't know what had hit him.

Okay, okay, if she really thought about it, it wasn't what she'd wanted. She hated that those bitches were free. And she hated that *she* had been the one to turn Nick in. But she knew what might have come next if she hadn't. As soon as she heard those sirens, she'd started to panic. She'd imagined the cops finding him . . . and then *her*.

Well, she couldn't have that.

And so she'd fled. The cops had found Nick, still

unconscious on the ground, Ali long gone. He'd probably told them she'd put him up to everything—which
was pretty much the truth. And if Ali didn't have solid
proof to stop them, the cops would come looking for her.
Luckily, she had the very thing to seal his fate.

That video. Nick never knew she'd taken it. But that
was what you needed to do to survive in this world. You
needed tricks up your sleeve. You needed to keep secrets
and release them at the perfect moment.

Still, when Ali shut her eyes, Nick swam into her
thoughts. The first time they'd met at The Preserve during group, Nick throwing a wadded-up piece of paper to
get Ali to talk. The first time he'd ever shown her that
secret attic at The Preserve that only the cool patients
knew about—she'd written the name everyone but Nick
knew her as, *Courtney*, in big bubble letters on the wall.
The way he'd listened to her when she'd explained the
horrible story about the switch. How he'd vowed to help
her get revenge.

She thought about Nick's figure looming next to her
over the hole in her parents' backyard that night Courtney
died. After it was over, he'd grabbed Ali and hugged her
hard, repeating over and over that he loved her so much
and he was so, *so* proud. That was true love, she figured:
Someone who would kill for you, over and over again.
Someone who would go to the ends of the earth to wrong
all your rights.

But now, something inside her turned to steel. *Only the*

strong survive, she incanted. Even if Nick, when on trial, professed again and again that Ali was alive, there was no trace of her: She always made sure of that. Besides, he *had* been the one who'd murdered Tabitha. That video didn't lie.

She rolled over in bed, poking her tongue into the space where her tooth was missing. "Screw him," she said out loud, testing out her voice. "It's time to move on. I'm Alison. And I'm fabulous."

And she knew, suddenly, and without a doubt, that whatever she did next, she would do it well. And someday, when those bitches weren't looking, she'd come for them again. But let's face it: She was impatient. She had a feeling it would be sooner rather than later.

She couldn't wait.

ACKNOWLEDGMENTS

Once again, I could not have written this book without the help of the team at Alloy Entertainment, including Lanie Davis, Sara Shandler, Josh Bank, and Les Morgenstein. Kristin Marang and her digital team have been amazing, too—don't know what I'd do without any of you guys. Also huge thanks to Kari Sutherland at Harper for your keen insights. Much love to my family, including Mindy, Shep, Ali, and Kristian, who now knows what a horse says and possibly isn't as afraid of *moo* anymore. Also a hug to Michael, who is beyond funny and patient, and who has many ideas for new book projects and random inventions—your creativity is very appreciated around here. Also, big hugs to all the readers of this series who have hung on this long—I love seeing you at book events and reading your letters. You're the reason I keep writing!

Finally, a huge shout-out to the lovely actresses who play Aria, Emily, Spencer, and Hanna on the ABC Family series *Pretty Little Liars*: Lucy Hale, Shay Mitchell, Troian Bellisario, and Ashley Benson. I thought you guys were perfect for the parts from the very beginning, and it's been amazing watching you grow and change with the show. I owe all of you a ton, and I am your biggest fan.